BIG ISLAND, L.A.

ALSO BY BOSTON TERAN

God Is a Bullet

Never Count Out the Dead

The Prince of Deadly Weapons

Trois Femmes

Giv - The Story of a Dog and America

The Creed of Violence

Gardens of Grief

The World Eve Left Us

The Country I lived In

The Cloud and the Fire

By Your Deeds

A Child Went Forth

How Beautiful They Were

Two Boys at Breakwater

Crippled Jack

BIG ISLAND, L.A.

BOSTON TERAN

Copyright 2023 by Brutus Productions, Inc.

All right reserved under International and Pan American Copyright Conventions.

ISBN: 978-1-56703-069-3

Library of Congress Control number:

Published in the United States by High Top Publications LLC, Los Angeles, CA and simultaneously in Canada by High Top Publications LLC

Interior Design by Alan Barnett

Printed in the United States of America

ACKNOWLEDGMENTS

To Deirdre Stephanie and the late, great Brutarian...to G.G....
and L.S....Miz El and Roxomania...the kids...Natasha Kern...
Alan Barnett...the Drakes at Wildbound...Melissa Brandzel...
Charlene Crandall, for her brains and loyalty...And finally, to my
steadfast friend and ally, and a master at navigating the madness,
Donald V. Allen.

ACKNOWLEDGMENTS

PROLOGUE

This is the child of the columnist William Worth—known professionally as Landshark. It is the accumulation of investigative reporting, clandestine surveillance, unnamed dubious politicos, and a forever plagued citizenry.

As in Landshark's first published work, *Never Count Out the Dead*—based on the infamous Temple Beaudry school scandal and ensuing murders—it is Landshark's voice at the heart of this work. It is through Landshark's eyes and commentary, because the manuscript is as much about the state of his Los Angeles and soul as it is about a pyramid of corruption and murder. And as in *Never Count Out the Dead,* this work is dedicated to G.O.—Birdhous gal.

CHAPTER 1

Landshark was the first to report in his "Big Island, L.A." podcast that a Covid mask arted up to mimic the Joker's heinous grin had been left at the scene of the robbery at the Los Angeles Police Revolver and Athletic Club gun shop.

Duffels of weaponry and ammunition—gone. Even a handful of marksmanship trophies had been clipped. So much for police security.

By the time the dream militants got their imaginations around this news, takeoffs of the mask began to appear almost mystically across the graffiti capital of America, and so we were gifted at some point with another little novelty moment from the City of Privilege.

CHAPTER 2

Popotla was a fishing village south of Tijuana. A roadside attraction that leaned heavily on color and local seafood. A slum, really, that had washed up on the shore of the last few generations. The beach was crowded with *pescaderos* selling their catch to restaurants and traveling vendors and trashy seaside shacks that served cold beer and ceviche.

But that's not all this sandy cinder block village had to offer, as it had a history of being a jump off point for illegals of all classes, breeds, and types. Where for seven to fifteen thousand, one could get themselves boated up the coast to El Norte. If you were lucky enough not to be robbed, raped, and dumped overboard for the price of admission.

From where Ana sat above the beach in a ratty Volvo, she could see up the coast about as far as the Fox Baja Studio. The partly sunk hull of the *Titanic* prop there, vast and mysterious against the silky dying blues of evening, as silent as the black tomb of water where the original lay, caused her to wonder: What had started out a hundred years ago as a freezing and horrible tragedy had been reborn and rendered into a beautiful and entertaining fraud. But maybe, she thought, the fraud was more real than the tragedy that had come before it and afforded it a life. Maybe it is the fraud that serves us better, because a beautiful, entertaining fraud is a means of wiping away the absolute desolation of our existence.

She was sitting in the front seat, smoking, partly coiled up, with one long creamy leg dangling out the open driver's window and decked out in the most slickly decorated handmade boot.

Then, along came this guy passing, one of those real sense of selfhood types. Great dark hair, breezy summer shirt, and jeans, and his stare skied down that long leg all the way to the designer boot, and he started singing, "These boots are made for take your pick...."

She looked up with her summer hair and dark eyes that there was no capturing, and he came cruising over and leaned against the car by the front door where he could look down at her.

"Great boot," he said.

"Are you the type that makes instant decisions?" she said. "Because I am."

"Me…no," he said. "I drag on for all of about two seconds."

"I know a place," she said, "down the beach. Where——"

"Everybody knows a place down the beach," he said.

"Now that we got that out of the way," she said.

She opened the car door. As he stepped back she swung out her other leg and he saw it had been amputated at the ankle. He had a flash of self consciousness. Didn't know how to get his head around the moment.

She hitched up her prosthetic with that fancy boot.

"I'm sorry about the crack before——" he began.

"It's no big deal," she said. "My name is Ana, by the way."

She stood. She was pretty tall. She swung her bag over her shoulder.

"How'd it happen?" he said, pointing.

"I cut my leg off shaving," she said.

CHAPTER 3

They were crowded in at the end of a long homemade table outside a shanty on the beach. There was music, beer in coolers, fish being cooked on smoky outdoor grills. Lobster, yellowtail, grouper, whatever else made for nasty tacos. Paper lanterns of painted colors, faces in shadow played up the romance of the moment, even where there was none.

Someone was passing around a joint, and the air had that earthy stoner smell to it.

"What are you doing down here?" said Jerry.

He'd told her his name was Jerry, but it wasn't.

"I'm plotting my future," said Ana.

"Looking to take that right turn?"

She downed a little cerveza with lime. "Fuck no," she said.

A Federale chopper came sweeping in low from the south, the rotor blades blowing sand over their dinners. Its searchlight scanned the beach like the eye of God Almighty himself, then it arced out to sea.

"You know what that's all about?" Jerry said.

Ana nodded. "They're on the hunt."

It was late when they walked back up the beach. They were both pretty smashed, or so it seemed. There was music from a bar down by the surf. Blues with a Mexican kind of flair. Their shadows merged and scaled the adobe walls of the shops together and she leaned into him and let him feel all that femininity.

"Am I gonna have to ask you?" she said. "Or are you gonna ask me?"

He grinned like he had no idea. "Ask what?"

She held up her motel key.

The room was dark. He was right on her tail, already had his hand snaked down the back of her shorts. They had hardly cleared the doorway when two men in masks took him down. Before he could get out a scream, a cry, any kind of sound, he was stun gunned.

With the door closed, the three stood over the unconscious body. The one with the stun gun said, "You did good."

"Wait till he wakes up," said Carter. "He thought he was gonna get fucked."

"He did," said Ana.

They drugged their prize. Getting him into the Volvo trunk was easy enough, but onto the waiting boat that had brought them there—that was another matter. There were still some late nighters hanging out on the dock on their boats.

They carried their prize like he was some passed out drunk, each of his arms slung over one of the men's shoulders, with Ana leading the way, cursing the shit out of this lifeless soul, acting like he was her wastrel of a husband.

They laid him down in one of the lower bunks and then they took their fifty footer out of the marina and north for the border.

CHAPTER 4

Carter was piloting the boat. The other man with them, named Ellison, was down below, working the GPS and charting a course.

They were making their way up the coast a few miles out. Ana was on deck with Carter. She was smoking and watching the darkened sea ahead.

"We should have hooked up, you and I," said Carter. "We still could. I'm reliable."

She glanced at him. He was reliable. He was that rugged, solid type, with a personality like unclouded light. He was not burdened with gravity. She could see him in the Thrifty Mart, stocking up on supplies for a barbecue. Living the dream.

"You can do better," she said.

"What if I don't want to do better?"

"You have no choice."

It got quiet again, except for the engines. Then Carter said, "What are you gonna do with the money you get for turning that rat ass below over?"

She looked down at her hands. They were filthy from tonight. No shortage of chipped nails.

"I'm gonna open up a manicure shop in Beverly Hills...or maybe West Hollywood. Real outré joint. Lots of chrome and vivid colors."

He gave her a look. Some things just don't compute.

"Are you serious?"

Her look suddenly said she was fucking with him.

Ellison shouted, "There's trouble!"

It was the Coast Guard on the radio with a mayday. Smugglers had been confronted on the open sea. There was a shootout in progress. There were dead bodies on the rising waves, survivors trying to flee the scene in a small outboard.

It did not take long before they sighted the chopper about a mile ahead. It was circling a sixty footer that was being consumed by fire. One Coast Guard cutter was already on the scene. They were closing fast and now could see smugglers imprinted against the flames firing at the authorities. Ana was the first to spot another Coast Guard boat with its two huge 650s coming out from the far lights of the coast. It wouldn't be long before it would cross their path.

"This," she said, "is either the worst that could happen...or the best."

A reality they all understood.

The cutter might just blow right past...it might slow enough to check them out...they could even board on suspicions, make sure all papers were in order, identifications checked out...they might even demand the boat help search for bodies, or survivors.

Hard core as they were, the Coast Guard coming at them did a real number on their guts. They were facing twenty to life, and when that searchlight bore down, when it bleached out everything around them, they had to shield their eyes.

Ana said, "I guess we should have brought dark glasses."

The cutter sped past, its bow rising. Not a thought more, not a moment. Just armed men on deck with weapons, deeply shadowed, there then gone.

Ellison, short and densely muscled with a fearless pug face, clasped the railing in relief and said, "Shit," stretching the word out until it was a mile long.

CHAPTER 5

William Worth, otherwise known as "Landshark" and the creator of the "Big Island, L.A." column and podcast, was a housebound agoraphobic and had been for well over thirty years. He had left his property about a dozen times and only when heavily medicated.

Worth had a four story retreat on Mount Washington. Originally two acres of hillside at the end of Andalusia Avenue, over the years, with his family's wealth, Worth bought up one adjoining property after another. Then, tearing the homes down, he created a Xanadu 2.0 of unrestrained eccentricity and loneliness. It was just him and the coyotes up on that mountaintop—except for the view.

One of the lower floors was all office with 270 degree walls of glass where he could see from Glendale to the downtown skyline, then east to Boyle Heights and Monterey Park.

The scene had all the trappings of a Hollywood VFX illusion, if not something a little less profound off Shutterstock. You know— chrome and glass skyscrapers and a snow capped Mount Baldy. A sky that is rarely so rich with color.

Of course, Worth couldn't see the homeless druggies and drunks from his windows. Or all that filth and poverty decked out in hopelessness. The tent cities with their blue tarps and personalized shopping carts that were now the rule and not the exception. Bloody needles and excrement marked their territory. Beirut meets Disneyland. And that wasn't counting the crazies.

Never mind that gas prices were through the roof, and *Roe v. Wade* was down the drain. There were protests and political hatred everywhere, and that was without the sixties music. Woke America meets the hard right…meets common sense…meets the soft center…meets social revolution…meets blunt force trauma.

He fed on these kinds of thoughts, even as he was tormented by them, because they pointed out the dichotomy of his life. He was trapped by his own self inflicted existence, and had been helpless to overcome it.

But inside him, somewhere, he was on the hunt for an escape and believed that out there, in that big island of a city somewhere, was a story that would free him, that would help him overcome the failure of himself, that would imbue him with the courage he needed to become that other, new self.

It had almost happened once. Back in '06, when he helped uncover the scandal around the Temple Beaudry charter school being built on toxic land in downtown L.A., and the murders they generated. His series of exposés had seen to it and had been collected together and published as *Never Count Out the Dead.*

He found himself staring at the wall where the citations and awards for his work on that story hung. Most people saw this "shrine" as one of those acceptable symbols of achievement and pride.

It was neither. They were there to remind him, if not flat out haunt him, that he'd once been shown the turnoff for the road less traveled, yet had missed it.

But keep one foot raised and ready to go, Mr. Worth, because there is another turnoff and it's coming on fast.

And as you know, every dream comes with its own special nightmare. And this nightmare starts with a former police officer named Luis Velez, who had a trunk full of weapons and a strange character in the shotgun seat he had strangled.

CHAPTER 6

It was about four miles from the Worth estate to Elysian Park, where the robbery took place. Luis Velez waited out in the hills north of the gun shop that was on LAPRACC property fronting Academy Road. It was a vast park above Chavez Ravine and Dodger Stadium. There was no game that night, so the surrounding hills were particularly dark and silent.

Velez had chosen a patch of undergrowth where the hiking trails converged so they had multiple means of escape in case things went bad. He watched through field glasses. He'd put his faith in that strange little creature, and why? Shared desperations is how Velez would describe it.

"You got the dark in your eyes, man."

That was the first thing Andres had ever said to him. And he'd said it as they were coming out of Sunday Mass.

Andres was a diabetic, a former junkie, a depressive, a real fly-weight who could barely carry his own emotions. But he'd worked at the Academy for years—as a repairman, janitor, attendant.

"The boys up at the Academy had nothing but bad things to say about you," Andres told Velez. "That's why I feel right approaching you."

Velez noticed Andres had had the tips of his eyelids tatted black.

"I got this thing wired in my head," Andres said. "Two years refining...and I need someone who..." He made a fist so tight his papery hand tremored. "...Who will take that step over the line."

Andres was pitching a crime, right outside church, to a total stranger, with parishioners walking past. It was fucking audacious or just plain mad—maybe both.

Velez attended Mass sometimes because his ex and kids were there and he wanted them to see him do that contact thing. Show them the old man was still on the straight and narrow and could be trusted.

The two men never saw each other after that. Andres never showed at church again. Everything done between them, all the prep, was done over burners.

CHAPTER 7

Andres was to handle the robbery, Velez how they would get away clean. Velez was caught off guard when suddenly there was Andres lugging his way through the underbrush with two duffels of weaponry, plus a couple of useless trophies.

Velez grabbed a duffel and led them along one of the hiking trails. They were ghostlike against the burning skyline, breathing heavily as they went.

"We dreamed the dream, man," said Andres. "We dreamed the dream."

A police siren somewhere.

"Be quiet," said Velez.

He stopped to listen. Andres was bent over trying to catch his breath.

"It can't be us," said Andres.

Velez took a burner from his pocket. He looked northeast of the park to where the L.A. River and Interstate 5 merged. He dialed a number, and seconds later there was an explosion.

Velez had planted a bomb in an abandoned van by the railroad tracks alongside the river, and when it exploded, the van went straight into the air, ignited, and came crashing down. They could see flames and black smoke rising up onto the freeway overpass with its endless graffiti.

"That'll keep them busy."

They started down a narrow hiking trail when from out of the undergrowth comes this wreck of a human, drunk or drugged out, barefoot, wrapped in a ratty blanket, who just got done relieving himself and he stumbled straight into Velez.

You talk about a moment. He's looking at Velez, at one duffel, then the other, at Andres, at the distant fire.

"What is all that over there?" he said.

He is barely holding it together. And doesn't realize he is going to die uninformed.

Velez took out a pocket automatic and shot the man. Then, for good measure, he shot him again.

They made it past the arboretum and playground. They'd hid a car on Park Drive in a maze of scrub oak and chaparral. They sat in the dark in that little grotto of trees and darkness. Andres was shaking uncontrollably. Velez held the steering wheel tightly and thought.

"Maybe he's not dead," said Andres.

"Better hope he is...did you ever tell anyone about this? Your idea?"

Andres stared at Velez. There was something he could feel in the man's voice.

"Think, man," said Velez. "This was a murder in the commission of a crime."

"I'll tell you when we're out of here."

"What?"

"I'll tell you when I'm somewhere safe."

That answer was answer enough. Velez lunged.

There were no houses close enough to hear the pitiful screams. His cries died on the night silence. He might as well have been on the barren wastes of the moon for all his desperate clawing and kicking did for him.

CHAPTER 8

There was a mobile home village in Chatsworth on Topping Canyon Boulevard. Ana Ride lived there in a two bedroom, right next door to her father's mobile home.

She pulled in late. Her father's trailer was dark, but through the window she saw the television light flash on the ceiling. As usual, the volume was all the way up.

When Ana was out of town, there was a widow who begrudgingly looked in on the girl's father. She was coming up the walk when Ana got out of her car.

"Fidelma...how's Elias?"

"I prayed he'd get bit by a rattlesnake."

Fidelma was a transplant from Ireland. Still had the accent.

Good thing, thought Ana, the old woman had a sense of humor.

Ana knocked on the trailer window. Elias didn't bother to turn around. Whoever it was, he waved in.

Ana had been away about a week, so she expected carnage—a complete state of carnage. As soon as she got a good look at the place, she mouthed the word "Fuck."

"You know who that is?" said Elias.

He was pointing at the screen. It was some archaic black and white movie with English soldiers somewhere in India. There was a little girl with long curly locks and a kind of soldier's outfit marching along with the troops.

"Well?" said Elias.

"Got no fuckin' idea."

She gave the room a scan. Count your blessings you don't have to face this much garbage every day.

"We watched this movie together when you were a kid."

"You mean you forced me to watch it with you when I was a kid."

She noticed a pair of his underwear on the floor by the stove. Why the fuck it was on the floor by the stove was anyone's guess. She used the handle end of a broom to pick it up long distance and dump it on the washer lid.

"*Wee Willie Winkie,*" said Elias.

"What is Wee Willie Winkie?"

He was pointing to the screen. "The little girl...Shirley Temple... don't you remember?"

The girl was prancing along, high stepping it, with her locks bobbing out the sides of her pith helmet. Utterly ridiculous.

"Biggest star in the world in her day…don't you remember?"

"I must have been in a coma," she said.

"That little trooper was a real movie star. Bigger than most of the fag stars they got these days."

"They don't use that word anymore, Elias. It's persona non grata. You know that and are just being a shit."

She went to the fridge and got herself a beer. There was a salt shaker in a leftover bowl of stew. She just shook her head in disgust.

"Just for spite," he said, "I could make you wear a Covid mask coming in here."

"And cheat me of the opportunity to infect you with something fatal?"

CHAPTER 9

She went and sat on the couch. Elias saw she was exhausted. He said only, "Whatever you were doing…did it get done?"

"It got done."

She drank her beer. Leaned forward and massaged her leg along the prosthetic. She sort of watched the movie. There was little Shirley Temple all bubbly and smiling in the face of death as the English fort in India was attacked by turbaned renegades.

"They shot the movie right here," said Elias. "This was the fort… see the rock formations…those are the rock formations at the gate."

It was true. The mobile home park had been part of the Iverson, one of the most famous movie ranches from the Golden Era of

Hollywood. How many times had her father pointed out scenes from some movie filmed there?

She glanced at Elias. His mood deepened. There was the calculating stare. He was still a good looking man at sixty. Sam Elliott with the profile of a bull shark. Mustache, goatee, and a deeply lined face from twenty years in the army, then twenty more with the LAPD.

"What?" she said.

"You're the real deal, you know that. Silver Star…two purple hearts. You outranked me…you outclassed me."

She did not know how to accept such things. She disappeared into the movie for a while. She actually remembered watching it with him, she only pretended not to just to fuck with his head.

"They couldn't make this movie anymore," she said. "The English would be white colonist villains and the Indians struggling people of color. And Shirley Temple—"

"She was a boy in Kipling's book. They changed it for the movie," said Elias. "Now she'd be a 'person of color'…or 'gay'…at least a tranny. Thank god for the Golden Era of Hollywood."

They went silent after that. At least until Elias just came out with "You got to find something you can build on. With people you can build on. You got to connect."

CHAPTER 10

It was true. She needed something to build on, to connect with, and so be at one with the world, and of the world. But it felt to her she was chasing after some shimmering heat on the desert floor. You can see it, but you can't get there.

She sat on her bed in the dark with her head propped up on a pillow. She had taken off her prosthetic and rubbed the painful flesh there.

She palmed a couple of valium and washed them down with a half bottle of wine. By the time she passed into that hot, dry darkness, Elias was shaking her.

"Get up and come with me," he said. "Now."

She cursed his ass, but obeyed. When she walked into his kitchen he was pouring her coffee. She was in her pajamas and boots and she did look the mess. He pointed at the television. Watch, listen, and keep your mouth shut.

It was the local news—about the robbery. The scene jumped from the Academy gun shop to where the van blew a half mile away by the river...the lingering question from the reporter—were the acts connected?

Elias's cellphone rang. He saw the number and answered.

"No," he said. "I haven't talked to her yet. She just walked in. Give me a couple of fuckin' minutes, will you?" He hung up.

Ana sat at the dining table. Elias held up the phone.

"Revenge," he said.

She couldn't make heads or tails of any of this.

"You remember Moe Orteig? He was here a couple of times."

She shrugged her shoulders.

"Black guy. Huge. Pissy beard. He had eighteen years on the force and was fired for an out of policy shooting. No one was hurt. Lost his pension." Elias made that slash motion across his throat. "And being black didn't help him. That woke shit didn't help him. Black Lives Matter didn't help him...he was a cop, so fuck him.

"He was stationed at the Academy for a while. After he was terminated, he worked at the gun shop. That shows you how two faced they are down there at the department. He gets a call this morning from an investigator he knew who was working the robbery, questioning him about where he was last night. It's bad enough to be fired and lose your pension, then they question your integrity.

"Here's where they make the next turn. They ask him if he's got names, numbers, addresses for any of the people that used to work in the gun shop since they fucked up their records.

"He's got address books and crap in his garage, but he needs help 'cause he's in such bad shape and I told him you might go over there and—"

"This is such a—" She put her cup down and stood. "I'm outta here for points unknown."

"What?" he said.

"You're hustling me."

He threw out his arms as if he were shedding a lie. "He's an old guy. He needs help. And I can't go climbing through—"

"You know what I'm talking about," she said. "Because I know what you're talking about."

"I don't have the slightest—"

"Not the slightest, no—" She headed for the door. "You want me to take those names and numbers and maybe—"

"Maybe you can help him get a little of his reputation back. Is that such a bad thing?"

"No…it's a good thing."

"He can't do it himself. Maybe it all goes nowhere. Maybe—"

"I hate that word…*maybe*. It comes packaged with such *attitude*."

"You feeling good enough to talk to me?"

"To you…or with you?"

"Either."

"I'm available," she said. "Once I get out of these smelly pajamas.

And what is the topic of this conversation?"

"Your life."

She stopped abruptly like she'd been grabbed by a mechanical claw. She leaned against the door jamb and looked back at her father.

"I don't ask about the things you do," he said. "I don't probe. I don't judge."

"We're not going down that road, are we? The one where you use me against me to advance your cause?"

"You know what your failing is? Your one egregious failing?"

"I don't know. I have so many. Which one do you think it is?"

CHAPTER 11

Elias slipped his hands into the waistband of his trousers. Those blue grey eyes of his bore down on her. She knew the look. It carried the weight of his good side and the measures of that other side. He went right up to her, got into her space like a real drill instructor would.

"You don't believe you have it in you to fix the world. That's your failing."

"I don't believe I have it in me to fix myself. That's my failing."

"You should demand the belief in yourself…especially when you don't have it. You did have it once…before you got it ripped away from you."

He tapped her prosthetic boot with the tip of his shoe. He started away. He thought his ending the conversation ended the conversation.

"I got it ripped away from me long before that."

The air was hot and dry that day and he turned and each tried to stare down the other.

"Maybe you remember," she said, "what I like to call our atomic days. I don't want to get too sensational about the past. I like to think of it as the light rain of devastation. You remember that someone we both know, crying themselves to death. And little phrases like 'adultery' and 'cervical cancer.'"

He looked like he wanted to knock her down.

"Don't start a fight you can't finish," she said. "It's bad manners." She started back for her place. "Now write your friend's information down and slip it into my windshield."

CHAPTER 12

Moe Orteig lived in Chesterfield Park, which was South Los Angeles. In the old days—the '80s —it was known for the 54th Street Massacre.

The neighborhood around the park had been cleaned up since then. The houses were painted, the lawns neat and trim. Moe's place was a tiny stucco box that needed some tender loving care. Someone was also playing music way, way too loud.

There were a few upset neighbors outside of Moe's house. The music, it seemed, was coming from his place.

Ana parked her truck, went right past the neighbors and up the walkway. A woman called to her, "Can you please get that man to lower his music?"

Ana knocked on the front door. No one was going to hear her over the music. The bell didn't work. She looked in the window. Called out. What good would that do?

She decided on the driveway. Opened the gate with caution in case he had a dog. It looked like someone had emptied the garage and dumped everything in the driveway. She continued around back, calling out Moe's name. And what did she see, sitting in a rattan chair with the two megadeath speakers flanking him? Moe Orteig.

He looked comfortable decked out in his underwear and a holster and toking on a joint. When he saw this stranger, up he came, reaching for his gun.

"Hey!" Ana shouted out in panic. "I'm Ana…Elias's daughter. I'm here—"

Moe spread out his arms and wrapped up the girl. He was a beast and almost choked the breath out of her, repeating her name and Elias's all the while. She was pressed up against his sweaty crotch and white Jockey shorts and his holster was pressed into her hip bone, and all she could think of was running her father over.

Moe let her loose and thanked her, and Ana could see beyond being stoned and amped he'd actually been crying, the whites of his eyes that pulsy red and watering, and he kept asking, like a kid, did Ana remember him, and she said she did over and over, but she didn't.

He hustled her inside. There was a shoebox on the card table by the sliding glass doors to the patio. He handed her the box and when he did, she could see there were a couple of lines of coke on the table ready to go.

"The names of the people…in the box," he said. "Put it in your car right now. Go on. I want it out of the house."

He got her by the shoulder and practically dragged her to the front door.

CHAPTER 13

By the time Ana got to her truck and had set the box on the shotgun seat, two squad cars had pulled into the driveway. She started back to the house when a neighbor of Moe's, whose property flanked his, shouted, "He's in the backyard…and he's got a gun!"

The phrase turned into something those there knew all too well. Decades of police and civilian confrontations from the purposefully malevolent to the pure mistake. That endless American loop of shootings, stabbings, suffocatings trailed by arrests, indictments, lack of indictments, lawsuits, convictions, and acquittals… all wrapped in the flag of tragedy and loss.

Ana hustled to the front door. It was left open when she went to the truck. She could hear Moe howling and the officers demanding he not resist. She could see the fight playing out through the sliding glass doors and the card table with the coke.

This was where people made "the mistake." The one that cost you your life. And it happened as quickly as it took to cross the threshold of a front door.

Just before stepping into the house, she stopped. She did not enter. Instead, she stepped back. Moe was railing against his self entrapment. She took another step away and down the walkway she went. To hear the plight in his voice, the unquestionable rage, it went right to the heart of her own world. He was tasered, but it did little to slow that locomotive of a man, so they tasered him again.

CHAPTER 14

He suffered a seizure and died shortly after the paramedics arrived. They cordoned off the house and waited on the coroner. There were drugs in the house, so this was now officially a crime scene.

An officer questioned Ana, as one of the neighbors said she had gone into the house.

"I never did," Ana said. "I went up the driveway is all."

If proven she was in the house, she could be legally connected to that scene, and the drugs. She would be brought in, questioned, and even arrested. Then the digging would start.

"The neighbor also said you came out the front door and that you were carrying something."

"My shoulder bag." She pointed to it up there on the dashboard. Ana was leaning her back against the truck door, her prosthetic up on the runner. She was smoking. The officer was trying to glance past her to see inside the cab. No dice the way Ana positioned herself.

"I also want to say politely...I don't give a shit what someone says. I was never in that house."

A crowd was gathering. Things were getting moody and loud. There was definitely a news truck in their future. Someone shouted out to the officer who was questioning Ana.

A man in an uptown suit had gotten out of an unmarked car. He was definitely part of the investigator class and about Ana's age. The officer went over and the two talked. He was an investigator alright. He had that long drawn out stare that said *I got this chick wired.*

The officer returned. She bore an impassive look. She was tapping her notepad with a pen.

"What were you doing here?" she said.

"My father was friends with Moe. I was coming downtown. So he asked I stop by and check on him. They were both LAPD together."

"And, if I may…where were you last night?"

Oh yeah, thought Ana, this is the beginning of the dig.

"I was with my father. We were watching one of those stupid old black and white movies they show on Turner…*Wee Willie Winkie*, I think it was called. Pretty pathetic, huh?"

CHAPTER 15

Luis Velez had breakfast at the Saugus Café. He sat at a table where he could watch the news of the robbery play out on a television above the counter.

He was just another nondescript customer—who had happened to recently dig a two foot grave in the desert. Who had stopped at his house beforehand to pick up a shovel and saw for the task. Who had cut off that strange creature's head and severed his hands at the wrists and buried each in their own little private cemeteries.

"More coffee, sir?"

He looked up at the waitress. He had been jotting on a napkin the tasks needed to destroy any evidence that might connect the men.

He held out the cup. "Yes, please."

It was said the Mojave Desert was the mafia burial site. But that was not the reality. Most of the dead out there were victims of a domestic disturbance or the petty quarrels between business partners.

CHAPTER 16

Luis Velez was to have met his wife, Maritza, at an ongoing protest in an empty lot in El Sereno that was the seat of growing unrest.

More than half a century ago, under the auspices of eminent domain, Caltrans seized property in El Sereno up through what was to be called the 710 Corridor. The plan had been to extend the 710 Freeway and connect Pasadena to Interstate 10. To that end, a huge number of homes, empty lots, and warehouses were bought up by Caltrans. But the Corridor never happened. It was killed by activists, though there was a belief that clandestine money was behind the defeat of the plan, so that the property could be bought up later by developers. Many of the homes and warehouses remained empty for decades and became a blight upon the landscape. There were few voices to change all that, as El Sereno was peopled mostly by those of Mexican heritage. And during those decades they carried little weight.

But now, L.A. was desperate for affordable multi unit housing and the governor, as with all governors, was intent on showcasing himself as a champion of the greater good. So he strapped on his best deeply committed expression and helped pass the Senate bill—the one where Caltrans was to sell the properties to developers for just such housing.

But the bill did not address the hundred or so tenants who had been renting the small house or apartment units for years, decades even, and were not going to benefit from the promises made by Caltrans. Promises that went back generations stating long term renters would be given first opportunity to buy the properties they lived in.

As Landshark wrote in an editorial when the bill was first presented, the promises made by Caltrans were very much like the promises made to the Native Americans about their lands by white men of no consequence and who were hardly indistinguishable from their own shadows. Promises that broke a record for brevity.

CHAPTER 17

She called her father from the freeway. "Moe is dead…Don't talk to a fuckin' soul till I get home."

Her father started throwing questions at her.

"I'm in the fuckin' car! I'm an accident waiting to happen, genius—"

She killed the call.

He waited on the porch with a bottle of beer, picking at the label, trying not to give off the stress that was eating him up, a smile that was purely phony for any neighbors who walked by.

Ana pulled up and braked hard. It was a hot, grimy day. When she got out of the car, she was carrying the shoebox.

"You alright?" he said.

She gave him the finger and went to her trailer. He followed after her.

She dumped the shoebox on the dining table. "I'm so fucked," she said.

"Just tell me what happened."

"What happened? You happened…I happened. He, she, and it happened."

"Get off it," he said, "and tell me."

She laid it all out for him while lighting a cigarette, taking swigs from a rum bottle, lighting another cigarette while the first was still burning away, pacing over her worn out carpet. She walked just like Elias, the same shoulder pattern. When she saw herself reflected in the sliding glass doors, it was like staring at her father and she could have just spit.

"You didn't go into the house," he said, "when the LAPD was there. Smart. You remembered what I taught you. That says something."

Elias had browbeaten his daughter as a child with the do's and don'ts of police procedure, like he was sharing with her invaluable secrets. They'd be in his pickup truck running errands and after he taught her, he would test her. He would actually test her with a kind of homemade multiple choice. When she told her girlfriends that, they almost spit up with laughter.

"My youth came in handy for something, didn't it?" she said.

"Being well informed comes out of being curious, and being curious grows out of being well informed," he said.

"I'd like to know who you stole that from," she said.

He had sat down at the dining table and was staring at that shoebox.

"They're gonna dig," she said.

"There's nothing," he said.

"There's never nothing...who taught me that?"

He knew who.

"You were watching a movie with your father," he said.

"There's earlier that night...and the week leading up to that night."

"But for them to get there—"

"They're gonna dig. I could see it in that investigator's face when I drove past. He was sizing me. He thinks Moe was connected to that robbery...and I'm connected to Moe. And they'll fill in the blanks later."

"They can't get there…because you weren't there."

"But they're gonna dig."

"I'm sorry I got you into this."

"Bullshit…Elias Ride does not do sorry. He never did."

"No…he never did."

She smoked and stood at the edge of the table. She and her father both were eyeing that shoebox.

"He emptied the garage," said Elias.

"Like a tornado."

"What are they thinking…about that and his actions?"

"Like he was guilty."

"Or just out of his mind."

"They're gonna dig."

He looked up at his daughter. "Yes," he said. "They're gonna dig."

CHAPTER 18

In an empty lot a few doors up from the Velez house, Assemblyperson Julia Domingo and members of the Tenants Association were filming a video plea for their cause, to be put on YouTube. Among the handful of residents chosen to speak was Maritza Velez.

She had asked her husband to be there to support her. She pleaded, really, and that was something she resented. He promised her he would be there. More than once he promised. But his promises—they were much like those of Caltrans.

When he arrived at the house, his wife's state of mind was in a risky place. She was in the kitchen setting out food for her mother.

The woman was a worn sixty. Too much work, too much smoking.

Maritza put her hands on her hips when Luis entered the kitchen. Her look went from resentment to hatred to just sheer disappointment.

"I ask you so little," she said. "And even so little is too much."

He stood in the doorway like the scorned child.

"I've been going over all that I could say to you," she said. "But I need to remember. This is not about me. Not about what I feel. Because my feelings are nothing to you. I am no more important to you than...that refrigerator. I needed you there because it is about the house. This house."

She swung her arm about, poking at the air with a fork in her hand.

"This is about our home. My mother's home. Remember my mother?"

He glanced at the woman. She sat with folded hands. A judge with sad eyes and whose stoicism was something to behold.

"I was born in this house," said Maritza. "My mother lived in this house fifty years. She let us live here when we were first married and never demanded, even asked for, rent. And you never offered."

"I was meeting with some people," Luis said, "about work I could do to make—"

"You are like a miscarriage," she said. She was completely frustrated and baffled. "Everything you do and say is like a miscarriage. I needed you there today."

"How did it go?" he said. "Your speech—"

"You're trying to skip over the subject." She turned to her mother. "He's trying to skip over the subject. Do you hear him?"

The mother sat there gravely, her nonexpression a pure condemnation.

Crossing the kitchen, Maritza noticed through the doorway and the living room window a strange car in the driveway. The one he'd suffocated a man in. The one with stolen weapons in the trunk.

"Whose car is that?"

"I…borrowed it."

"Where is your car?"

"It was acting funky."

"Like its owner," said Maritza.

He suddenly couldn't look her in the eye. And this rubbed her curiosity the wrong way.

"Something is off," she said.

He kept from looking at the car. Afraid somehow she'd see a man being suffocated in there.

There was a man being suffocated alright.

CHAPTER 19

The shoebox delivered about a dozen relevant names, numbers, addresses. In a day book, on a scrap of yellow legal pad, a restaurant napkin—a haphazard array if ever there was one. Spread out they were on the dining room table, with Ana and Elias sitting across from each other.

There were also, surprisingly, some photos in the box. A letter, a picture of Moe's mother and father, a former wife or girlfriend, medals he'd won as a shot putter in high school, medals he'd won on the force for marksmanship.

"What kind of statement is this about a person?"

Elias sounded like he was feeling sorry for himself. He had a hangdog expression, as if seeing his own life there.

"He had a garage full of crap that could flesh out his life," said Ana.

"You directing that at me?"

"Damn right."

"Feels very last will and testament to me," said Elias.

A shot of Moe with a date at a birthday party. He's dressed as a Mexican bandit with fake mustache and gaudy sombrero.

Ana held up the image. "This will get you tossed out of Wokeland."

"What are you gonna do with the stuff I leave behind?" said Elias.

"Burn it all."

"Nice."

She tossed the picture aside. Picking through the last of the crap at the bottom of the shoebox, something catches her eye. It's an article from the *L.A. Weekly*—the "Big Island, L.A." column. There was a hotline number circled. And a second number below it, scribbled in pen.

CHAPTER 20

William Worth got a call about the murder before it hit the news. A homeless man had been discovered by joggers just off one of the trails in the park behind the Academy. They had no hard facts as to the who and why of the murder except that his time of death could fall into the hour of the robbery.

Worth wrote down the facts on an index card. He kept about a dozen freestanding corkboards in his office where he pinned details and updates on stories he was working. He put this new bit of information on the board he sarcastically named THE JOKER MURDER.

He went back to his desk and sat. He cued up YouTube so he could watch it on his wall flatscreen. He wanted to see the Open Letter From the Tenants Association about the El Sereno issue with Caltrans.

The first representative to speak introduced herself as Maritza Velez. She was petite; an "everyday type" is how Worth would describe her. She brushed her hair back a bit before she spoke because of a breeze, and Worth noted a plain wedding ring.

"To all justice loving communities of peoples," she said. "To our governor and representatives, this is a goodwill letter—"

He made a note of that—*A goodwill letter.* It all started out that way. *Life,* he meant, *that is the ultimate goodwill letter*—pregnant with possibilities—

A phone rang. He wheeled his chair to the far end of the enormous half moon desk.

He had phones alright: a dozen cells, a couple of hard lines, a hotline.

The phone that rang was a private cell he only gave out after he talked with someone, and was reasonably sure of them.

NO CALLER ID came up.

He did not answer. He let voicemail kick in. He waited. A message was left. He played it back. A woman's voice—"I got your number from a former policeman you talked with recently. I'd like to follow up with you on that."

She left a number that Worth jotted down. Then he sat back.

CHAPTER 21

There was something about these moments, just before what was out there became part of his reality, that Worth felt this near prurient excitement. He'd be ashamed to admit to it, and that the more brutal the potential of the story, the more radiant the feeling. Every story, in that respect, was god.

He dialed the number. "Landshark here."

"I hope so."

A woman, young probably, with a crisp, slightly deep voice.

"You called me," said Worth.

"That I did," she said.

Then nothing more.

He waded through the silence that followed.

"Can I help you?"

"I don't know yet."

"Would you care to share with me how you got this number?"

"Not yet."

"I see. I have to know why you called. Otherwise—"

"I'd like to meet with you."

"I see," he said. "Convince me why we should."

She did not answer. He listened to her quiet breathing. It was slow, not the least anxious.

"I don't know what you're playing," he said.

"You will," she said.

"This call is taking on a troubling tone."

"Then hang up," she said.

He sat tapping his fingers on the glass tabletop.

"I don't get hysterical so easily," he said.

"Good," she said. "Neither do I, for that matter." Then, out of nowhere, she said, "Safety first. That's where I'm at."

"Yours or mine?" he said.

"Both," she said.

Her tone had eased a bit. But he was still this side of wary.

"Good," he said. "How do we proceed?"

"I know your name from a former police officer."

"I know any number of former police officers."

"This one is recently deceased."

Alright, he thought. Alright. Could it be—

He was up and hustling over to one of the corkboards with the header *CHESTERFIELD PARK DEATH*. He reviewed his index cards. A woman had been questioned at the scene. He didn't have a name or photo.

"You still there?" she said.

"Chesterfield Park," he said. "Sound familiar?"

"More than that," she said.

"Right…let's meet."

"I have to be able to trust you," she said.

"Trust is a two way street."

"I don't take mistrust lightly."

"Is there any other way? When do we meet?"

"Now," she said.

"Zoom call?"

"Fuck Zoom calls."

"I don't leave the premises…ever."

"That's of no concern to me."

"When, then?"

"Now."

"Now?"

"Right now."

She was so definitive, and the timbre of her voice such that a feeling went through him, one bordering on threat. He quickly crossed the room to a bank of security cameras—the long, tree lined dead end of a private road to his estate, the gated entry, the driveway, the front door, angles of the walled compound and property surrounding the house. He searched the screens closely, his fingers moving from image to image.

"You're here, aren't you?"

"Yes."

"Where?"

"On your patio."

CHAPTER 22

One screen favored the patio, but the lights were off and all was just shadows hiding shadows.

In a file cabinet he kept a Walthers. He checked the magazine and chamber. He went downstairs as if to face a reckoning.

He crossed the darkened den. At the glass doors to the patio he peered out. Under an arbored overhang he picked up the faintest outline of someone sitting in one of the rattan chairs. Light from a cigarette for a moment flared and a trail of smoke shaped out a face.

"It's quite the place you have here," said Ana.

"I think so," said Worth.

"Your security system is for shit, though."

"I gather," he said.

"You were watching me while we talked on the phone, weren't you?"

"Yes," she said. "I was."

"Did you get the answers you want?"

"I don't know yet."

"I'm going to put a light on, if you don't mind," he said.

"I don't think you'll need the gun," she said.

He flipped on an outdoor switch and just like that, the patio was subtly touched with soft, well placed pools of light.

"Mood lighting to perfection," said Ana, with just a hint of bite.

As he approached, she stood. She was decidedly not what he imagined. She was wearing a black sleeveless tee shirt and black jeans and black boots that went well up her calf. And all that topped with super short hair.

"How long were you back here?" he said.

"About an hour."

"How was the show?"

"Boring."

"Do you have a name?"

"Ana…Ana Ride."

He noticed a USMC tat on her shoulder.

"Is that for show? Or the real deal?"

"Lieutenant Ana Ride," she said. "Retired."

He ran his fingers along the collar of his cardigan pullover. "You're rather young to be retired."

"The road is long…with many a winding turn…."

Her tone was quietly dismissive. Her eyes warned of something else.

"Shall we go inside?" he said. "And get to why you're here?"

"As long as we're off the record."

CHAPTER 23

She sat on a leather and chrome chair in his office. A real specialty item, like everything else in the place, that must have run in the five figures. She handed him a list of names she'd written up, some with addresses, some with phone numbers. She laid the whole story on him, starting with Moe's phone call.

He stood at the window looking out over the city and listening. He was one tall fucker, she thought. Six foot six and not a hundred and fifty pounds to him. He was totally androgynous, fiftyish...with perfect short grey hair and this artsy braid down the back of his head. He looked like he'd been peeled off one of the pages of *Vogue*.

"They questioned you, and you told them none of this."

"No," she said.

Ana got up. The bulletin boards had caught her attention.

"You didn't tell the authorities that Orteig reached out to you... did you?"

"No," said Worth.

"So there we are."

He hadn't noticed before...the way she walked...it was hardly noticeable...and the boots...it wasn't your standard issue prosthetic...but one of those personalized hipster models you see all over the internet.

She scanned *THE JOKER MURDER* and *CHESTERFIELD PARK DEATH* boards.

"I'm sure you have people," she said, "that could cull the list for you, fill it in. A lot faster and better than I could. Then there'd only be the high percentage possibilities to search out...question."

She crossed the room and stood behind him and she looked out the window. He was studying her all the while and she saw he was studying her and she just stood there in profile and let him turn this all over in his mind.

He finally said, "You didn't come here just to hand a list over and walk."

"I'm not the handover type."

There they were, with the great expanse of the city at their feet.

"What do you want?" he said.

When she spoke, it wasn't off the top of her head, no, she had thought this out. It was obvious to him.

"It's not that I failed with my old life…I just don't have a life to go on with from there. You see, I'm short on faith and light on hope."

"Survival needs relevance," he said.

A police chopper came out of the blackness and swept across downtown with its track of lights, past the office buildings and high rises and for a moment she flashed on Mexico.

"Clarify your terms so I can decide," he said.

"I take it out there," she said, pointing to the downtown skyline, "I'm the warhorse."

CHAPTER 24

Investigator Jayden Miller skipped dinner to get right to his favorite feeding ground—the Hollywood Park Casino—and settle into a night of No Bust Blackjack.

He was on a neat little run when he got a text from his superior: URGENT.

There's nothing worse than having a streak skyjacked by your straight assed superior.

Miller didn't answer. The cards, you see, were god. So he got another text: I HOPE YOU'RE NOT BLOWING ME OFF.

So now Investigator Miller had to pry himself loose and it was especially bad as he was juked on Adderal and exquisitely high on focus and low on impulsivity.

He called in from the lounge.

"Yes, sir."

"Where are you?"

"I'm at my regular therapy session."

"That's bullshit," said his superior.

Jayden was checking out the asses that went by and he was not being subtle about it.

"Yes, sir…it's bullshit."

"Listen…update…boot tracks on the trail where that homeless man was shot…"

"Yeah…"

"…match tracks at the exitway behind the gun shop."

"Great, sir…I'll get to it first thing."

"That's not all."

He's gonna keep me here all fuckin' night, thought Jayden.

"The girl at Chesterfield Park…the one questioned…"

"Oh…that one."

"I'm gonna send you a picture."

CHAPTER 25

Elias was on the internet doing searches about the robbery when headlights flared past his window.

He was on the porch as Ana was getting out of her car. She did not even acknowledge him.

"How did whatever you did go tonight?"

She walked into her place without answering.

"So that's how it is!" he shouted after her.

She was sitting on the couch taking off her prosthetic when Elias came in.

"Don't knock or anything," she said.

She took off her other boot and tossed it across the room.

"Don't leave your door open or anything," he shot back.

She sat back. "I'm exhausted...my leg hurts...and I'm pissed."

"I put on my LAPD cap tonight."

"Don't you hear me?"

He went on, "We have to organize our answers. And we better have a good one for that."

He pointed at the shoebox, which was now on her coffee table.

CHAPTER 26

Velez was trying to drink away his anxiety. Las Ranas was an upscale Mexican joint near where, of all places, the 710 ended and the Corridor was to begin.

He had stashed the weapons and was now playing out in his head the task of dealing them. Andres had had the connection who was to handle the sale, but he'd never named the dealer to Velez.

He was morose when he walked out into the parking lot. And his wife dumping on him only added to his misery and shame. Not that he didn't deserve the beatdown.

"Hey...do I know you?"

Velez turned to see this gent about thirty. He was wearing tony glasses and leaning against a Lexus. He was smoking.

"You look familiar," he said. "Do I look familiar to you?"

Velez shook his head. "Sorry."

"My name is ChiChi."

He put out his hand. Velez shook it. He looked the man over carefully.

"My name is Luis."

"You sure I don't look familiar to you?"

"I'm bad on faces...and worse on names."

"What was your thing?" said ChiChi.

"LAPD...once upon a time."

"Ohhh." ChiChi threw his head back. "You didn't arrest me or nothing. And I'm not some heat seeking missile looking for revenge. Though I have been arrested a few times."

ChiChi changed the subject. "The food's pretty good in there."

Velez kind of nodded. He wanted to be done with this guy.

"I'm waiting for my old lady," said ChiChi. "You know how they are when it comes to the bathroom."

"I know."

"I could grow roots by the time she gets out."

Velez smiled.

"What line of work you in now?"

Velez froze on that for a moment. "I'm...between gigs."

"Sorry I brought it up. Something will come along," said ChiChi. "It always does. And when you least expect it."

Velez said goodnight, got into his car, waved, and drove up Valley Boulevard.

When he got about two blocks or so and couldn't see the Las Ranas parking lot, he made a quick U turn.

He turned off his headlights, drove about a block, and pulled over. He could just see the man. He watched and he waited.

When ChiChi finished the cigarette, he got into his Lexus alone…and drove away.

CHAPTER 27

The doorbell rang at six thirty in the morning and unpleasantly awakened Ana. She thought it might be her father venting. But it was a messenger with a package courtesy of William Worth.

Ana sat naked at her dining table, smoking, with her bad leg propped up on the chair.

Worth had delivered back to her that list of names with updated phone numbers, whereabouts, nonwhereabouts…even imprisonment and death.

In another packet, bound up bubble wrap held a stylized crucifix. She held it up to the light. It had a built in mini camera and could be worn around the neck.

He'd included a note:

Got a crew of researchers who work 24/7.
As for the crucifix—there's no charm bracelet
to protect you—but a watchful eye never hurt.

CHAPTER 28

Ana had a simple enough pitch. She was working for the "Big Island, L.A." column, gathering information about Moe Orteig from anyone who worked with him at the gun shop. The truth—she was hoping to circle in on the subject of their whereabouts the night of the robbery.

One of those she contacted worked in a box making plant and had broken his leg the week before in a car accident. Another was a night manager at a mini mart in Torrance. Another was down with Covid. Another was unemployed and on antidepressants. The lover of another told Ana to go fuck herself.

It went on like this. She was making her way through a landscape of people you never notice from the cradle to the grave, and who were strangling on gas prices and groceries they couldn't afford but couldn't do without, and any one of them she could imagine might try to score off a robbery.

And who could fully blame them? After all, the Brinks truck known as America was in dire need of an overhaul before the wheels fell off.

The next one on the list was Antonin Andres, who lived in a rooming house called Maggie's Farm. It was in the heart of Skid Row, on a block of recently built low income housing. The building was designed for damage control and against the likes of graffiti and human excrement. Maggie's Farm, on the other hand, was a three story throwback to 1906 with one of those cantankerous cage elevators.

Urban legend had it that Bob Dylan lived there for a time and composed his classic—"Maggie's Farm"—while a guest. But then again, Los Angeles was noted for its urban legends. Landshark had even mocked in one of his columns that all of Los Angeles actually was one vast urban legend in desperate need of a reality.

CHAPTER 29

There was a desk clerk in the tiny rooming house lobby who also served as assistant manager, janitor, repairman, and all around security guard. He was a work in progress, so to speak, with his tuck and roll wig and a pair of oversize breasts he'd picked up in Mexico. He watched Ana intently as she entered the building and approached.

Ana was neatly dressed and all polite and businesslike. "Hi... maybe you could help me. I'm looking for Antonin Andres."

The clerk's painted on Joan Crawford eyebrows rose decisively. "And what could you want with that...cocksucker?"

Well, that set the tone for Ana all right.

"I need to...talk with him."

"He lives in 206...but it should be 666...the devil's number. He went out two days ago. Gone. Does this have anything to do with that take it up the ass crowd on the third floor?"

"No...How do you like to be called?" said Ana.

The clerk smiled. "Well, thank you for that. My name is Felis. Felis Pope. It was Felix, but I changed it when I moved on."

Ana told Felis it was a nice take on a name, and this loosened up the woman's empathy.

"When you came in," said Felis, "I noticed...." She pointed to Ana's boot. "What happened, girl?"

"Afghanistan happened."

"Thought it was something like that."

Felis started to undo her blouse, making sure no one was around, and Ana thought, *What the fuck?*

Then Felis flashed a U.S. Army and star tat on one of her industrial size breasts.

"I was Army," said Felis. "NATO. Aide to the supply chief in Germany."

Ana gave the tat a good looking over and showed Felis the USMC tat on her own shoulder and the two of them tapped fists.

"I don't get much girl talk in this place," said Felis. She took out a pack of cigarettes and offered Ana one. The woman's fingers were yellow from decades of nicotine.

They chatted on about everything from the pathetic state of California to how difficult it was to find a proper fitting bra and panties.

Finally, Felis said, "I hate Andres. He's a liar, a cheat, he sold me bad weed. If he's involved in something criminal, and I wouldn't put it past him, I'd love to help you fuck over that little cocksucker."

CHAPTER 30

Ana texted Worth: *We might have something. Will email you footage later.*

When she pulled into the trailer park, she had to drive past the office, and who was there talking away with Fidelma but the investigator for the Orteig place.

No sooner did she get in the house than a call came in from her father.

"He's here."

"I know," she said. "Did you talk with him yet?"

"No."

She peered out the blinds. There he was, coming up the sunny gravel driveway.

"Time to armor up," she said.

Miller was just about to knock on the screen door when it opened. He was going to flash his creds when Ana said, "Don't bother. I saw you yesterday at Orteig's house."

She invited him in. He gave her his card. Without looking, she discarded it on the bureau with the rest of her junk mail and bills. She continued on to the fridge where she pulled out a half bottle of triple sec.

He was looking around. "Nice place you've got here."

There was no way of knowing if he was being sincere or full of polite shit.

"Yeah…it's perfect for grannies and drug dealers."

"I want you to check this out," he said.

He had a picture on his cell. There was Ana, coming down the walkway of the Orteig house. The front door open, her carrying that shoebox.

"You were coming out of the house," he said.

"You can think so, but it doesn't show so," she said.

"And the shoebox? You didn't get that in the house? You mind telling me what's in it?"

She pointed with the bottle of triple sec and he followed along behind her.

"I checked you out," he said. "No Facebook, no Twitter, no Instagram, no etcetera, etcetera, etcetera."

"I don't believe in things that make you stupider," she said. "I bet you're on them."

"No comment," he said.

She pointed the bottle at the dining table and there was the shoebox—open.

He went and started to look through it. There were the photos, snapshots. Everything else had been pulled. While he picked his way along, he said, "What kind of work do you do?"

"Security…surveillance…bodyguard…I freelance it. I work a lot of concerts, political gatherings, the usual Hollywood crap."

"Why would he give you this?" he said, pointing at what could only be described as a mess.

"Ask him!" she said.

His look stiffened.

"Oh, I forgot…you guys killed him."

She sat on the couch and hiked her boots up on the coffee table.

"The Irish lady at the office said you were away for about a week before the robbery. And only came … in late that night. You mind telling me where you were?"

Ana rubbed her leg. "I snuck off and was fuckin' a friend of mine's husband."

Miller's nostrils flared a bit 'cause he almost smiled. "You're a counterpuncher, aren't you?"

"One of the best," she said.

Miller started out. At the door, he posited a thought. "Let's see how good a counterpuncher you are after you carry the weight of my questions around for a while."

CHAPTER 31

Once Miller was gone, Ana took a shot of triple sec and then rubbed the cold bottle against her temples.

Her father came in. Saw his stressed out daughter sitting there, leaning forward, like she was just about to tip over.

"Bad?" he said.

"He's got questions…I got wisecracks. This is a losing combination."

"The Orteig business is gonna get swallowed up."

"What do you mean?"

He turned on the television to CNN.

"There's been a mass shooting in Buffalo. At a supermarket. A black supermarket."

She could see on the screen the usual shots of a mass shooting. There'd been so many, the news had its coverage of these things almost down to a science.

"There's only so much goodwill to go around," he said. "They'll have investigators looking into every possible lead here on a copycat or some other crazy."

She didn't want to hear what she was hearing and just kept on with the cold bottle against her temples.

"This is good news…considering the situation," he said.

"You know, Elias…sometimes when I hear what comes out of your head, I think…I can't be related to you. Somebody must've gotten into Mom ahead of you."

CHAPTER 32

Ana had emailed her footage from the room to a secure Landshark site. He'd been waiting, watching the news on multiple cable networks.

America, it seemed, was in a perpetual state of madness. It could barely stitch up one wound when here came another. It was as if some malign electricity was running through the hearts of the end-lessly unhappy, lost, and broken, connecting them to some faithless, empty prison of a world, where once lived a soul.

At times like this, Worth wondered if his cowardice and fear was not a better life choice than having to step out in all that sickness.

CHAPTER 33

The camera in her crucifix picked up on a door with a 206. She opened it. "I picked up the key from the desk clerk," she said on film, "which I will explain later."

Once inside, she gave the room a pan with the crucifix so Landshark would get his bearings.

"I thought it would be a dump," she said.

Frankly, Andres kept a neat and tidy place. There was a bed, a television on a bureau, a kitchenette, a desk against the opposite wall, and a chair.

The room was spartan but for the desk. She went through the stacked papers there slowly, dutifully. You could hear voices in the hall every now and then. Ana would stop, nervous it was Andres.

Then back to searching. Suddenly, she said, "Ahhh."

She held up a plane ticket.

"Bangkok," she said. "And check the date."

She held it close to the camera.

"The ticket was for yesterday…What does that say?"

She went through the desk drawers. "Look what I found here," she said. She held up a cellphone, which she set down. Then she pulled out another…and yet another. "Burners," she said. "I say we take these too."

She sat there at the desk now. She'd gone through everything. Her fingers made a slow pass again through the scraps of paper, the bills, just junk really.

Then her eye caught something because her fingers snaked through a stack that was off to one side.

Landshark could partly see what she was pulling out with two fingers.

It was a church program, of all things. One of those two page flyers they hand out for the Mass of the day.

CHAPTER 34

Velez lived in a small guesthouse behind a fourplex near Woodrow Wilson High and less than a mile from his ex-wife.

He needed to think through how to get clear of those weapons. To find someone to sell them to so he could help his wife and kids have a down payment for the house, because he didn't believe for a minute Caltrans would come through. And he needed to get straight with what that character in the parking lot was all about, though he had an idea.

He was making for Ascot Hills Park. He liked to jog there around dusk. They described the park as an urban retreat with hiking trails and panoramas of the city. Disregard the occasional rape and assault, it was a pretty fair description. Of course, every time he saw a park now, he thought of that homeless bum he shot in the face. It left him queasy and pissed him off he even had a moment of conscience.

He was sweating it along Multonah when a Lexus came gliding up alongside him, and who should be behind the wheel? Yeah... only now the guy had two sturdy looking youths with him. With the sunset glaring off the roof, Velez couldn't make out their faces, but who cared?

"I've been looking for you," said ChiChi.

"Yeah?"

"I had a thought about a business deal."

Velez looked the scene over. Not good.

"Can we talk later? I'm running."

"Five minutes."

Velez pulled a cell out from his windbreaker. "Give me your number and I'll call you when I'm done."

"Just five minutes...."

ChiChi angled the car now so he'd start cutting off Velez's pathway.

Velez played it like it was nothing.

"I don't stop when I'm running."

He gave ChiChi a wave and a smile and darted around the back of the car, leaving a long shadow as he crossed the road and was on up toward the empty hills.

He didn't bother to look back because he remembered what happened to Lot's wife.

CHAPTER 35

The sound was off, but the news on that flatscreen was wall to wall the Buffalo shootings and the tragedy therein. And as for Moe Orteig—he was now back of the bus.

Worth was sitting at his office desk. "Just got an email," he said. "Andres didn't refund the ticket. Didn't exchange the ticket."

Ana was watching the bay of surveillance cameras.

"He's dead. Or gone where—"

"I vote dead," said Ana.

"The burners," said Worth. "I have people who can deal with these things. If there's anything on there."

Ana kept to the surveillance cameras. Any light, any motion, anything cornered her interest.

"What really intrigues me," said Worth, "is why this intrigued you."

Ana craned her neck around. Saw Worth was holding up the Mass program.

"All Saints Church…in El Sereno," said Ana. "A long way from him downtown to that church. If he was the type, and there was nothing in his room to suggest that he was church. Except that… and from one Sunday two months ago. Something is…off."

"You think this connects him to…what?"

"Just a feeling. I think it's the atheist in me. I'm suspicious of all things…especially when they don't fit."

"Like the cross you're wearing."

"Exactly like it."

"You don't believe in the Big Soul?"

She went back to that bay of cameras, lighting a cigarette. "I am untainted by sensationalism. And I only believe what's between the goalposts of good and evil."

"You keep looking at those screens…you're making me nervous."

"That investigator, Miller…he's the type that is gonna take the sharp turn. Authorized or not. And life's disorder isn't gonna slow him down."

"How do you know? About him, I mean."

"Because one rattlesnake always recognizes another rattlesnake."

CHAPTER 36

Maritza got a call. She was in her kitchen doing dishes and listening to dance music. She answered the cell with wet hands. It was her husband.

"Luis?"

"I need to see you…tonight."

"Not tonight."

"Just for a few minutes."

"No."

"Please. I'm begging you."

There was such urgency in his voice.

"I'm in trouble, honey."

She lowered the music. "What's happened?"

"Are the kids in bed?"

"Yes."

"Your mother?"

"In her room."

She ran her wet hands through her hair, disgusted and afraid for what she did not yet know.

"I hate this. I hate you. Where are you?"

"In the backyard."

"The backyard...?" She rushed to the window. The yard was dark all the way to the tiny, listing garage.

"Turn out the lights," he said. "Do it."

She turned off the kitchen lights. Wiped her hands one at a time on her tee shirt.

"I'm coming in the back door. Is it locked?"

Standing there in the dark, she said, "No...I mean, yes...I'll unlock it."

She unlocked it.

"The rest of the downstairs," he said. "Shut the lights."

She went from room to room like a crazy woman. She was by the stairs when she heard the back door open. She was as terrified as she was confused.

"Where are you?" he said.

"By the stairs."

He was coming up the hallway and grabbed hold of her.

"What's wrong?" she said. "Tell me...goddamn it."

The way he held her, she thought, was like the old days when they had meaning together. There was a succession of small moments— an embrace, a kiss, his head resting against her neck, then the hint of a sob.

She felt pity for him and was enraged that she did.

"What's happened?"

"I've done something...bad."

"Oh no...you've got to leave now."

"I did it to make money for you and the children and—"

"This is too much to bear."

"I was desperate to help you get this house."

"Desperate. You don't know what desperate is."

"And ashamed."

"You were never about anyone but yourself."

"That's a lie."

"Go home. Please. Have pity on your children." Her voice almost hissed as she spoke.

He shook her hard. "I can't go home."

She pushed away from him. Could not see the terror in his eyes because of the dark.

"What does that mean?" she said.

"The gun I left here for you. Get it."

CHAPTER 37

Inspector Jayden Miller had paid into a No Limit Hold 'Em Tournament. He was performing well for a while, but had the gambler's dramatic failing for betting until it hurt.

Miller was also an Adderall junkie with an ongoing prescription as he suffered lifelong ADHD and depression. He preferred to parachute the drug and kept a pestle and mortar in his SUV and he'd grind up the pills to a fine powder and bundle it in a bit of toilet tissue, then down the chute it went with a neat shot of whatever liquor god had been kind enough to leave handy. If he was out of Adderall, Vitamin R or ephedrine would do. There was one side effect he had to watch for—the drug made him want to chew through the black leather pants the cocktail waitresses were wearing.

Once he'd torched his playing stash, Miller went to the bar to drink away his disgust.

He'd received a text from his superior:

SUBPOENA—NO GO

"The gods," he said aloud to anyone, "are tampering with my f'in soul." He got a burner phone from his suit pocket. As a bartender walked by, Miller corralled him with a wave: "Give me something that really earns a DUI."

Miller dialed a number. The phone was answered.

"It's me," said Miller. "Where do you think I am?…Yeah…I got a shopping list. I need phone recs of last week for an 800 tipline… It belongs to the columnist for the Weekly…'Big Island'…you're not allowed to say 'flamer' anymore. Haven't you kept up with your Woke Handbook?

"I also need last week's recs for an Elias Ride and Ana Ride… They live in Chatsworth…No, father and daughter…At least that's what they claim…What.…"

The voice at the other end of the line rattled along and the bartender came by and set down a drink.

"This is sure to get you arrested," said the bartender.

Miller made a sign of the cross over the glass.

Then Miller got this sudden burst of one Ana Ride and he got tight right where you go vulnerable and he saw her sitting there on her couch, laid back, with all that female working for her and he hoped to Christ this was only the Adderal, otherwise—

"Listen to me, you half witted genius," Miller said to the voice at the other end. "They don't indict or convict murderers anymore in this fuckin' city…So I'm gonna get shy over what I'm askin'?"

CHAPTER 38

Luis Velez crept out of the house the same way he crept in. He hid alongside the garage amid the garbage cans and rats, watching the alley a long while for any whisper of a sign they were lying in wait.

When he thought it right he took off, sprinting up the alley toward the street, ready to take a fence if necessary. His wife had watched all the while and only got a glimpse of him for a moment. Then she just sat at the kitchen table after that, mired in a world of lost values and bad choices.

Velez kept a grip on the gun in his windbreaker pocket and knew if he made it to Alhambra Avenue, at the end of the alley, with all the lights and businesses, it would be a lot tougher to take him down.

When he did make it to Alhambra, nothing had changed. He was in that great big bad world of the night and the bars and the businesses and the occasional person passing were not worth a consoling shit. And every headlight that climbed up his back had the bile churning in his stomach.

Velez prayed even though he was sure they wanted him alive—if not, they could have done him in a drive by how many times.

He prayed Maritza would hold up with all that he had laid on her, even though he didn't tell her he killed that homeless bum. He prayed that god forgive him and he felt like a fraud for exploiting god that way, but better to take a chance for the payoff of a little help and forgiveness.

And then a set of headlights slowed, really, really slowed, and he didn't look but he had the gun ready and then a voice said, "Hey, Luis…that you?"

You want to talk about a world turn. A voice he recognized.

He stopped and came about. There was a squad car.

"Luis, it's me. Charlie Engel."

Of all things. An officer he knew and served with.

"What are you doing?"

"My car," said Velez, trying to get the shake out of his voice. "It went out on me. So…I'm walking home."

Charlie looked around.

"Get in. I'll give you a lift."

CHAPTER 39

You can die for a long time up in Kagel Canyon and no one will be the wiser — A little graffiti wisdom painted on a garage door that faced the road.

Kagel was an unincorporated community at the edge of the San Gabriel mountains along the northern tip of L.A. It was mostly remote homesteads, small ranches, truck storage depots, and prefab warehouses. The perfect place for people who liked to keep their secrets up long dirt roads. There was a bar in the canyon, aptly named The Hideaway.

When Velez came to, he was lying on the floor of a van with his hands and feet bound.

He had been taken down without even realizing. He was getting out of the squad car and Charlie Engel stepped out to shake hands when he put Velez down with his taser.

The first thing Velez saw through his haze was the pitch outline of that gent who called himself ChiChi sitting on the wheel hub staring down at him. The two sentries he'd traveled with from before were up front now.

"Bad break for you that Charlie Engel is one of ours," said ChiChi.

Velez didn't bother begging, pleading, crying, trying to connive or be hard. Through the windshield the dark of spare trees his pallbearers.

He thought of his wife and he thought of his children, and he said to himself, *You fucked up, boy. It's time you decide about dying well.*

"I bet my boys here," said ChiChi, "that when we got your ass, you'd have some story worked up."

Velez lay there, silent, trying to see how restrained he was by the zipcuffs.

"Andres fucked up, you know. He wasn't supposed to rob the place, but he went off the reservation. Thought he could outsmart his handlers. Then he found a fool to go along with him."

As Velez lay there, he tried, very carefully tried, to see how much flexibility and strength he could manage, bound by those zipcuffs, to lift and drive himself into the back doors and use his head to ram the handle.

The canyon road was rising, getting steeper. That would give him just a little more force.

Every now and then headlights passed.

He took a breath.

Better to die on the road.

He managed to rise up enough and throw himself.

ChiChi shouted as Luis hit the back doors.

They flew open. The van braked and swerved. Luis slammed against the asphalt, face first. The van skidded onto the shoulder. ChiChi tumbled into the roadway and came up furious, grabbing at his hand. Luis tried to caterpillar away. His nose was broken. He'd lost teeth. He was dazed and trying to breathe through the blood draining down into his mouth.

He looked to the darkness for headlights. From far up the road the trees lit, then darkened. A vehicle was making its way down the winding canyon. The three men lifted Luis to get him back in the van and he fought them, twisting wildly, screaming, striking out with his bound legs.

They just about had him when oncoming headlights flooded over them, and for a moment the men froze, and then a pickup truck went past, leaving only the hot red of the taillights—there, then gone.

CHAPTER 40

Inside the van ChiChi was furious and he kicked and kicked and kicked Velez. ChiChi was holding one hand. He'd broken two fingers—they were bent at the knuckles.

The van turned off Canyon Road and started up on a steep and rutted driveway. The shocks taking a beating, on and on the van shook and swayed before it finally stopped.

Dust drifted across the halogens and then all was dark.

They dragged Velez from the van. He was conscious and suffering and bloody, and they dragged him past three boats on trailers to a corrugated hangar of some kind with sliding doors.

ChiChi had gone on ahead. The hangar was a repair shop. He went to a workbench and dragged a chair from there to an open area. There were portable lanterns and he took one and turned it on and set it on the floor so the chair was all lit up.

ChiChi was so enraged he could barely contain himself. He kicked over trash bins and empty cans of paint and thinner. He told his people to cuff Velez to the chair as he walked along the corrugated walls of the shed, searching....

Finally, he bent over and came up with a rat dead in a trap. He dangled it, then dropped the trap in Velez's lap.

He went back to the workbench, looking among the tools, then came out of the half shadows holding a small butane blowtorch.

He fired it up.

"Let's get this show going," he said.

Velez's terror was so great he wished he'd die that fuckin' moment.

ChiChi held up the rat by the trap and put the blue white flame to its skull, turning it into something hideous.

He threw the rat aside.

"Well," said ChiChi.

Velez spit out blood. "You'll never get them. They're in a frozen meat locker I rent. And not in my name. And you know how many businesses there are in L.A. where you can rent lockers...Good fuckin' luck."

"Hold his head," said ChiChi.

Velez tried to bite the men's hands, their fingers. He spit in their faces but they eventually caged him with their arms around his throat and skull.

ChiChi leaned down.

Velez was looking into the face of unspeakable menace that was about to dish out a case of well dressed rage. He was going to die like the poor homeless bum he'd shot in the park and the strange creature he'd strangled, only his death would take a lot longer.

Velez could just make out that venomous stare at the edge of the flame and then the voice that spoke, "Let's start with one of your eyes."

CHAPTER 41

Ana had barely crawled out of bed, dragging along a hangover, when there came a knock at the door.

She called out, "Elias…if that's you…go fuck yourself."

"It's not Elias. It's Inspector Miller. We talked. I gave you my card."

Just what I need, she thought. She was still in her pajamas and didn't have on her prosthetic, so she crossed the room grabbing doorknobs and bureau tops for support. Then she leaned out a little bit from the waist up so she could see through the screen door.

"Can we talk?" said Miller.

"I'm in my pajamas," she said.

"Well, I could wait until you—"

"This isn't a fuckin' bus stop. You want to talk? I can hear you from in here."

She left him there on the porch like something unwanted and she went to make coffee. He followed along the porch because he could sort of see her through a grimy window.

"So…when do you start talking?" she said.

"I was up all night thinking through our conversation. Can you hear me alright?"

"Too well," she said.

"I call Orteig to ask him a few questions and he goes off the rails on me. And not long after he calls, the 800 tipline of that columnist at the *Weekly*…Why?"

Her answer—she turned on the water and filled the Melitta.

"Not long after, he calls your father, and a few hours later you're seen leaving Orteig's with a shoebox."

The water turned off.

She didn't say a thing.

"What's in the shoebox...some bullshit pictures you show me. I don't think so."

She appeared at the window. He could just make her out through the filthy screen. Her eyes a direct hit on him, the cig hanging from her lips, a hand rubbing the back of her bare neck. And he realized—it wasn't the Adderal, 'cause he had the same feeling he had last night.

"You and your father took something from the shoebox. Don't know if you were helping cover for him, were involved with him. But you're involved now. Well...tell me something!"

"Why not?" she said. "I have a couple of questions to throw at you. This is the third...fourth time I've seen you and every time you're in a different suit. And they're always expensive. You got a scam going on somewhere? Maybe working a sugar mommy? Or are you one of those hot and cold racetrack boys?"

"You load the gun, don't you?" he said.

"And that hotline. If Moe had done something criminal, why call the hotline? To confess? And when it came to Moe calling my father...Did you subpoena the phone records? I'll bet not. I told my father the first time I saw you, this guy is an outside the box type. He'll gas pedal it right off a cliff."

Miller stood there like the proverbial hanged man.

"And you came up with all that," he said, "while you're standing in your pajamas?"

"I'm not done yet. Here's the last of it. Are you ready?"

"I'm hanging on by my fingernails from anticipation."

"Some of what you said is right on point. Utterly true. Yeah... Now...what the fuck are you gonna do about it?"

CHAPTER 42

Ana entered her father's trailer unannounced.

"Ana…that you?"

"Yeah."

"Go fuck yourself."

She went to the breakfront and opened the top drawer and removed a Colt semi-automatic. He came out of the bathroom, his face covered with shaving cream. He was in his underwear, and those bony legs. She shook her head in dismay.

"Did you hear us?" she said.

"I heard."

She checked the weapon to make sure it was empty.

"You're not gonna kill him, are you?"

"Hadn't thought about it."

"I checked him out. Facebook, Twitter. Once upon a time he wanted to be an actor."

"He's got a look."

From the drawer she took two magazines for the automatic.

"Actors…they all take it up the ass," he said.

"That's one of the prerequisites, huh?"

"Yup."

"Even John Wayne."

Elias held up his razor like a scepter. "He was fuckin' Ward Bond for years."

She rummaged around in the drawer and found a box of shells.

"You plan on it getting bad?"

"I think so," she said. "Don't you?"

"You want the short answer?" he said, as he walked back into the bathroom.

CHAPTER 43

Landshark had a shooting range on the bottom floor of his estate. It was a premier job with bullet traps and ventilation so gas and shell fragments could be sucked out to avoid lead poisoning.

He even had beside it a two lane bowling alley, a real Brunswick classic piece of workmanship. *It's better to be rich and happy than it is to be rich and unhappy* — this he had embroidered into a huge mock needlepoint that hung on one wall.

He and Ana took turns at the target. He proved to Ana to be pretty damn good with a revolver.

"I don't sleep," he said, "so I need lots of interests. Especially ones that flatter my fake masculinity."

"You don't have a personal life, do you?" she said while reloading.

"No...and you don't seem to have one either."

She gave him a blunt look of agreement.

"You ever fuck a woman?" she said.

"Once...but they hadn't completely tranned yet."

With the gun loaded, she said, "I got this idea how we find Andres...if he's alive. But I need help to pull it off."

"What kind?"

"Money."

CHAPTER 44

Carter and Ellison had not seen or talked to Ana since their "excursion" into Mexico. But that was not unusual.

They ran their security and surveillance company out of a building downtown on Main Street, about a block from Amtrak and the river.

This was an industrial section of town and all the buildings were heavily secured. They got few visitors, and then usually by appointment. And they didn't recognize the man they saw on camera working the front door buzzer.

Carter hit the intercom. "Can we help you?"

Miller flashed his credentials. He was buzzed in.

Miller looked the place over. Talk about spartan. It was a large open space, with brick walls and plenty of high tech equipment. There was a partitioned office, kitchenette, bathroom, and shower.

Carter and Ellison both looked like they could handle any kind of business. Carter had a scar that went from his ear down into his shirt collar. They offered Miller a seat, they offered him coffee, they waited.

"I checked out your website. Ex-Army. Your creds are deep."

"We cover a fair amount of ground," said Carter.

"I bet," said Miller. "You work much with Ana Ride?"

The men glanced at each other. Miller picked up nothing in their expressions, and he was hunting.

"We hire her," said Carter, "when the situation calls for her expertise."

"She's quite the piece of work," said Miller. Then he waited.

"If you don't mind our asking," said Ellison, "how'd you come to connect us with Ana? We don't list people we hire on our site."

"You handled security for the Bieber concert at Universal…She got a thank you on the Bieber Twitter page for her good work…along with you guys. Google…it gets us all in the end. Harmless enough?"

"I guess," said Carter, "that depends on how you define harmless."

"Translation," said Ellison. "Why are you here…" He looked at Miller's business card. "Mr. Miller?"

"From the sixth of this month to the twelfth," said Miller, "was Ana Ride in your employ? Particularly the twelfth."

CHAPTER 45

It was seven o'clock on a Sunday morning and Ana Ride stood on the steps of All Saints Church in El Sereno. She was quite the lady that morning in a long skirt, conservative boots, and a beret. She was passing out flyers to every churchgoer.

The flyer had a picture of Antonin Andres—driver's license, Facebook—and Ana was asking each parishioner in a polite and quiet manner if they might know or at least had seen Andres at the church.

There was a hotline number on the flyer and the promise of a reward from the *L.A. Weekly* regarding information on the man's whereabouts for an article in the "Big Island, L.A." column that dealt with gun crime in Los Angeles.

Before each Mass she passed out flyers, talked with parishioners, and for each Mass she sat in the rear of the church and took in the service.

Nothing of interest or import happened until the ten o'clock Mass. A woman came up the church steps with two small boys in tow and an older woman alongside her. When she took the flyer, Ana saw the woman was adversely affected. She wouldn't make eye contact after that and silently walked away.

But before services began, the woman came out of the church and approached Ana. She was a statement of trepidation.

"I have a question," she said.

"Yes?"

The woman was holding up the flyer. "Information given to you would be…safe? I mean…protected from—"

"From anyone," said Ana.

"And the money…"

"Solid."

CHAPTER 46

Ana watched the woman from her seat as the last of the parishioners filed in. The woman glanced back once, then twice. Ana maintained eye contact as someone sat down beside her and said, "I almost didn't recognize you."

Ana looked to see it was the inspector.

"I like the beret," he said. "It's a good touch. Very Audrey Hepburn."

"Who?" said Ana.

He looked Ana over. "Perfectly impassive," he said. She was fuckin' with him, he was sure of it.

He had a flyer. "One of the parishioners dumped this," he said.

The Mass began and everyone stood.

"You want to talk to me about this?" he whispered.

"You got all of LAPD at your disposal. What the fuck do you need me to explain anything?"

CHAPTER 47

All Saints was on Portola Avenue. The parking lot and school were just across the way. It was a narrow street and, when church let out, crowded.

If there was a shooting to be done, it had to be done fast, and escape assured. The vehicle to be used was an older Plymouth with a painfully chipped paint job but a bully of an engine. It was also wearing stolen Arizona plates.

The shooters parked down Portola where the street curved but they could still see the front of the church. The windows were tinted and rolled up even though it was hot. There was a driver listening to music on a headset, and the shooter in the back, barefoot and smoking weed. They were both Catholic boys. And as far as killing on Sunday—it was a paycheck.

CHAPTER 48

Ana saw Miller knew the Mass, that he seemed genuinely connected to the spirit of it—that it wasn't just polite lip service.

The priest talked about the mass murder at the supermarket in Buffalo. And how human isolation and the breakdown of our institutions have created a deformed breed of humans who believe they can escape the emptiness of their existence through acts of violence, and that their personal desires, drives, demands to correct the real or imagined wrongs inflicted upon them, caused them to become harbingers of death.

And the weapon they carry is not an AR 15, or a handgun, knife, explosive device—the weapon is a loss of faith, and it not only is responsible for the death of the hunted, but that of the hunter.

CHAPTER 49

Julia Domingo, the assemblyperson for the district and a hard-core advocate for tenant rights in the 710 Corridor, made a special appearance near the end of the service. She was introduced by the priest with the promise of something "joyful and uplifting" to close out the service.

As Julia Domingo joined the priest up on the altar, a huge flatscreen television mounted on a high platform was rolled out from the sacristy, and followed by the All Saints choir, who lined up along the railing. You could see the flatscreen all the way to the back of the church.

Julia Domingo held up the remote and asked, "What is it we all need most?"

She flipped on the flatscreen. They were on YouTube and there was a freeze frame from the animated Netflix series Beat Bugs, about five humanized and hipster insects who live in a large backyard where they have had all kinds of adventures—usually to the accompaniment of a Beatles song.

Julia hit play and the scene came alive in all its gaudy wonderfulness and super wild set pieces to the Beatles classic "All You Need Is Love."

The choir rocked along with the characters, and kids in the pews began to clap to the music and some stood and a few sang the refrain and others stumbled through lyrics they didn't know or couldn't remember, and even some adults were clapping and standing and rocking to the music.

The scene, thought Ana, could look silly and infantile in its sweetness. Some, she thought, could even see it as a cynical and clumsy attempt by a politician to gain brownie points for themselves with their voters. Ana certainly did.

But she wondered, all this around her—were the people genuinely feeling god inside them? Did all this really connect to something grander? Or was it just...? Did they believe? And Miller there beside her, clapping to the music like the rest, an expression of sincerity on his face. She was almost tempted to ask him...almost, anyway.

CHAPTER 50

Ana was one of the first out of the church and stood on the top step in the blazing heat and lit a cigarette while parishioners began filing out. The kids, you could hear them back there, still going full throat with the *Beat Bugs*. And who could blame them?

The woman from earlier came out with what had to be her mother. She passed silently and on purpose within feet of Ana.

"Any time," Ana half whispered. "It will be alright."

There was a slight flicker to the woman's face muscles before she looked away from Ana.

Miller stepped from the darkness, and once beside Ana, said, "It came to me in church. You know what I think about you?"

Ana blew smoke out her nostrils. "I don't believe I can dig that deep."

"You're a displaced person, Ana Ride. That's the key to you. You're not exactly on the main highway of life…but you can see the main highway from where you are. Yeah…if Thelma and Louise had a kid, you'd be it."

CHAPTER 51

She was just about to thank him for the "rare and gifted personality profile" when she heard something that felt wrong. Something like she'd felt a thousand times when she was in combat. It was a car engine, a rough and nasty growler shifting gears and coming on way, way too fast for the narrow street and the people there.

She was probably the first to see the Plymouth coming up through the curve as she stood on the top of the church steps closest to the street looking over Miller's shoulder.

The car sped into the curve with its tinted windows, and then through a shaft of sunlight there was the barrel of a long gun— maybe an AR 15—starting to neck its way out the open window behind the driver and Ana's body went into professional overdrive.

Ana started to shout, "Get down! Gunman! Get down!" She shoved Miller from the steps and he toppled to the sidewalk and in all that panic she crouched, shoving people toward cover while others scattered and scrambled back into the church as the front walls of the adobe church was sprayed with bullets.

CHAPTER 52

Elias was outside his trailer listening to Fidelma rant about inflation and gas prices and what it cost her at the supermarket that morning when he heard through his living room window—breaking news on Fox. There had been some kind of drive by at a church in Los Angeles.

He tried to politely cut Fidelma loose and when that didn't work with the old bitch, he resorted to "You get what you vote for, girl."

She knew what he meant and shouted at his back, "White supremacist loser!"

He gave her the power sign as his parting shot.

CHAPTER 53

He was watching a scene that had played out in an endless loop of police cars, yellow tape, and a trim and prim reporter, relaying the news in how many American cities. This reporter explained how three people had been wounded, one seriously, in what looked like a drive by.

Elias called Ana every five minutes, only to end up in voicemail, until she finally called him back.

"I'm looking at the news," he said. "Was that the—"

"Yeah. We'll talk when I get home."

"Where are you?"

"Liquor store."

She'd hung up before he'd had a chance to ask if she was alright and he was furious with himself because it should have been the first thing out of his mouth as it was the first thing in his heart, but his heart did not have much of a vote in how he acted because his expertise was in being heartless.

CHAPTER 54

She came into her father's trailer still dressed like a lady, but all drained out and a little drunk, carrying a bottle of triple sec she'd been drinking from.

Elias stood as she entered.

"I didn't get to ask you on the phone," he said, "if you were alright. Everything went so fast and—"

She waved him off.

"I didn't want you to think I—"

She was miles away.

"There were a lot of kids in the church," she said. "They were having this thing with music from an old cable series." She was pacing. "It was moving, in its own way, and...forget it. There were a lot of kids in the church and the next moment...It was combat all over again."

She kept pacing. Slugged from the bottle. She had a lot on her mind.

"They said they thought it was some kind of drive by," said Elias.

She stared at him like that was the stupidest fuckin' things she'd ever heard.

She walked over to a photograph on the wall of her and her mother from way back when—a mother, a daughter child, a Christmas tree all decorated up, and a pair of smiles lost to the unpleasant dust of time.

"I wonder," said Ana, "what she'd look like today…What she'd be like…With all those extra years under her belt. What she'd feel about things. You ever wonder, Elias?"

He didn't know what to say to avoid what he knew was coming.

"All you need," said Ana, "is a piece of wood hung around your neck by a rope with the words burned into the wood: GUILTY AS HELL."

CHAPTER 55

She took another drink of triple sec.

"They didn't keep you there for questioning? Or to give a statement?"

"Change the subject when it's got you in a clinch…I slipped their noose, Elias. But they'll show up. He'll show up."

"Miller?"

She thought of what he'd said outside of the church.

"Did you know there's a thought going around that I'm a displaced person?"

"Displaced from what?"

She let out a tight laugh.

"Elias, you think you could kick my ass right now? Even with my handicap? The way you kicked Mom's ass?"

He sat. He rested his forearms on his thighs. Bowed his head. He didn't want any part of this.

"I think I could kick your guts out. What say you?" She sang, "When I was younger…I should have known better…."

She kicked the coffee table with her prosthetic foot.

"Look up…let's do the eye contact thing," she demanded.

He looked up.

"Do you have faith?" she said.

"What?"

"Faith…do you have faith?"

"Faith?"

"What am I, talking Chinese here?" she said.

"What kind of faith?"

"Jesus Christ. Plain old straight off the shelf faith."

"Faith in what?" he said.

"Forget it. You answered my question."

She started out. But she was not done. She came around like a prizefighter.

"I wish I believed in all the stupid things I saw today. I wish I had faith in them. And you know why?"

"I'm afraid I don't."

"Because then I could forgive you for…for your malicious mal-treatment of my mother…or I could forgive myself for not killing your stinkin' ass way back then."

CHAPTER 56

Ana was at her dining table eating a couple of fried eggs and drinking triple sec from the bottle. She kept checking the hotline for the call that didn't come.

There was a knock on her screen door and she called out, "Come on in, Miller."

When the screen door shut behind him and he saw Ana across

the room at a table, eating, he said, "How'd you know it was me?"

"We hope for the best, but expect the worst."

"You got right out of there, didn't you?"

"You want a couple of fried eggs? A drink?"

He slipped his hands into his pockets, kind of cruised the place, looking at photos, family stuff on a breakfront. Whatever would give him insight into her.

"Did they ask you what you were doing at that service?" she said.

"I made up a story. They bought it."

"You didn't tell them you followed me there?"

"I'm waiting to see if you have any answers about the flyer that satisfy me."

"I don't," she said. She then took down a fried egg in one swallow.

"We're gonna have to deal with this," he said.

"That's what I'm doing."

She got up. She was wearing a black tee shirt and black jeans. There was red lettering on the tee shirt that said HERSELF.

She wasn't wearing her prothesis and used the table to keep her steady. She pointed toward the couch right near where he was standing.

"My boot there. You want to toss it to me, please?"

He picked it up, looked it over. It was a slick specialty item. And real snakeskin. He walked over and handed it to her. She sat and went to work putting it on.

"What's the word on the people that were wounded?" she said.

"No deaths."

"That…at least…is good news."

She got up and motioned for him to follow her. Outside, she held up her car remote.

"You know how to drive a stick?"

"No," he said, somewhat embarrassed suddenly.

"My leg hurts from today," she said. "You'll have to drive."

"Where we going?"

"Does it matter?"

It didn't really. He pointed to a worn and dinged up Explorer.

They both got in. As he started up the engine, she scanned a dashboard that was a mess of files, notes, paper cups. And the floor, no better. Then she noticed something. "What do we have here?" she said.

She reached down and up she comes with a mortar and pestle.

"Perfect for grinding up those pills and drugs. You got your own little apothecary here, Mr. Miller."

He grabbed for it, but she was too quick.

"Stainless steel," she said. "Those powders can't get down into the grooves. Very nice."

She noted there was some residue, which she ran a wet fingertip over. Put to her tongue. "Let's see what we got here." She tasted. "Adderall...?"

CHAPTER 57

Ana had Jayden pull into a bare strip mall just off of Topanga Canyon Boulevard. She led him into a bar called *The Rabbit Hole*.

"Alice in Wonderland in the western Valley," she said, opening the bar door. "Only in L.A., man. Only in L.A."

When you entered, sure enough, you were greeted with a hedge maze and the looking glass, and there you were, taking this funky, deep dive into literary atmosphere with hand carved bar seats and life size chess pieces, the Ace of Spades, the Queen of Hearts, and bartendresses all done up like characters straight out of Lewis Carroll's treasured imagination.

"Everything about Los Angeles is something else," she said, "isn't it?"

He took a moment to really look into her barlit stare. "And translated," he said, "that means…everyone in Los Angeles is someone or something else."

She gave him a good, on point smile.

"You're all right," he said.

"All right hardly describes me. Let's order me a drink, then you start firing away."

CHAPTER 58

Jayden sat with a club soda watching Ana across from him at the table drinking down some jet fueled concoction they specialized in at the bar.

"Don't be jealous, Miller," she said. "If there's ever a next time… I'll drive."

He unfolded the flyer he had saved in his pocket. "What's this about?"

"I'm working for William Worth…aka Land—"

"I know who he is."

"—as a researcher slash investigator in training."

"Why is Andres so important to him?"

"Is he?"

She played with the crucifix she now wore around her neck.

"You're offering a reward for information—"

"My employer is offering the reward, not me. Why is he so important to you?"

"You know what I was told on my way to your place?"

"No idea," she said.

"Andres worked for a time at the gun shop that was robbed."

"You got that from the flyer?"

"I was curious after seeing the flyer, so I called in."

He kept on. "Here's what I feel…Orteig told Worth or he told you about this man. For what reason…That's yet to learn. We got people going downtown right now. Andres has a place on Main Street, but you've probably been there."

She sat back. Her look expressed real plausibility to that statement.

"Why did you go to the church with this flyer? Were you looking for Andres, or someone connected to him?"

"I went to the church for the same reason you did."

"Are we gonna be part footrace, part prize fight?" he said.

Before she could answer, Ana was cut off by a text. When she read it, she told Miller, "I have to deal with this. So I'm gonna cut you loose for a few minutes."

She left quickly. Too quickly.

She was in the parking lot that fronted Roscoe Boulevard, calling a number. As cars sped by, she picked up a woman's voice.

"Hello…?"

"This is Ana Ride, getting back to you."

"I'm the lady from today at church. We talked."

"Yes."

"I want to meet, but it has to be so I'm protected. And it's secret.

As you can see I have two children."

From her shoulder bag Ana got out a pen to write with, but she had nothing to write on, so she used her palm. "Do you have a place? A time? Or do you want to get back to me with a few ideas?"

"I prayed about this all afternoon," said the woman. "There are reasons to be very afraid. For you also."

CHAPTER 59

Jayden Miller had come out of the bar as Ana just finished writing and started back in. She smiled at him. "Wrong number," she said.

He grabbed her by the arm with the hand she'd written on. She fought loose from his grip before he got a look. But there was writing there alright.

"You just go right for the deep water, don't you?" he said.

"And what about you? Now…you want to go back into the bar and pick up where we left off? Or call it a night?"

"Call it a night."

They didn't speak for the few miles from *The Rabbit Hole* until she said, "Is this the sizing up phase? Where we each make the list of pros and cons about the other?"

He braked at her trailer, leaned across her, and opened her door. She got out and leaned back in. "I think we almost had a good time tonight. I feel we were *that* close." She held her thumb and index finger just a breath apart.

"If you think you're getting out of here tonight," he said, "I'll be watching. And I'll have your ass DUI'd."

He pulled away.

CHAPTER 60

It wasn't twenty minutes when Ana's truck swung out of the trailer park and started down Topping Canyon Boulevard. Jayden had parked across the way at Stony Point, that shitass Explorer of his tucked back in a reef of shadows. He'd done a little Adderall when he'd parked and started to feel that gambler's focus. He sat back and waited for the dopamine to tone down his impulsivity—and here came the girl's pickup.

She was either behind the wheel—or she'd enlisted Elias to drive the truck and hopefully bait Jayden into laying chase.

Miller believed it would be her behind the wheel. That she was slick as those rattlesnake boots she wore. He didn't lay chase, though. He had an idea of his own. He wanted her to feel she was smarter than him.

Just to be sure, he drove back to the park and cruised their trailers. Through the slatted blinds there was Elias, carrying a plate of food and a beer to his trusty recliner and an awaiting television.

CHAPTER 61

Ana followed Maritza's directions. She parked a block from the house and instead of coming to the front door made her way down the unlit alley. She had on a black leather coat and a black newsboy hat, and with her black jeans and tee shirt she went along from shadow to shadow unseen, like the trained soldier that she was, until she reached the garage with its slight list and stark graffiti. She came up the narrow walkway alongside it to a ratchety gate Maritza left open.

The back of the house was dark, but Maritza must have been watching because when Ana was about halfway across the yard, the kitchen door slipped open slowly and silently.

The women met in the unlit doorway.

"No one saw you?" said Maritza.

"No one saw me."

Ana followed Maritza into the kitchen. There was a single light on above the breakfast table. The television was the only light in the rest of the first floor. Maritza seemed smaller and more fragile than at church.

"My boys are upstairs. My mother also. I told them a woman would be coming over who might need some help with making a dress. I'm a part time seamstress…plus I work at the church."

CHAPTER 62

Maritza had Ana sit at the table. She offered her coffee. She peeked out the blinds.

"I'm sorry to make you go through all this," said Maritza. "But you see, I believe the shooting was meant for me."

"How do you know such a thing? It could be just as the news reported…a drive by. And I heard coming over here your assemblyperson…Domingo…is having a press conference down here in the Corridor about the shooting and what she suspects."

Ana said all this, but she did not believe it.

They sat there afterward in silence. Like people alone and playing solitaire.

"Do you want to tell me?" said Ana.

Maritza got up. There was a table in the hall with a small statue of the Holy Mother and another of Christ. And there were candles, which she lit. She was, Ana suspected, praying.

Maritza went and peeked out the blinds one more time and then sat. She folded her hands and then told the whole story of the last night with Luis in this very kitchen.

How this man—ChiChi—approached Luis in the parking lot outside Las Ranas. And how, along with two other pumped up thugs, he followed, then chased Luis when he was jogging. She described the man—ChiChi—as her husband described him. She described his car as her husband had described it. And then Maritza took a few moments to compose herself and told Ana about the crime. And how her husband swore all things true that he spoke. Only they were not. He'd said Andres had killed the homeless man and then he and Luis fought and he killed Andres in self defense.

"I believe," said Maritza, "he was lying about these things for my sake and the children's sake. I am sorry to say this, but I say it."

"And you haven't heard from him since that night?"

"I saw him walk up that alley to the street...and then he was gone."

The next logical question: "Where do you think he is now?"

"With god, I hope."

"You didn't take this to the police?"

"Would I be here with you now if I had?"

"Why not...really?"

"I have my reasons...the money among them."

"Do you think they want you dead because you might know things...like about this ChiChi?"

Among other things.

"Such as the weapons?" Ana continued.

"Of course."

"I don't know how to say this without it being harsh. If they caught your husband, wouldn't they go to any...extreme...to learn of the weapons' whereabouts?"

"Yes, but in this they failed."

"And you know this because...?"

Maritza sat back. She looked around the room as if someone might overhear, then said, "I have the weapons."

CHAPTER 62

Maritza got up and went to the counter where there were two mini torchlights. She handed one to Ana, who stood. They had been right there the whole time, thought Ana, and she'd never noticed.

She followed the woman out and down the walkway to the back of the garage, where there was a tear in the chain link fence around the abandoned house next door. Maritza bent down and squeezed herself through, with Ana clumsily negotiating the opening behind her.

"It's empty," said Maritza. "Been empty a year. And all fenced off."

At the kitchen door, Maritza took out a key. "I used to know the people that lived here. They were very old and friends of my mother...We looked out for them."

Ana was led through the pitch dark house. Maritza stopped at a door that led to the cellar. Ana tapped Maritza's arm. "I wear a pros- thesis," whispered Ana, "so I have to be careful."

"Lean into me," said Maritza.

Once down in the cellar, with the door closed behind them, Maritza turned on the torchlight. The cellar bloomed up out of the nothingness.

"It's alright," Maritza said. "Luis blacked out all the windows for the people that used to live here."

Ana flipped on her torchlight and panned across the windows. They were blacked out alright. As for the cellar, those windows only added to its utterly rank atmosphere. It was a living, breathing fire hazard down there that smelled like a sewer. There was garbage everywhere and wadded up blankets and tarps with clusters of animal unnameables.

"Where are the weapons?" said Ana.

Maritza pointed her light down through a pyre of ruined furniture, drawers, paint cans, sections of roof composite, PVC piping, a TV dish, and other indistinguishable refuse from your basic middle class life.

But beneath all that was a section of wooden slats covering a hole in the flooring, and with that light Ana leaned down and could just make out what had to be the zippers and shiny bordering of a canvas duffel.

CHAPTER 63

The women were back in Maritza's house and Maritza had pulled out a bottle of wine to calm the nerves. She opened up to Ana about her life, her kids, her fatally flawed husband, when there came a knock at the door.

A startled Maritza rose from her seat and peeked out into the hallway. You could see through the living room curtains a police car parked out front.

"I'll stay back here," said Ana.

When she answered the door there was Officer Engel, who Maritza knew, as he was friendly with her husband.

"Is something wrong?" she said.

"I was just checking on you and the boys. We know you attend All Saints, so my wife thought—"

"It was terrible," said Maritza, "but we're okay. And thank you both."

"Well...you have our number."

He turned, then stopped. "By the way...I've been trying to get hold of Luis for the last couple of days. I even stopped by his apartment."

Maritza gathered herself and rested a hand on her chest. "The last we talked he was going upstate to see about a job. But, of course, with Luis that could mean anything. Including some girlfriend he has stashed away."

He went to leave, then stopped again. "One more thing...Did you get one of these? My wife did."

It was the flyer. She felt suddenly pale and sick to her stomach. She wondered if he would see this in her.

"I got one."

"Do you recognize the man...or know what it might be about?"

She had to struggle to look him in the eye. "No," she said. "Why do you ask?"

"Because everyone's on edge, that's why. So...be careful."

CHAPTER 64

A half hour later, Engel pulled into a gas station so he could hit the head.

He latched the door and stood in that flat white tile light with water from the toilet on the floor and made a call.

It was ChiChi who answered.

CHAPTER 65

The sun was spidering up the windows of Landshark's office. He sat at his computer, an exhausted Ana sprawled on a leather couch.

She had remoted Worth the secret footage of Miller taken by her camera in the bar. She had done the same with the footage of Maritza Velez.

"He's a nice looking man," Worth said of the investigator.

"As far as nice looking men go," said Ana.

"They go pretty far," added Worth.

"Yeah," said Ana. "But they're real gas guzzlers when it comes to self gratification."

Worth laughed out loud. "That's a direct hit if ever I heard one."

Worth replayed the footage taken in the basement. "I've emailed one of my attorneys that we need to construct a deal that will work with Velez and her situation...but we've got to be sure what we're doing."

Ana sat up and started to shed her boots.

"You saw the weapons, you heard Velez," he said.

The images were inconclusive. Vague. And Worth said so.

Ana admitted that was true as she took off her tee shirt and jeans.

"Velez didn't leave any prints, did she?"

"Her husband is LAPD. He warned her."

"And you—"

"No."

He looked up from the computer and there was Ana, stark naked and holding her jeans.

"How…did you get into the duffel?" said one very surprised gentleman.

She took a stiletto from her jeans pocket and snapped open the needlepoint blade.

"Perfect for zippers…What's the matter? Never seen a naked chick with a stiletto?"

"Only in my dreams."

She pointed the blade toward the bathroom. "I'm gonna get a shower."

"I'd say make yourself at home," said Worth, "but…you already have."

Ana rabbit hopped from the couch to the desk, then on to the bathroom door. "Remember," she said, "we don't officially know those weapons are stolen or part of a crime. Until their serial numbers are reported. After that—"

"We qualify as accessories to the crime," said Worth, "if we don't report them."

Ana leaned against the bathroom door. Worth was caught up in a thought or two.

"Is it about the money?" Ana asked.

"I have money to burn. Besides, there is something here. Why didn't they just pay off Velez and be done with him?"

Ana was leaning against the doorjamb, only now twirling the

stiletto in her fingers like some kind of majorette.

Worth was staring at this bit of action. Ana saw it.

"When I was in the Marines," she said, "and I was edgy and thinking, it got to be a habit. Now...what's on your mind?"

"You."

CHAPTER 66

Julia Domingo lived in a three story house in the 3200 block of Tampico Avenue. The house was in what was known as the Elephant Hill section of El Sereno. The Hill was twenty acres of open space that overlooked the city. It was mostly grass and brush that burned brown in the summer.

Her house was on a two acre lot. It was old California, built of clapboard around 1900, and belonged to her grandfather, who was a recurring character on the old black and white television series *The Cisco Kid*. The upper two stories had decks with a commanding view of those magnificent Los Angeles sunsets.

The main floor served as the assemblyperson's headquarters, the top floor her residence. Her brother, Daniel Domingo, lived on the bottom floor where he served as his sister's campaign manager and de facto chief of staff.

It had been a long and harrowing day. Julia leaned against the deck railing and looked out into a familiar nightscape of small bird-cagelike homes nesting on the hills. This scene always fed her with serenity. But tonight there was a squad car parked in her entry, and another at the far end of the property.

Everyone had been ushered out. There was only her and her

brother, and he sat in an easy chair working his tablet, preparing for the next wave of demands.

"How are you?" said Daniel.

"Sometimes I feel it will all come to nothing."

Daniel was not a Homeric character. Just a small, slim, smart man of thirty five whose life and career was his sister's life and career—or so everyone either thought or believed. He got up and joined his sister at the railing. They shared the night air.

"When you speak tomorrow, you come out with pure passion," said Daniel. "No buildup. This was an attempt on your life."

"We don't know that."

"See down there?" He was pointing to the squad car. "What does that say? And remember...Caltrans and the developers, the builders, the money hawkers, the mayor, the tax collector, they're not going to let you carry a few hundred tenants to victory so they can be out a few hundred million...or more. You're sticking it to billionaires."

"We still don't know if it was true."

"They could have hit the nine o'clock Mass, the eight, the eleven, the noon."

"I understand."

"There's been rumors," said Daniel. "Right...LAPD said so."

"Which you helped spread."

"I don't instigate. I retweet."

"You know what everyone will say. What the press will insinuate. That we are exploiting this tragedy for our selfish purposes."

"We are," said Daniel. He held up his arms as if the heavens had opened. "That's exactly what we're doing. And our selfish purpose has a purpose that is not selfish...and what is that? The good fight. Tenants who were promised by Caltrans in the 710 Corridor that the houses and apartments they lived in and paid rent on and maintained for half a century…earned them…the right to buy into those properties in first position. And not be shoved aside because of America's greatest enemy: corporate greed."

He had gotten passionate and grabbed his sister by the arms to make his point. He calmed himself. "Listen…these are the kinds of moments, situations, events, tragedies, whatever you call them, however you frame them, that can turn a little known but hardworking assemblyperson into a national figure."

"Especially one they tried to murder," she said.

"Just act like it's true, girl…and it will be. Remember…no one can flaw you for showing courage."

CHAPTER 67

The news conference was to take place in the front yard of an empty house in the path of the 710 Corridor. The house was just across the street from one Maritza Velez and the fenced off Caltrans property beside it, where the weapons were hidden.

Ana stood there smoking at the rear of the gathering of press cameras and locals and thought not only about the sheer irony of it all but the threat of potential violence that could come visiting. The LAPD thought so, from the excessive number of officers.

Ana was quietly filming the crowd with the crucifix camera on the chance she and Worth might learn something, see something— or someone—who would prove to be another "brick in the wall" as the song says.

Maritza was already there with her children. Ana had learned their names were Javier and Jorge, ages ten and nine, respectively.

They looked very much like their father, but thankfully that's where the similarity ended, or so said Maritza.

She passed Ana without so much as a glance and joined the other tenants who had been part of the video plea on YouTube for their cause. Two black SUVs showed and out stepped Julia Domingo and her brother with their aides and security. Daniel Domingo made a show of extra security to heighten the feeling of threat.

Julia Domingo walked to the microphone, thanked the people for coming, thanked god no one was killed at the shooting, and then followed her brother's advice and struck right at the heart of the matter.

"The reason for this gathering is a complete and utter disgrace. And another study in violence.

"Rumor suggests I was the target...the reason...for the shooting at All Saints Church.

"Whether true or not, let me say this clearly: I would rather these creatures that came to a place of worship do make me the target of their depraved behavior.

"And why do I suggest such a thing?" She pointed to the tenants and complainants of the Corridor standing behind her. "To bring awareness to the cause they're fighting for...."

CHAPTER 68

"She's full of shit."

Ana turned. It was Miller...unfortunately.

"It's you," she said.

"You say that like you've just been diagnosed with a fatal disease."

She took a long drag on her cigarette, as if that were answer enough. Then she said, "So why is she full of shit? *Illuminate* me."

"Her…the queen of self aggrandizement. *'Make me the target'…* She's already running for mayor…in her fuckin' dreams. And don't think she's not making a not too subtle pitch that Caltrans or some developer might snuff her out because of her stand on the tenant issue. Joan of Arc, she ain't. This is her brother talking too…he's a slick. You know I've heard for a couple of years now the two of them fuck each other."

Ana took another long drag on her cigarette.

"Seriously," he said.

"Thanks for the gossip," said Ana.

"What are you doing here?" said Miller.

"What are *you* doing here?" said Ana.

"I'm working."

"So am I."

"What a coincidence."

She looked him over. "Is that another suit?"

"I have six suits. One for each day of the week."

"The week has seven days."

"No kidding. By the way…I tried to get a subpoena to search yours and Miss Landshark's place."

"No luck?"

"He knows every judge, prosecutor, their wives, husbands. He's donated to all of them. Besides…this is California, where the criminal has the upper hand."

He tapped the *Weekly* press pass she had clipped to her belt.

"I have a reporter question. What if the shooters yesterday were after you?"

"I could say…better me than the others."

93

"You suddenly remind me of Julia Domingo."

"You mean I'm self aggrandizing...or that I sleep with my brother?"

CHAPTER 69

The news, as always, can't keep up. On the runway of humanity one tragic flight after another lifts off into a maligned sky. People are murdered, beaten, robbed, raped, destroyed for—fill in the blanks.

Over the course of a day or two, the flyers passed out at the church were chased down by reporters and police alike. What came of it: Antonin Andres had worked at the Academy gun shop for a time. Antonin Andres had been in any number of illegal and sleazy enterprises. Antonin Andres had been missing since just before the robbery.

Everyone was at ground zero after that. Well...not everyone.

CHAPTER 70

Worth was not at all surprised when he received a phone call from Julia Domingo. His attitude in these matters was more a state of affairs than a state of mind. She asked if they could meet, and knowing his phobia—it wasn't exactly a secret—suggested she come to the estate. That she would be alone except for a driver.

He had the meal catered, but performed the task of server himself, with Ana's help, so as not to leave any channel open for word to leak out.

The lunch was in his formal dining room, which had been a centerfold picture in *Architectural Digest*. The magazine, of course, had seen fit to remove the photograph of William Worth posing as Saint Sebastian, naked and being martyred by arrows.

They talked politics and they talked L.A. and it was all foreplay and drivel as far as Landshark was concerned, and that was essentially what he said to the assemblyperson.

"I couldn't agree with you more," said Julia. "So if you should learn of or suspect a threat against me, I will respect your secrecy in this matter if I can at least be forewarned."

"As for me," said Landshark, "if you learn or suspect certain information that may further my attempt to uncover this robbery and murder, can I count on you to feed me such information through any back channel of your choosing?"

"I think we understand each other," said Julia.

They shook hands.

Ana and Worth stood in the doorway as the assemblyperson was chauffeured home.

"What do you think?" said Landshark.

"I hear a rattlesnake in our future," said Ana.

"She is quietly charming...demure...intelligent. So I ask," said Worth, "can you see her naked and sucking her brother's dick?"

"I can not only see that," said Ana. "I can see her slitting his throat afterward."

CHAPTER 71

The Landshark flyer hotline ticked up with alleged tips. Most were crackpots or people venting. A lot like Twitter and other social media in that respect. But there were always a few that loomed with possibility—or threat.

One of these felt queerly true, substantive—the caller left no name, no number. Stated only that he had been witness to what looked like a fight by a parked squad car between a policeman and a suspect. And that the subdued suspect was placed in a beat up white van.

Ana drove to the location on Valley Boulevard and judged, if true, would be close to the night and time that Luis Velez left his wife's house on Shelley, never to be seen again.

Landshark called a contact he had at the department. There was no such fight reported, no such arrest, no such incident where a suspect was placed in a beat up white van.

The caller, it seemed, had not reported this to the police but had come to the hotline.

"Why?" said Ana, sitting in her parked car on Valley Boulevard. "Why would the caller connect that incident to the flyer?"

Worth stood in his office near the windows. He could not answer this. He looked out over a city, bright, warm. The kind of day that flooded one with good feeling. But he did not have a good feeling.

CHAPTER 72

There was no wind that night and the air had all the hallmarks of a bad omen. That California dry and brittle air, you know, the one that rendered everything with such clarity that the skyline from Mount Washington all the way to the airport was like something created out of Technicolor.

It was the perfect night for arson.

Ana always kept extra clothes in her truck. She stayed over at the Worth estate. She was tense and moody and did not answer her father's calls or texts. She could not sleep and wandered the house like something feline.

"What is it?" said Worth. "What's going on inside you?"

"The rattlesnake," she said.

"What does that mean?"

"It means...when I hear a snake rattling in my head...it says...'Warning.'"

"That come from your time in the war?"

"Long before.

Landshark was standing over her. She seemed as vulnerable as she did tough.

"The call..." said Landshark.

"Yeah," she said. "The rattlesnake tells me we're in play."

CHAPTER 73

She lay in bed stiffly. She fought to keep her eyes closed and find peace. Thank god she failed. She had been weaned on night sounds, on sounds that just don't belong. Like footsteps somewhere nearby on dry, dead camellias.

She slipped on her prosthesis before she sat up so the blood would not swell the stub and make the prosthesis unfit. She slipped on a shoulder holster and stood.

She called Landshark on the intercom.

"What it is?" he said.

"Something outside the wall on the fire road side of the house."

He looked at several surveillance screens. He was about to say, "I don't see—" when there was a burst of flames. Something had been tossed over the wall. A gazebo near the back corner of the compound was suddenly engulfed in flames. The bougainvillea that draped the roof burst into leaflets of fire; the olive tree beside it burned with a choking smoke.

Landshark came running out of the house, barefoot, a rangy freak in a silk kimono carrying a fire extinguisher and calling the fire department in a wailing birdlike voice.

Ana grabbed him as he rushed past. "I'm going to try and find out who's there."

She ran as best she could up along the compound wall to a gate by the patio. She slipped out and peered down the dusty fire road, then hustled across it and on into the trees. She had capture or killing in mind.

The air stank of gasoline and the sky was alive with cinders of light.

She held her position in a stand of trees and listened. With the gun at her side, knowing. In all likelihood for anyone escaping the scene, this might not have been the safest way out, but it was damn well the quickest.

Then she heard not one, but two bodies thrashing their way through the brush and with some distance between them.

She fired a shot in their direction.

The shot was answered by a flurry of rapid flashes in the darkness and the report of gunfire echoing across the hills.

She returned fire, not at them but behind them. More shots sparked far up the hillside.

She fired again. But she was not trying to hit them.

She was driving them toward the fire road.

CHAPTER 74

Worth came running out of the gate, out of breath, speckled with ash, his kimono flapping wide open.

Ana stepped into the fire road and ordered him to stay where he was and she fired, but she fired off into the trees.

"What are you doing?"

"Fire department on the way?"

"Yes."

"Police will be right on their tail."

Ana fired again.

There was no return fire.

"Come on," she said.

Once in the house they reviewed the surveillance tape of one camera that had been hidden in trees along the shoulder of the fire road that led to the street. As the tape rewound, through the night stillness, a sudden rush backwards of shadows.

Landshark played the footage forward and slow—what did they get? The two shadows passing through the most obscure patch of street light were men—youths really—dark skinned. There, then gone.

"You were trying to drive them to the fire road and the camera," said Worth.

Ana nodded.

On another screen a fire truck was turning off the road. Ana looked up at Landshark. "We have a decision to make," she said.

He understood. "Do we show them the footage...or withhold it?"

CHAPTER 75

While they put down the flames and made sure nothing spread to the brush across the fire road, Ana and Landshark were in the office being questioned.

Miller arrived about that time and was led to the office through the dining room and past that photo of a naked William Worth being slain by arrows and thought, What the fuck?

Miller entered the office as Ana was explaining about hearing the noise outside, then seeing the flames and calling to Worth while she strapped on a gun—she still had on the shoulder holster.

Miller listened but kept to himself, pacing the office, checking the room out, the most minute details warranting his attention, particularly the surveillance cameras. Ana watched him as she went on about going out to the fire road. Miller had walked over to a wall of photographs of Worth with celebrities from movies, music, politics, many of which were taken in that very office.

He was going over those photographs for a long, long time, she thought.

"You fired at them," the officer said to Ana.

"I fired at the trees where I heard they were."

"And your intention was to—"

"You bet," she said.

Miller had drifted over to the bulletin boards with the cases Landshark was working on. As he checked them out, he picked up a look that passed between that bizarre character in the kimono and one Ana Ride.

"You say you saw them on the fire road, near the street," said the officer.

"For a heartbeat," she said. "Vaguely. Two youths…late twenties, tops…dark."

"They wouldn't be the shooters from the church," said Miller from across the room.

"I couldn't quite say."

Then Ana excused herself and went to the bar, where Miller joined her.

It wasn't just a bar—it had the most expensive coffee maker, espresso maker, cappuccino maker.

"It's like a fuckin' movie set," said Miller.

"Sorry for pulling you away from a card game. It was a card game, wasn't it?"

"I should thank you. You probably saved me my rent payment."

"What do you want? Espresso, cappuccino?" she said.

"I want to live like this."

She nodded. "You'll need an espresso for that. Lots of it."

She made him an espresso.

"You're good," he said. "You know that?"

"Excuse me?"

She treated him to a stare that could cut right to the heart of you.

"Like ice," he said.

CHAPTER 76

A call came in on Worth's private line, but it was for Ana. He held off telling her until everyone, including Miller, had gone. Then he handed the phone to her. "The Domingo campaign called."

An aide named Marcus wanted to set a meet for Ana and Daniel Domingo the following night. The time was late, the place in question was The Rock Inn.

It wasn't exactly like it sounded. This was not some faux hipster club in Los Feliz, Echo Park, or DTLA. This was a tavern out by Lake Hughes, an unincorporated area northwest of Palmdale in the Angeles National Forest.

It was built back in '28 and made all of river stones. The clientele were misfits and misbehavers, motorcycle gang members, and a lot of the crowd you find around a pool table.

"Did you ask him why the meet had to be out there?" said Worth.

"What's the point?" said Ana. "You won't get the truth."

CHAPTER 77

Ana agreed to a truce with her father, at least for the time being. Elias watched as his daughter got ready for the meet.

"I know The Rock Inn. Been there, got drunk there. I could drive out and keep watch."

"I'll be alright."

"You sure going alone is the right move?"

"I won't be alone."

She pulled up a pant leg. Had a nasty revolver tucked in her prosthesis boot.

"I regret sending you to Orteig's place."

"You and I have more serious regrets to deal with."

She started out. He followed.

"I feel like I should ask you again," said Elias, "about why you're taking this on."

She stood in the dark by her truck door.

"I'm trying to jump past the lost years of one Ana Ride. I'm trying to erase my…irrelevancy."

But it was more inclusive than that. In her car, playing her music loud, driving through the pure darkness up through Castaic to her destination at Lake Hughes. It was the fix of life, even the threat of life she needed, wanted to confront. It was being there, being in it, so you feel a little straighter when you walk, the limp a little less noticeable. Where you test your own brand of momentary permanence against the inevitable impermanence of existence.

It was like being back in the military—only better. Where death, like life, is complete. And you are in command.

CHAPTER 78

The inn was pretty much what she expected. A couple of HiTone choppers out front, super trucks in the lot across the narrow roadway. She took a seat at the quiet end of the bar and ordered a beer. As she waited she looked around the joint.

A guy slid into the seat beside her carrying a tablet. She thought he might be the one she was waiting on, but he struck out with "You ever Google the most popular suicide sites in the world?"

"One of my favorite pastimes," she said bleakly.

"Look here," he said. "Bridges, forests, cliffs for jumping…hosts of sites by continent, by country. The Golden Gate is a big deal… And check this building in Africa…number one jump site."

"What are you about?" said Ana.

"The future is a short ride from the present, so you better watch out for oncoming traffic."

He kept looking her over. It was a distasteful look at best.

"You are oncoming traffic," she said, "so beat it."

"You're not wired, are you?"

Oh, she got it now, who he was.

"Before I take you upstairs to meet with Mr. Domingo, I got to check if you're wired. Do the search. So start with the fuckin' cross."

CHAPTER 79

There were a few rooms up on the second floor as this had been a tavern. They were being remodeled now, so there were just stripped down walls and exposed beams.

Mr. Oncoming Traffic turned out to be Marcus. He patted her down, had her take off her shirt, unloosed her jeans. He found the weapon in her prosthesis, but that was no big deal.

A door connected one room to the next. She was led in, and there was Domingo sitting on a chair in this dusty spare shell of space. There was nothing else but an empty chair that faced his.

"She's good to go," said Marcus. He then left and closed the door.

"Now we can say we never met," said Daniel.

He had her sit. And there they were, the shades drawn, a single light in the lamp on the floor, each casting larger than life shadows on the ceiling.

"Interrogation central," she said.

He was not interested in her humor.

"I've heard you do high end security work," he said.

"Some," she said.

"I hear that sometimes you…push boundaries."

She didn't get baited into that query.

"It's like that, huh? Okay," he said. "Ground rules are good."

He crossed one leg over the other.

"What I am about to tell you comes from a trusted source. And I'm telling you this off the record. Agreed?"

"Agreed."

"And that Landshark character. Off the record."

"Agreed."

"The robbery was a fuck up. And the weapons stolen are the tip of a political and criminal enterprise that has been long standing."

Daniel leaned forward, his shadow on the ceiling moving right across Ana's.

"When the weapons are discovered, they will show that the serial numbers do not match the serial numbers in the Academy gun shop ledgers."

"You mean," said Ana, "that LAPD management and accountants that handled the paperwork—"

"For years," said Daniel. "They're bringing in a forensic expert because the records are such trash."

She sat back, her huge shadow moving with her. She could hear the rattlesnake in the back of her head. Daniel Domingo had piercing eyes and he knew how to use them. But that rattlesnake.

"Question," she said.

"Ask," he said.

"How does this, what you told me, connect to you, the campaign, or your sister, for that matter?"

CHAPTER 80

Ana had started back down the Lake Hughes Road. It was pitch dark the whole way. The hills on both shoulders a spare brown, patched with creosote and scrub. The land exactly as it had been a hundred years back, unclaimed and still. But not without its share of threat.

She called Landshark.

He answered with anticipation.

"I got a boatload to tell you, brother. For starters...Domingo claims, through a source, the robbery must have been a fuck up... that the serial numbers on the weapons won't match the gun shop log...Yeah...And catch this: He says this isn't the first time...Well, his source does...And that there's been a scam going on for—"

A momentary flash of headlights in the rearview caught Ana's attention.

"Ana...?"

"Hey, wait a minute here."

"Ana...?"

There were no headlights, then there were headlights miles back, but coming on so fast. Could be a drunk...could be a couple of hot-shot kids...could be a crazy...could be...fill in the blanks.

"Ana...Ana...?"

"Someone is coming on fast, alright," she said. "And it's making me look like the slow crawl."

"You seeing the rattlesnake?"

"I don't see him, brother...just hear him. But no. I'm just quietly paranoid at the moment."

"What are you gonna do?"

"What am I gonna do?"

She shut off her headlights and kept driving.

"Ana?"

She had been doing a mellow seventy. Now she kicked it up a notch. She watched the speedometer climb past eighty.

"Ana...you can't not answer me."

She was intent on the road, because the road disappeared in the dark turn of the hills so fast it could cancel you right out.

"Ana?"

"I hear you."

There was no moon, so in places the sky blended into the hills, turning into a single impossible landscape. She had an idea and it finally came to pass. Where the shoulder was flat she veered off Lake Hughes and into the darkness, slow riding a slight rise over the crest, the chassis heaving from one side to the other.

She had not gone a hundred yards when she pulled to a stop. The dust from the tires settling in around the pickup, she got out and made her way up to the hilltop and got down on one knee and waited.

The vehicle, she saw, had picked up speed, but then it began to slow and slow. Her only guess—it had seen her headlights go out and her pickup disappear altogether.

Finally, she saw the headlights pull off the road and come to a stop along the shoulder. Its headlights went out.

She could see enough to know it was an SUV. She thought of what Maritza Velez had told her—a man named ChiChi who drove a grey Lexus SUV.

There was no way to tell through all that darkness what make and model SUV it was. Most looked like clones of each other anyway.

But then the driver's door opened and the interior light went on and the driver stepped out and the door closed and the interior light went out.

The driver was a man, and the man was alone.

CHAPTER 81

He stood there by the SUV. He was sure she had not flipped off her headlights and kept on pressing it. She had pulled off the road, of that he was skilled certainty. And he'd bet it wouldn't be beyond suggestion that she was watching him at that moment from some patch of scrub.

So he deflected the obvious, took out a pocket flashlight, knelt down, and pretended to scan the undercarriage and wheel well.

Through all this, he made a call.

"Talk to me."

"She's slick, Mr. Salamone. She's tough and slick."

"She met with—"

"The brother. Up in Lake Hughes if you can believe that."

"I don't even know where Lake Hughes is," said Salamone. "The sister earlier, the brother now. Do you think she knows where the weapons are...or actually has them?"

"You'd have to ask yourself why is she holding them back from LAPD."

"Is she gaming the system?" said Salamone.

"I guess your next actions will determine that."

"I stay out of your day to day operations. And as far as strategy to use," said Salamone, "do what you feel will work."

"I understand."

"It's a shame," said Salamone, "that you never caught up with Velez and confronted him."

"Certainly was, Mr. Salamone."

CHAPTER 82

James Salamone was a graduate of Yale Law, but he did not practice law. His career path could be best described as a business advisor visionary or new age corporate concierge.

You want to keep your hands clean, your breath sweet, your future intact. You bring in someone like Salamone and you're now bubble wrapped in plausible deniability.

At present, Salamone was advising the DON Group, helping

them leverage their desire to develop parcels of land in the 710 Corridor against the Tenants Association's demand that Caltrans commit to its promise and that long term renters be given priority when prices were agreed upon and bids submitted.

Salamone lived in the Flower Street Lofts—that was the South Park district of downtown. He owned two penthouses side by side. One served as his living quarters, the other as his office.

It was the old UPS building. Home now to writers, artists, entrepreneurs, and other forms of living matter making the big climb. It was between 11th and 12th streets and walking distance to five star restaurants, the Crypto.com Arena, the Disney Concert Hall. After the call, Salamone tripped it over to the Elevate Lounge so he could think through the failure he was facing.

The Elevate Lounge was on the 21st floor of 811 Wilshire Boulevard. You didn't get a view of the downtown skyline from there—you were the downtown skyline. It was a sleek and architectural mood scene with a dance floor and open air patio and private lounges bathed in well appointed, ambient shadows.

This was the kind of place people came to feel dramatic and special. Salamone didn't go for all that manifest futility. He knew it was a lie. All restrained, intelligent, forthright souls knew that much.

He went there because he liked the view and he liked the drinks.

He sat alone in a small lounge where the shadows were manufactured palm fronds that fell across plush sofas and chairs. He had one thought that needed answering: Why did Domingo have a meet with this woman, and by proxy William Worth, at some off the map bar?

And was there a way to exploit or derail them because of it?

CHAPTER 83

"Do you think the man on the road was this ChiChi character?" said Worth.

"I don't know," said Ana. "I could have just been paranoid. He *was* checking under his car as if something was off."

"Could he be that…plotting?"

"If he is, we'd better up our game."

She was sitting at Landshark's desk. He'd brought her something to eat. He stood by the bulletin board, which they'd remantled after the police and investigators had left. He was adding index cards of new information as they talked.

She was sipping at a beer. "Does the meeting feel wrong to you?" said Ana.

"It feels like it should be in black and white. That this all should be in black and white."

"It's all old, right?" said Ana.

"New headlines are just old headlines…with different players, different costumes, different music. They're remakes with a little more horrifying gloss." Worth took a breath. "This whole city is a remake, that's how I see it. It was a black and white classic of frantic energy that lost its way. And now a feature length disaster of punitive anxieties that are never gratified. But…I would rather be here than anywhere. And why? Because I am everything that is wrong with a place like this."

Ana had been picking at her food, sipping her beer. She listened, and when Worth was done, said, "We're sitting on evidence now, aren't we?"

"If we leak the story."

"Are we gonna leak it?"

CHAPTER 84

Elias came up startled from sleep by strange metallic noises and bursts of light. He pulled a revolver from under his pillow and when he got it together, saw his daughter was stripping the window curtains from their rods.

"Put the gun away," she said.

"What the fuck do you think you're doing?"

"These need to be repaired…then fumigated."

"What? Why?"

"Because I say so."

She was heading out with them, then stopped. "I might have a job for you."

"I don't need a job. What do I want a job for?"

"You don't want to end up an unwashed recliner rat who spends the rest of his days drinking and watching old movies."

"Speaking for me and two hundred million brother Americans… Fuck, yes."

CHAPTER 85

Ana didn't give a rat's ass if the curtains were repaired or not. This was all just a front. She pulled up to the Velez house and parked. The two boys were out on the front lawn, zipping a baseball back and forth.

Ana came up the walkway with the curtains, just another client for a seamstress who worked at home. Ana had to pass between the two boys. As she did, the ball buzzed right past her head.

She got it. They were letting her know whose turf this was. Kids with reckless fathers was an old and personal tale to her.

She stopped. "You're Javier," she said, pointing. "And you're Jorge. I'm here to see your mom, and I might be around some. We can be friends or not. But ripping a ball past my head is a nonstarter. Do it again…I kick your ass."

The front door was open and Ana called out. The boys were on her tail, scoping out Ana's slight limp. The grandmother had seen what went down and was reprimanding the boys in machine gun Spanish.

"Are you the lady that's crippled?" said Jorge.

Javier nudged his brother to cut it.

"That's a fair description," said Ana.

Maritza heard that and railed into her sons. It was obvious they had been told about Ana.

Jorge asked if he could see the leg.

"It's my foot," said Ana. "Not my leg."

Maritza swatted at her son but he was too quick. He followed up with "Could we see the foot?"

Maritza swung again and missed again.

In the den Ana sat. She set aside the curtains and an envelope she carried, and said, "Check it out, *hombres*."

She slipped off the boot. The boys crowded in around her. They felt it, they tapped it, they prodded at her prothesis. And if that weren't enough, they wanted to get a picture of it with their cells. Maritza wouldn't hear of it, but Ana was cool. They even wanted a group shot with the both of them. All the while the mother burning with upset and the grandmother thrashing at her own daughter for not stopping it.

This, thought Ana, was America. In the state of loud and

somewhat ruthless. Outstanding at how quickly kids cut through the crap. Kids know what relevance is—it's whatever interests them in the right now.

CHAPTER 86

Once they got rid of the kids, the two women got down to business. Ana took the envelope she'd set down and handed it to Maritza.

"This is the contract. I've included the name of an attorney who will take care of you in this."

Ana glanced out the window. "You may hear some noises out back over the next few nights. Disregard them."

"It's all gonna come out," said Maritza.

Ana did not answer.

"I may have someone stay here after that," said Ana.

"There's going to be violence."

"Probably not, but—"

"What are you going to do?"

Again, Ana did not answer.

Maritza took Ana's hand in hers. "Maybe you should reconsider—"

Ana bypassed her statement. Told her about the phone message on the hotline about a fight by a squad car parked on Valley Boulevard. And how the victim was put in a van instead of the squad car.

"Did you hear about this?" said Ana.

"No…Do you think it could have been Luis?"

"William hasn't been able to confirm the incident even happened.

There's no record of it."

"The night you were first here," said Maritza, "the officer that showed up asking about Luis...His name is Engel...Would you want to talk with him?"

"Were he and Luis close?"

"No...not particularly."

"Did it seem odd him showing up like that? At night? In his squad car?"

"I didn't think of it at the time. Does it seem strange to you?"

"Say nothing to him until we know more. If it happened...And there's no record of it—"

"Yes," said Maritza. "I see."

Ana stood to leave. Maritza took her by the arm. "I'm fighting for my family...my mother...this house. I'm fighting for forty years of sweat equity. Why are you doing this?"

"Because I'd rather be you...than me."

CHAPTER 87

Landshark sat with dark glasses on at dusk by the burned remains of his beloved gazebo, enraged. He wanted to draft his column in that state. The words and thoughts came easier in his case when there was hate involved.

He intended to open with the tip that came in on the hotline about an "alleged fight off Valley Boulevard" where the police were involved and a man was taken away in a white van.

This would serve as a teaser or tantalizing rumor since the incident came just days after the robbery and murder at the Academy gun shop. This would connect by inference to information he received from a "source close to the investigation" about the gun shop scam and the missing weapons.

Then he added the torching of the gazebo to the article, which he described as an attempt to burn down his estate by "parties unknown" as an unsubtle threat to desist from the story.

Of course, he was taking liberties with the facts. The article was long on conjecture but short on certainty. "It does make for dramatic reading," said Worth.

As Ana reviewed what he had drafted, Worth offered, "I'm using the *New York Times* model of truth in journalism…which means swing for the fences."

He wasn't done. "When it comes to the weapons," he said, "we are now in the flightpath of legal jeopardy."

CHAPTER 88

Miller was sitting at the bar in the Hollywood Park Casino. He was not gambling that night. He was doing Adderal with scotch, scotch, and more scotch. He was in a black mood for being fucked over by the Living Aberration and Ms. Ride—fucked over, not outsmarted—by the sleight of hand those two burners had pulled.

He had tried to get a search warrant based on the information he presented to a judge, but Los Angeles was Woke Fuckin' Central, and the prosecutors were *The Price Is Right* on steroids when it came to crime.

Then, the God of *Sticking It to You* presented him with a treat.

Ana Ride slipped down onto the seat beside Miller, wearing a refresh smile, a men's fedora, fishnet top, and trashy jewelry.

"I was thinking about you," said Miller.

"Yeah…how was it, Jayden?"

"I was cursing you out…What's with the hat?"

"I'm keeping all those bad thoughts under wraps."

"You didn't outsmart me, by the way."

"I didn't…?"

"You may have outsmarted that crew I was with at the Aberration's house."

"Was I even trying to outsmart you? I don't believe I had you—"

"I'll give you a dose of clarity."

CHAPTER 89

He grabbed her by the arm, hustled her outside half against her will. They stood out front, away from the security and the people milling about until they were alone and awash in flashy neon.

"You ever look at the photos in Landshark's office?" he said.

"I don't make a habit of it."

"In a number of those photos, the surveillance monitors are in the background…In all those photos there are nine monitors… Nine. But there's only eight monitors on the cabinet in the office. And there's a camera in the woods at the edge of the entrance to the fire road…And there is no surveillance monitor in the office for that camera.

"And those bulletin boards with details from the articles he's working on…Not one about the gun shop robbery."

He got right in Ana's face. "You pulled the monitor before fire or police got there. You pulled the bulletin board. You're withholding evidence."

Buzzed as he was, Miller was riding a wave of determined focus.

"I tried to get a search warrant for that fairyland Worth lives in, but I got Woke'd out. No matter…I'll get you."

She took out a cigarette and lit it and Jayden got an answer he did not expect.

"I'll bet you will," she said. "But that's only because you're right on with pretty much all you said."

She caught him squarely with that answer. And his response—he didn't have one.

He reached into his coat pocket and took out a flask. "Scotch," he said. He offered her a drink. She turned it down.

He drank, she smoked. Nothing was said. People came, people went. The casino doors swung open and there was a rush of cold air and music, then the doors closed.

"This is what I call the face off phase," she said.

He took a drink.

"You got a boyfriend?" he said.

"Jesus," she said.

"A girlfriend?"

Back to back Jesus.

"I had a girlfriend last year," he said, "but she blew me off when she found out I gambled away all the savings she was hoping to take me for."

Ana threw her head back and cracked up.

"I never," she said, "heard that reality explained better."

He smiled himself. He went to lean back and rest against the hood of a parked car, and that was the last he remembered.

CHAPTER 90

When Jayden came to, he was in Ana's pickup truck. His head was resting against the closed window, a folded up coat of hers wedged between his head and the glass. He organized the scene around him.

"Where are we going?"

"You live on Chicasaw at Highland View?"

"Yeah."

"That's where we're going."

"How did you—"

"I went through your wallet. Are you really six foot two?"

"Did I go completely out or just wobble?"

"You took a ten count."

"Great."

He lived in a funky Eagle Rock neighborhood. Small apartments and houses. Some had been reclaimed from the nicks of time, some were desperately calling out.

They parked in front of the property. There was a shitty chain link fence that opened to a shitty empty lot. Behind it was a hill and maybe forty, fifty steps up to a shitty wood frame house, with more steps yet.

"Can you make it?"

He said he could. He was lying. She gave him a little guiding hand.

Then about halfway up the stairs he stopped and leaned back against the railing. Ana thought he was too wasted to go on, but it was not that at all. He wanted to take in this moment.

You see, there was music floating down from one of the houses up beyond the trees. Slow beat rock and roll, straight out of yesteryear, from when times were simpler, when people said what they meant, and meant it. When mood and romance were not life's discounted trappings. He couldn't even remember the name of the song, or who sang it, he only knew the feel of it.

And it was not lost on him, then and there. The music being right, the breeze being right, the unclouded sky, the slip of moon, the very night itself, all being right.

"Some people," he said, "only believe in punishments. Not ever rewards."

"Never truer words, Miller."

She picked up what was going on in his eyes and in what felt like a current passing between them. *Yeah,* she said to herself, *I'm not immune to it either.*

"I'm going to get you," he said. "Eventually."

"Yeah, I know."

"It wouldn't be good."

"It never is, even when it is."

He leaned away from the railing and kissed her. He could hear the tinkling of her jewelry as her hand snaked its way around the back of his neck.

She whispered in his ear, "I'll fuck you if you make me one promise."

"I hate promises."

"Who doesn't?"

"What is it?"

"That you'll forget it ever happened."

CHAPTER 91

Ever since the amputation, whenever Ana had sex there was a sense of incompleteness, or a melancholy disconnect, even emptiness. She and her body were not one being.

Yet on this night, for some reason she could not explain, when she was aroused she could feel her phantom foot. When he pushed into her vagina, her foot was there and alive. All those nerve endings destroyed on the battlefield, there and alive and filling her with uns-carred wholeness. She was, for those moments, the woman she had been once upon a time. It was a breathtaking shock.

She said nothing to Miller about this as they lay up in the sheets. It was a secret she would have to unravel to understand.

CHAPTER 92

His cellphone woke him. Jayden had been dreaming about a ghost town in the desert. It was a patched world from pieces of a min-ing community known as Darwin that now boasted a population of forty.

In the dream he wandered lost down rubbled, listing streets with their vagrant, dried out buildings, calling to someone. But who that someone was and what he was calling out...was never answered.

It was Ana on the phone.

He looked across the dark to where she had been.

"Where are you?" he said.

"In my truck...about to pull away."

He wanted to ask, was that literally or figuratively?

He said, "You don't have to—"

"But I do," she said.

She then asked he just listen and she confessed all that would appear in the article.

CHAPTER 93

Julia Domingo was at her open kitchen counter working through a speech for the Chamber of Commerce in Compton, rehearsing as she went. It was late, she was alone. In her bra and panties with a glass of wine and wielding a slice of pizza.

"Hispanics and African Americans make up about half of California's population. About a third live in poverty. And many of the rest damn close to it...."

She circled the word damn.

A generation ago the Reference Bureau stated that California was creating a two tiered social system with Blacks and Latinos at the bottom and whites and Asians at the top. The 710 Corridor was living proof of this reckoning. The underprivileged and poor would slave their lives away paying rent year in and year out while development companies that wanted the properties fed money to the campaigns of city and state officers to achieve the outcome they desired.

"It's a tried and true plan. And a plot you've seen on endless cable dramas because it is true...It is the bleak realization in the bad faith of men."

She was so intent on her notes she was not aware her brother had come in and was listening silently.

"We now live with the Woke Movement...the world is going

Woke…Woke ideas now want to teach our children ethnic studies courses…make them woke conscious. But what is the good of it when you can't read? When you are illiterate?

"I have a better idea. Forget ethnic studies courses and teach them welding. Welding can get you to the middle class. Ethnic studies cannot."

She stopped. Made a note. Mumbled. Jumped back to her notes.

"And remember this," she said. "With the Fourth of July coming fast upon us—"

Daniel cut in before she finished, "America is the greatest experiment in self governance there has ever been."

When he spoke out, he'd startled her.

"The speech is coming together," he said. "I'm not sure about the wardrobe. And the pizza has got to go."

He came up behind his sister and handed her his tablet. "Read this."

She set down the pizza. Licked her fingers. It was a draft of the Landshark article. He was offering the Domingos a chance to comment "on the record." As she read on, her brother slipped a hand around her waist. She was in no mood and armed him away.

She was enraged at what she read. "Where did you get this information?"

"Where do you think?"

"All this?"

"It's true. It will come out."

"How did you—"

"No questions."

"Why didn't you tell me?"

"I don't want to engage in unnecessary fights you can't win."

"We stand for something or we don't."

"Yeah, and right now you're the assemblyperson they probably didn't shoot at outside the church."

"I hate the fact," she said, "I'm at constant war with my conscience."

"You want to run for higher office? It all comes down to a bank account or heavy duty recognition."

She went to reach for the glass of wine but he bested her to it.

"It's billionaires going after these crackpot jobs. And as of right now, you're a little short on heavy duty recognition."

He took a sip of wine.

"And it's my job," he said, "to supply you with recognition."

CHAPTER 94

Two unmarked police cars made their way up the few hundred yards from the street to Landshark's private driveway. To their surprise the front gate was open. To their further surprise the front door was open. Miller had just reached the entry with a forensic team when Landshark's voice sounded through the intercom: "Mr. Miller, come in, please. You'll find me in the dining room."

Sure enough, there he was in the smooth morning light, having cappuccino and some sort of expensive brioche. He was dressed in black slacks and a black turtleneck and black Italian loafers.

The agents with Miller could not help but stare at the nude photograph of William Worth, shot to hell by arrows.

"I have a search warrant here," said Miller. "It's only limited to your office, so—"

"Please, you know where the office is."

Miller led the team to the office. To his surprise the surveillance monitors were gone, the computers were gone, the bulletin board with case information also gone. To his further surprise, at the desk sat a well dressed lady with bleached white hair and wearing a man's suit. She had a leather briefcase and stood.

"Mr. Miller, my name is Paige Hughes. My firm represents Mr. Worth in this matter. May I see the warrant?"

He handed it to her.

At this point, not to his surprise, from her briefcase she took out her own papers, which she served him with. "These are challenges to your warrant. And a stay. They have already been submitted to the court."

As the forensic team made their emptyhanded way back to their cars, Miller took a moment in the dining room with Landshark.

"That was quick," said Worth.

"You're one on top of it fucker."

Landshark sipped at his cappuccino. Miller would have liked to hit him over the head with one of the fancy objets d'art he had lying around, but that wouldn't be good manners.

"I'm just a retired businessman...living on a pension," said Worth.

"I saw that movie," said Miller. "And I get it. But we're not done here."

"I should hope not," said Worth. "Maybe by the end of this we can shake hands like gentlemen and be...something."

Miller had about a dozen comments he'd have liked to throw at the son of a bitch, but decided against any of them. On the way out, Worth said to him, "How was your evening?"

CHAPTER 95

Miller knocked on Ana's screen door, but she didn't answer. Her truck was there, and with a tight throat, Jayden wondered if he was about to face some wolverine form of wrath.

"Hey Miller…she's not there."

It was her father.

"Do you know where—"

"For a walk," said Elias.

"Can I—"

"Walk down Topanga. First street, look down to where the train tracks go into the tunnel. She sits up on the rocks above the tunnel entrance when she's pissed. Can't miss it. It's where Jimmy Cagney jumped from the tunnel onto a moving train he was gonna rob at the beginning of *White Heat*."

Miller had to pass Elias, who grabbed hold of his shoulder when he did.

"You carrying a search warrant? Subpoena?"

Miller nodded he was.

"I may have to take it under advisement one day to kick your ass," said Elias.

"Seems everyone in your family is an ass kicker."

"Damn right," he said. "And we don't believe in participation trophies either."

CHAPTER 96

Ana was exactly where Elias said she'd be, sitting on the wall above the tunnel entrance, the road coursing behind her. She was still as a statue in thought and saw him coming a long way off.

"I know exactly what you're thinking," she said.

"Christ, I hope not," he said.

She lit a cigarette. "It's that next day conversation. The one after you've done just about every hedonistic sexual act known to man with a person and you're choking on your thoughts." She took a swig from her beer bottle, then set it back down. "Orgasms are not nearly as tough as conversations, are they? I mean real conversations, not real orgasms."

"A sobering thought," he said. He reached for her beer. "May I?"

"Is it a subpoena or a search warrant? Or both?"

"You sound just like your father."

"He called me right after you talked."

Jayden looked down the thirty feet or so to the tracks.

"It's not far enough to kill yourself, unless a train flashes by."

"I'll bring a box lunch and wait," said Ana.

"Let's get on to the nature of this call. And skip a few kind words altogether. We got a picture from a cellphone just as you were coming out of the Orteig house."

"Well," said Ana, "do I go with you in handcuffs or do we save those for the party afterwards?"

CHAPTER 97

The Culture of Rot.

That was the title of the speech Julia Domingo was to give. It was to take place on the Cal State downtown campus. It had been set up by the Students for a Better America, which was a progressive, left wing group the Domingos hoped to rally for their door to door reelection campaign.

Salamone was there. He made it an essential to be at all his adversaries' speeches. He'd read the Landshark article and knew it would become pivotal to her reelection. He also knew his political strategies were reduced to one—violence.

A speech was where Julia Domingo was at her best. Soft spoken, intelligent, with a kitchen counter vibe, she opened with: "The weapon of love has devolved through time to be...the love of weapons. It was the crucial truth at the core of the Culture of Rot."

CHAPTER 97

Julia stole snippets from the Big Island L.A. article: "Weapons stolen, then sold from the police gun shop, a conspiracy that has allegedly been going on for years. Sold by whom, to whom. LAPD involved. Think of all those weapons and the carnage that may have been committed in the hands of such committed.

"Were they sold to gangbangers, thieves, murderers, MS-13, white supremacists? This...is the Culture of Rot.

"Were some of the weapons the ones used at the All Saints Church, or any other such violent attacks? And who were the weapons meant for? Was it an assault on the church itself and what the church stands for? Was it an assault on the parishioners and what they stand for? Was it an attempted assassination of me and the people I work with in the 710 Corridor? Was it an attempt to intimidate through slaughter? Another aspect of…the Culture of Rot. And if it was…who is behind it?"

The reelection committee was handing out tee shirts that had on the front:

TAKE DOWN
THE CULTURE OF ROT

Salamone was handed one of the tee shirts as he approached Daniel Domingo.

"You wrote that speech," said Salamone.

Domingo was unmoved.

"My sister wrote it."

"It's got all the Domingo touches. The jump cuts from a half fact here to a quarter thought there, insinuations, character assassinations. That phony columnist pushes an unverified lie and you advance it a little more."

"What you really mean is we're getting traction," said Domingo.

"What I mean is you'll be on political life support before you know it."

Salamone walked away.

"The election is a wrap…or haven't you noticed?"

CHAPTER 98

Once Salamone was back from the crowd, he made a call on his burner phone.

"Did you get my text?" said Salamone.

"Got it. Read it. Article too."

"We have a leak somewhere."

"You have a leak somewhere is closer to it."

"Yes," said Salamone, "I have a leak. But if I have—"

"I know when I'm downwind of bad news."

There was cheering and applause in the background from something Julia said.

"What is that?"

"Julia Domingo at Cal State. Inspiring the student body with a speech on the Culture of Rot."

"Culture of what?"

"Culture of Rot."

"And what the hell is that?"

"That's us...and people like us."

"The Latinas are taking over the world."

"But they're all running Republican," said Salamone. "Except here in Wokeland. Listen—"

"Do me a favor, Salamone, and hang up so I can get us upwind of this thing."

CHAPTER 99

When John Rabel got off the line from his call with Salamone he was one deeply troubled soul. The trappings of others' stupidity ruled the day. The simplicity of the original plan had been lost to them when Andres decided on some foolhardy venture to outwit those who hired him. It got worse when he clandestinely brought in Velez, and worse yet when Velez withstood a remorseless torture without divulging what he knew, swearing only that Andres had stolen away with the weapons and disappeared. Rabel, of course, knew it to be a desperate lie, because he might have confided what he knew in someone close to him, like his wife, and was willing to die for her safety. If so, why hadn't she gone to the authorities once he disappeared?

Add to that another question: How did a former Marine, the Ride woman, appear at All Saints with a flyer for Andres? How did she know anything about him at all? How did she get to the same church the Velezes attended?

The costly and stupid failings of others is why he had never used his real name when dealing with the street trash necessary for any conspiracy. Why ChiChi and his silver Lexus would be relegated to the ghostyards of failed crimes. Even the John Rabel that Salamone knew…did not exist.

He had been below deck on the boat where he lived in Marina del Rey. He came up into the sun, knowing that from here on, there would be a hard run of violence ahead of him. He was already lining up the dead, and the order they were to be taken down.

He wondered about the article, how much energy it would unleash in Los Angeles, how may desperate wannabes with information, how many holes in the dyke he did not yet know about.

Then, what he saw as good news shined down on him.

He heard the people on the boat moored beside him. There were a handful watching the news, a wave of shock and dismay passing between them.

It seemed there had been another school shooting, this time in a Texas town named Uvalde.

CHAPTER 100

"This is you, correct?" said the prosecutor.

She slid a tablet across the table with a photo Miller had shown Ana. She and Paige Hughes, her attorney, both looked it over.

"Correct," said Ana.

"This photo puts you inside the Orteig house."

"It suggests, that is all," said Hughes.

"I was under duress," said Ana. "Mr. Orteig was acting crazy. He was high. That had all my attention."

"What all was in the shoebox?"

"Miller can tell you," said Hughes. "He examined the contents."

Miller sat off to one side in the tiny room with a number of other investigators.

"I examined the contents," he said, "that Ms. Ride had laid out on her dining table. Whether they were all the contents I cannot say."

No glances passed between Ride and Miller.

Then Hughes said, "But she gave you free access to the contents."

The prosecutor changed gears. "How did you come to know of Antonin Andres?"

"That information is privileged," said Hughes, "as it is part of a story she is working on."

"And what is that story?" said the prosecutor.

"That is privileged. Do you have any factual evidence to connect your questions to a crime?"

"Mr. Orteig and Andres, we have learned, both worked at the gun shop for a time. And about a month before the robbery exchanged a number of phone calls."

"They could have been commiserating about their love lives," said Hughes.

The prosecutor addressed Ana. "What can you tell me about the weapons stolen from the shop? Do you have any—"

"Ma'am, if I may," she said, addressing the prosecutor. "I'll tell you nothing. No one rules me."

The sense in the room was pretty obvious. The interview was unquestionably over. The prosecutor closed up her case file, then went into a cut and dried legal riff.

"In criminal matters," she said, "there should be reasonable grounds to believe, based on public information or information from non media sources, that a crime has occurred. And the information sought is essential to a successful investigation or prosecution."

The prosecutor stood. "In other words, Ms. Ride...you are under arrest for withholding information."

CHAPTER 101

Ana sat quietly in the main room waiting as Paige Hughes handled her bail situation. All the televisions across the room were turned to cable news. The mass shooting at the Uvalde school. The attempt to get the viewer up to speed on another atrocity. It would suck up all available airwaves. Like the school shooting in Buffalo ten days before that, and the school shooting before that, and the one before that, would lay rights to the hours. The Domingo speech and its claims would be back burner stuff.

Miller approached Ana carrying two cups of coffee.

"Ma'am, if I may…I will tell you nothing…No one rules me." He offered her a cup. "Very well said…Dramatic. But not exactly—"

"It was as much for you," said Ana, "as it was for all the others." She took the cup.

"Yes…I feared that."

"I knew you would," she said, sipping coffee.

"Well," he said, "they're gonna take a bite out of you now."

"They? What is this? Who is they? Do I need to get out my pronoun guide? You're part of *they.*"

"Right," he said. Like she'd just bitched his heart with an ice pick. "*We're* gonna take a bite out of you. How's that?"

"You already did," she said. "Forget? Will you tell all this in confession?"

Paige Hughes was coming down the hall.

"Where do we go from here?" said Miller.

"We do all the obligatory scenes, then we shoot each other."

Hughes could see she interrupted the uninterruptable. "Do you both need some more time alone to have at each other?"

CHAPTER 102

While Elias was watching the next American tragedy that was unfolding in Texas, Ana walked in.

"You alright?" he said.

She headed for the fridge. "Who knows what secrets lie in the heart of man?"

"Your bail?"

"Worth took care of it…two hundred thousand, thank you very much."

"Fuckin' Wokeland L.A.…if you had robbed a bank…beat a homeless man to death…ransacked a nun…or burned down a car dealership in protest of white supremacy…you'd have walked without bail."

"You're not gonna start running your mouth about politics, are you?"

She opened the fridge, picked through a mess of food containers and half drunk bottles of beer and soda and who knows what else. It looked like the province of a schizoid, or a slob. She finally located one untouched beer.

The all too human news was awful. It emotionally owned both of them. The confusion of those poor parents not knowing, incapable of getting answers…then the crushing sorrow when word came that their precious ones were taken by a mad dream.

"They should have a Marine at the front door of every school in America."

"Armed Marine, you mean," said Ana.

"Fuckin' right. With a flag decal on their shoulder so people know."

He was on one track; she quite another. And they only met in passing.

"Elias," she said, "you ever wonder what kind of parent you'd be in that situation?"

He sat back. His daughter had gone to the heart of all that mattered.

"Better than the parent I was, I hope."

She started out. "Thanks for the beer."

It was all she had to say.

"What about that shitbag, Miller?"

"He's not a shitbag, Elias. As a matter of fact, he's a lot like me. Except for the fact he has a dick, while I *am* a dick."

"What now?" he said.

"Take the fight to them, of course. Whoever 'them' is."

CHAPTER 103

John Rabel drove those few dark miles up Kagel Canyon, then veered onto a rutted roadway through the trees to the corrugated warehouse where Velez had met the kind of self imposed end no man should, no matter how vile.

In the throes of lamplight he collected his instruments of death—chainsaw, handsaw, ax, tarp, tape, rope, drugs to sedate the soon to be dead—all of which he packed into a large duffel.

There was faded blood on the floor where Velez had once sat that Rabel stepped over. He called the two thugs who had been serving as his professional field hands. Muscle and violence being their stock in trade.

He picked them up in downtown L.A. at a particular location in a run of blocks where the homeless, hopeless, futureless played out their existence. Where they shot up and shit on the sidewalk, got drunk and urinated in alleys. Where they slept on their cardboard magic carpets, asses sticking out of shabby pants, their faces defined by schizophrenia.

Everyone was no one down there, no one and nothing there, just breathing death pots, so no one was looking.

CHAPTER 104

Rabel drove to Marina del Rey. He had the two men wait in the white van while he loaded the boat. When he was ready to depart, he phoned them. Rabel did this so their leaving together would be as inconspicuous as possible.

They started out for Ventura. They kept a few miles out from shore as they boated north. Rabel had a thermos of coffee so they would be awake and sharp. He laid out the murder they would commit. There would be risk.

He handed each an envelope with their payment. "On the chance something happens to me," he said.

When he saw the lights of the harbor he cut the engine. They were to wait for the appointed hour. While they did, Rabel watched the two men.

One of them had become ill. He was bent over, puking into the sea. The other man sat with his pale and ill looking friend. He thought it was seasickness his friend was suffering, but the illness took him soon after.

It was then he realized. He looked at the thermos lying there on the deck. And then to Rabel, who stood in the shadows of the night sea. In one hand he bore a weapon with a silencer.

"What have you done?" said the man.

CHAPTER 105

In desperation the man threw himself overboard as Rabel rushed to him, firing. But the boat rising and dipping with the tide skewered his aim.

Rabel shot the man lying on the deck in his own vomit, killing him. He then leaned over the port side and there was the other, his arms flapping wildly, trying to get away. Rabel fired at him time and again, the bullets making long strafings through the water. He fired until the gun was empty, though the man still floundered.

Rabel rushed down below deck while the man, ill, bleeding from a bullet wound, choking on saltwater, powered by adrenaline, screamed, howled, pleaded, begged for help, his voice out there on the night sea, hopeless to all but god almighty himself.

Rabel came back up from below with a harpoon gun. He leaned over the side, aimed the weapon, and fired. He could feel the staccato rush of the rope and the man was speared through the chest.

Rabel then went about the business of reeling him back on board. One hard foot at a time, trying to get that dead weight up and over the side, grunting, bracing his feet against the deck wall, muscles tremoring, cursing, hands scored by the rope, until finally he had the bastard halfway up and over the deck wall. Their faces not two feet apart, he saw the man was not yet dead.

His mouth was open, blood pouring out. He was trying to make words. When there was enough slack in the rope, Rabel wound it around the man's neck.

Rabel struggled to his feet and hoisted the man over his shoulder, and like a fuckin' mule, pulled the man aboard. When he had him there, flopping on the deck, he went below again. He came back with an ax, and standing over the Mexican, drove one blow down and through the man's skull.

It sounded like a piece of wood splitting.

Rabel then dropped down on the deck beside the dead. He fought to catch his breath.

The easy part, he knew, was over. Now came the real work.

CHAPTER 106

Rabel lay both bodies on a tarp he had spread across the deck. He removed each skull using a handsaw, severing them just below the windpipe.

He did not worry about the blood, which he would hose down. He did not worry about some imaginary investigation where luminol would come into play. The boat would be history by tomorrow, gone into a vast corruption that worked both sides of the border.

He never owned the boat anyway.

He pressed a weight against where he'd severed the skull and tied it in place with industrial tape. He bound up the whole skull. He did this for both, then threw them into the ocean. He watched the mummied remains slip beneath the waves.

He did the same with each hand after he amputated them.

He folded up the tarp and hosed down the deck. He then stripped down and rolled his clothes up, placing them within the folded tarp, and added a weight. He then bound all of it with the tape and overboard it went.

When done, he hosed down his naked body.

CHAPTER 107

Ana and Landshark were together in his huge television room that was a blend of NASA and Hollywood. At an imported Mandarin bar that was a thousand years young, Landshark made breath stealing margaritas.

All six of the wall televisions were dedicated to the slaying of those poor children in Uvalde. The chaos that ensued, the search for truth via absolute confusion that changed by the hour, deepening the catastrophe.

"It's quite a vision," said Worth. "Those people there like that, us here like this. I feel guilty. But I always feel guilty."

He passed her a drink.

"They're lethal," he said.

"Promise?"

"When I'm downstairs in my office…I'm a real person," he said. "Everywhere else…it's like I'm impersonating a real person."

She understood. True connectedness can move in and out like the tide.

"I have an ache that never goes away," she said. "That's why I'm here."

"You mean…" he said, pointing to her prosthesis.

"No," she said.

"I'll tell you a story," she said. "Once upon a time, there was a make believe family." Then Ana got into the cold blooded facts about how the father, Captain Elias Ride, took out his private, personal griefs on an innocent bystander called his wife. And how after one fight while the mother was dying of cervical cancer, the daughter put a hot skillet on the father's back. Just to give him a little taste of fury.

"Here's the real kicker," said Ana. "The father dragged the daughter into the bedroom, threw her on the bed, undid his belt, unbuttoned his jeans, pulled down his zipper. And just as he was about to slip the belt from his pants there came a shot heard around their world."

"The mother, it seemed, had put a .45 shell into the ceiling. The father, now visibly shaken, left the room."

Ana was quiet after that. She sat at that thousand year old bar staring at her untouched drink.

"You didn't know, did you?" said Landshark.

"Whether the father was going to beat the daughter with the belt...or rape her out of rage?...No."

"My parents were sexaholics," said Worth. "Fucked anybody, everybody. I had an aunt that took me to the movies when I was a kid. Disney crap, you know. We'd sit in the back of the theater and she'd go down on me."

Ana raised her glass. "Let's toast our lives."

They toasted their lives. Then they proceeded to get toasted.

"Now...let's figure out how we continue to take the fight to them," said Ana. "Whoever 'them' is."

"You're facing possible jail time," said Worth.

"Free room and board," said Ana. "Free medical, free dental. How can you go wrong?"

CHAPTER 108

Rabel took to tracking the "Big Island, L.A." column while he determined a new course of action. The weapons were a must. They had to be located, taken, along with those who had them.

Then Worth put out a query in his column, podcast, and on his Twitter account: *Does anyone know a man named ChiChi who drives a Lexus, as he might have pertinent information in the police gun shop robbery and murder?*

Rabel's timing had been right. His tactics in this matter intensely acute, which is why he still thrived.

And now this. He knew what this was. They were trying to bait him out.

CHAPTER 109

Calls came in on the hotline Landshark had set up just for this. All proved to be junkers, really. Ana had a physical description of this ChiChi that Velez had passed on to his wife, and she in turn confided to Ana.

The description they never released and was the first question they asked every caller. One of these was Rabel himself. He gave a phony story about a ChiChi and a Lexus. No sooner than he was done, Ana asked for a description of the man and when Rabel offered a wrong one, she ended the call. This assured him they had a true description.

His question now: Where did the Ride woman get it?

CHAPTER 110

Miller made an unofficial guest appearance at Ride's trailer. Her truck wasn't there; neither was she. But he was greeted by a not so happy, not smiling, not hardly polite Elias Ride.

"Do you know where—"

"You got a phone. Fuckin' call her."

"Listen, Mr. Ride—"

"Come to serve another warrant? Subpoena?"

"No. This is...informal."

"Informal. Let me see. Does that mean you want to question her...or see about fuckin' her?"

A woman with a stroller passing along took notice. Miller just stood there in his nice suit thoroughly embarrassed. This kind of verbal bad blood, well...he hadn't imagined it would start out this way, but there it was.

"I just wanted to tell her," said Miller, "informally...we have discovered your friend...Orteig had a number of phone calls back and forth with Antonin Andres in the weeks and days before the robbery."

"What's that got to do with anything?"

"We have evidence now that Andres was key to the robbery."

Elias put his hands on his hips. Looked over Miller with disdain.

"I get it," said Elias.

"Get what?"

Elias started to approach Miller. He put his hands out as if he was to be handcuffed.

"Come on...do it."

"I'm not here to arrest you."

"Fuckin' arrest me."

143

There were a few people around their trailers who could hear this disquieting confrontation and it sure piqued their curiosity.

"I have no interest in…no reason to—"

"You fuck up my daughter and I will run you over. And then I will set you on fire."

"I guess I can't half blame you. But the other half will have something to say about that."

"Let's have it out right now," said Elias.

Elias Ride kept approaching Miller and it sure looked like he was ready for a fight that Miller didn't want.

"Don't be crazy," said Miller.

"Crazy…crazy enough to see right through you."

"I'm gonna leave now," said Miller, "as politely as I came here."

"I ought to go inside and get a gun and run you out."

Miller turned on him. "Let me warn you. I was the best shot in my class."

"Shooting class and the street are two very different forms of validation."

Miller had had it. Waved off Ride.

"You and I both know you did not come here to see my daughter."

"No?"

"No. You came here to dangle that Orteig business in my face. To see if I would tell you something because I'm concerned for my daughter. I read you. I'm a Marine. I was LAPD when they were LAPD and not some subservient WOKE bullshit like you all are."

Miller stopped and dug in. He wagged a finger at Ride.

"The last part, at least, is untrue," said Miller. "And I did come out here to see you. I came because I was sure your daughter was not here. Your daughter is in the shit because of you. Yeah…you. You're the one Orteig called and you sent your daughter instead. Rather than go yourself. Because if you had, it would be you who'd be out on bail. Or worse."

CHAPTER 111

They were still fielding calls on the original hotline. One came through with promise. A man left his name and number with a telling message.

"The incident in El Sereno where a man was taken from a police car to a white van…The same night, I witnessed a fight by a parked van between a number of men."

Worth played the message for Ana. It was she who made the call back. The man wanted to know if the reward was still valid. She said it was.

"I was driving down Kagel Canyon…A white van was parked by the side of the road and still running. There was a fight…a bloody man was being dragged into a van."

"Can you describe the man?" said Ana.

"I only saw them for a few moments…everything was happening so fast…."

The descriptions were off…but for one.

Ana had recorded the call and played it for Worth.

A meet was set for that night. The Hideaway Bar, partway up in Kagel Canyon.

Ana would go well armed, and then some.

CHAPTER 112

Miller pulled up to the Velez house. The boys were playing on the porch under the watchful eye of their grandmother. Maritza was inside working, but could see out the window, past the porch, where two men in suits were coming up the walkway and looking the place over. This did not feel like good news.

Miller flashed his ID toward the porch. "I'm looking for Maritza Velez."

"In here," said Maritza.

Miller came up onto the porch. He could not see too well through the screen. He showed her his ID. "My name is Jayden Miller. Investigator with LAPD. Can we talk?"

She went to the screen door, as did he. She did not invite him in. He held out the flyer.

"You were given one of these at the church."

"Yes," she said.

"And you talked with a woman named Ana Ride."

"She talked to me."

"Did she tell you she wanted to find out about Antonin Andres?"

"Yes."

"Why?"

"She said she was working on some story."

"This Andres...what do you know of him?"

"I don't know him."

"Did you ever see him?"

"Once, I believe."

"When was that?"

"Weeks back...maybe longer."

"At the church?"

"Yes…at the church."

"But he was not a member of the congregation. So we were told."

"I can't answer that."

"You never saw him anywhere else?"

"I did not."

"Did he talk with your husband? You are married?"

"I am separated."

"And your husband was once with LAPD?"

"At one time."

"He was fired."

"He was."

"Did this man talk with your husband?"

"I believe he did."

"What did they talk about?"

Maritza shrugged. Her kids were close up around Miller, checking him out.

CHAPTER 113

"Might I come in?" said Miller.

"Do you have a warrant to demand it?"

"I do not."

"Then you cannot."

Miller held up a picture of Ana on his cellphone. "This is the woman…Ana Ride."

"Yes."

"Can you tell me about this woman?"

The brothers had squeezed in. The younger said, "We have better pictures than that."

"Do you now?"

In spite of their mother, they flashed the pictures they'd taken of Ana, including the group shot with her prosthesis.

"Seems like you are all quite friendly."

"She brought me some curtains to repair and clean," said Maritza.

"That's how you make your living?"

"I have other jobs...part time."

"Our mother works at the church," said the older brother.

"Do you know where I can find your husband?"

Maritza made a noise like this was the most ridiculous question of all time.

"Does he have an address?" said Miller.

She gave him an address. The other investigator wrote it down.

"When was the last time you saw him?"

"A few weeks back."

"Around the time of the robbery?"

"Around that time. Why don't you ask Officer Engel? He came by looking for him."

"Officer who?"

"Engel. He stopped by a few times."

The investigators took a few moments off by themselves.

"Run down Engel," said Miller. "Set an interview."

"Already texting in."

"Then see about a search warrant."

"Right...check this out."

The investigator led Miller to the house next door. Fenced off, boarded up, doors bolted.

"You think this could be something?" said the investigator.

Miller called up to the porch. "What is this?"

"It's a house, man," said the younger brother. "Any fool can see that."

The boy's grandmother scolded him hard. Maritza called out from inside. "Caltrans owns it."

CHAPTER 114

Kagel Canyon was much like the winding road out to Lake Hughes. There were long passages through scrubby hills and lonely blocks of light here and there in a world silent as a cemetery. Not a good place to break down, not a good place to be alone. You could feel the likes of the Hillside Strangler in the night around here.

The Hideaway Bar was exactly its name. A local watering hole in a pocket of space among the trees just off the road. A handful of parking spaces. A mural of John Wayne. Trashy signs that said DANCING.

Ana ordered a drink and sat at a table and waited, occasionally giving the thumpers looking a little squirrelly with her the polite brush off.

She watched the regulars come and go as she waited. She overheard the conversations, the laughter and loud talk, all the while eyeing the front door like Wild Bill Hickok with the Cowboy Junkies on the sound system doing a Lou Reed classic.

Real music never went out of style, never died. It was like the kite that carried all the tales of you into the sky. Nice thought, but the wait....

She flashed on Mr. Jayden Miller. She wanted to call him and let him know he was missing the whole story. She looked at her phone to check the time.

She finally realized the meet was not to be, and with a feeling she was about to confirm a nightmare, walked out of there and into the night.

CHAPTER 115

Ana sat in her truck and collected her thoughts. She was wary to watch the shadows. She called Worth.

"How'd it go?" he asked.

"The caller was a no show."

"What? I don't like it."

"I got that rattlesnake in my head."

"Just get out of there."

She checked her semiautomatic and set it on the console. She had a flare gun and a bandoleer of flares on the shotgun seat. The bandoleer she swung over her shoulder. The flare gun, with a rope loop attached, she slipped over her head and onto her neck.

"What are you doing?"

"I'm prettying myself up."

"Don't. Not with me...not now."

"Sorry...I'll try to clean up my act."

"Just go. Leave."

"He's around here somewhere I bet," she said. "He might have even been in the bar sizing up his competition."

"That's what I mean. Get out of there."

She looked up toward the road. She made sure the cross she wore was recording, for whatever good it might do.

"Ana?"

"I'm looking at a mural on a garage wall of John Wayne...and that scene from *The Wild Bunch*...the one at the end of the movie when all the actors are walking together...You know the scene?"

"Who cares? Get out of there."

She started up the engine. Landshark could hear the engine kick.

"Stay on loudspeaker," he said, "will you?"

"Sure, boss."

She swung out of the tiny lot and onto the road.

CHAPTER 116

Ana didn't push it or gun it. She drove at the same cool, healthy speed she had coming there. Though it's never dark enough not to know your hands are sweating.

"Everything alright?" said Worth. "It sounds alright."

Ana didn't answer. Then she yelled out, "Holy shit!"

Landshark panicked. "What?"

"I just saw a coyote in the road with an AR-15...Should I worry?"

"Fuck you."

She gave out with a gravelly laugh.

Ana watched every dark hollow, every roadside swale.

"Talk to me," she said. "Ask me questions to keep my mind occupied."

It didn't take Landshark but a heartbeat.

"Besides wanting to serve your country, why'd you join the Army?"

"Marines," she said. "I wanted to show my father I was a better man than he was."

"What's it like," said Worth, "missing a foot?"

"I pretend I'm the girl I was…and I pretend I'm the woman I'd like to be. That helps keep the person I am at bay."

"Did you have a dream?"

Where the road turned, this amped her the most, because she could be hit from a number of blind angles. If someone was going to shoot at her.

"I didn't catch the question," said Ana.

"Do you have a dream?"

"No dream," said Ana.

"You're lying. I can hear it in your voice."

"I'm like Los Angeles," said Ana.

"What's that mean?"

"We're both one dream short of a royal flush."

CHAPTER 117

A shot came through the windshield. It made a nasty hole. It spidered the glass all the way to its borders. The bullet hit the rearview mirror. It caromed and scored Ana's cheekbone, then went through the cab seat.

She was blinded momentarily and the car swerved. The second shot might have killed her except the car now was out of control, turning like a top as she cut the wheel and braked.

Ana tried to wipe the blood from her face to clear the spatters of it out of her eyes when she realized her right arm burned and there was a hard knifing pain from her elbow to wrist. She had been hit there too, but how bad, she had no idea.

Her truck was skidding backward off the shoulder. She cut the headlights so she was not quite the target.

The truck went straight down into a ditch, ass end first. The chassis bounced and lifted, then Ana was slammed against the cab wall when the pickup hit bottom.

Ana was stunned. The space around her turned black. She could not hear. She shook her head. She tried to gather in her breath. She called to herself, *Get it together, girl.*

It was then that she heard Landshark on loudspeaker. "Are you alright? Ana? Can you hear me?"

"Call 911," said a disoriented Ana. "Call 911."

She shoved the driver's door open and threw herself out. She was crawling over rock and sand. There was another shot. It tore into the front end of the truck. There was the loud cut of metal. The shot came from across the road, of that she was sure.

CHAPTER 118

She crawled her way along the decline until she came to a place where she thought it safe enough to make a fight of it. She loaded a flare. She aimed at the hill across the road where, by her best guess, the shot had come. She aimed for the crest of the hill and fired. A long trail of phosphor cut across Kagel Canyon. The flare exploded along the ridgeline and for a moment there he was—whoever he was.

A black outline. Man with rifle. A still shot amid burning colors. There, then gone. The hillcrest darkening again except for small patches of burning embers where the brush had been torched.

She got this extraordinary rush of the past. Adrenaline pumping through the system like a jolt of pure emotional electricity, and she was thousands of miles away. A young girl in uniform in a dirty battle for God, flag, and country.

The war never leaves you.

Another shot was fired. She heard it. She heard where it hit. Nowhere close. She had the edge, at least, for however long it would last. She loaded another flare and fired just as a car was speeding up through the canyon. The trail of phosphor went shooting right over its roof.

What the fuck must the driver be thinking?

That she had a moment to think that shocked her.

Again she saw him. Against this black outline. Man with rifle. Only now moving at a trot. Athletic, lean—log that—disappearing now into a backdrop of muted hills.

Then she saw what he must have from way down in the canyon. The lights of a police cruiser coming on fast up into the winds of the road. Its lights burning against the night, almost phantom like.

In the cool moonless night she heard the truck engine. It was still running, and there was Landshark on loudspeaker.

He was calling out to Ana. Pleading, desperate. "Can you hear me?...I've called 911...Jesus Christ, are you alright?"

She walked over to the truck, spent. The front end was protruding up from the gully. She could lean against the chassis.

"I'm here," she said.

Worth's voice flushed with anticipation. "Ana...is that you? Answer me, girl."

"It's me."

"You alright?"

She looked at her arm. Blood was trailing down over the backs of her fingers. She used her other hand to wipe at the blood trickling down her cheek.

"I'm alright," she said.

"The police are on the way."

"I know. I can see them down the canyon. Thanks."

"What happened?"

"I'll share it with you later. Right now…if you don't mind…I think I'll pass out for a little while."

CHAPTER 119

Miller and the investigator with him ate at a fast food joint near downtown that Miller trafficked from time to time. The burgers were bitchin', the chili on steroids, but at night it was a bit of a freak show of druggies, losers, homeless crazies. It would keep you wide eyed, especially now that no one got arrested in this town. Somebody had spray painted GOD BLESS GASCON on a brick wall. This Miller pointed out with grim humor.

They sat alone at an outside patio table chasing away beggars and working up what they knew.

Andres had been a serious "person of interest," but now they added Velez to the list. The two being connected, the two having disappeared around the same time as the robbery.

Could they have skipped together? Might one have offed the other and blown out of dear old L.A.?

"It wouldn't surprise me," said Miller, "if both are fertilizing some bleak corner of Wokeland."

A text came in—the meeting with Engel was set for the next day.

The search warrant for the Velez house would be granted in the morning.

"What about the place next door?" said the investigator. "It would be perfect for the two men to meet clandestinely and plot."

"We'll never get a warrant...yet...for that."

"Who said anything about a warrant?"

"I didn't hear you say that."

CHAPTER 120

Then a headcase two tables over went off on a major rant. He looked like a former beach boy, now a burned down sixty plus, with white hair to the shoulders, dog pound teeth, ratty shorts that barely concealed a jiggly crotch, his feet unwashed since the time of Christ, literally standing on the stone table gyrating as if he were surfing the big wave. He was screaming about the seventies and seventies television and Fonzie and his wuss puddle of a sidekick and Laverne and Shirley and how he'd fucked both of them and how this whole city was in decay and needed to be Terminixed with bug spray.

Then he pulled a bread knife and started wielding it and threatened to move his bowels right then and there.

Here's where Miller thought—enough. "Watch my back," he said to the investigator with him.

Miller asked surfer boy to put down the knife and he responded by slashing the air and Miller pulled his ID and ordered the man down from the table.

And what happened next—a slow march of voices started. *Kill the Piggy...Kill the Piggy.* Soon it was a whole chorus of crazies, losers, druggies, drunks…*Kill the Piggy…Kill the Piggy…*slapping their hands on the stone table.

CHAPTER 121

By the time Elias arrived at the medical center in Sylmar, Ana was being prepped for surgery. Miller was in the emergency room with a couple of officers who'd answered the call and a few news crews that were lurking about. As soon as Jayden saw Elias come in, he pulled him aside before the news hounds realized who he was and took him down.

"Thanks for calling me," said Elias.

Miller put out a hand. "Peace…for the time being, anyway."

"Peace," said Elias.

They shook hands.

"How is she?"

"A bullet fragment in her forearm. It'll be a cakewalk."

"What happened?" said Elias.

Miller gave him his phone. Let him see part of an emergency room interview he'd filmed. Ana was still bloody and thoroughly wiped out. She had an IV in her arm to sedate her.

"I was driving Kagel Canyon. I had been at a bar. The Hideaway. And someone took a shot at my truck. Then at me."

"You live in the canyon?"

"No…I was up there looking for property. I was thinking of moving there. Maybe get a small ranch. Put a little space between my father and I."

"And someone just shot at you?"

"This is L.A., man…They're shooting at everybody these days. Or hadn't you noticed?"

"Did you get a look at the shooter?"

"Not for what you need. But I'm pretty sure it was a man."

"Could it have anything to do with why you are out on bail?"

She shrugged the question off.

Miller could see Elias was pretty roughed up by that comment she'd made. *Put a little space between my father and I.* It was probably the meds that cut the comment loose.

"Mr. Ride," said Jayden, "take what I'm gonna say as a compliment. Your daughter is an Olympic grade liar."

Elias said nothing.

"And that riff about looking for property and buying a ranch, etcetera, etcetera, etcetera…You and I both know why she was up there."

"Do we?"

CHAPTER 122

LAPD had two choppers in the air working the trails that spidered out from the scene of the shooting, their searchlights panning the night, bearing down into deeply dark ravines. But the shooter was gone, disappeared like one of those winds over Los Angeles that can still you to death.

Jayden was in Ana's room taking updates from the Kagel Canyon investigation when Ana began to regain consciousness. Her eyes fluttered, then opened, then cleared somewhat as she drifted from her father to Jayden to Landshark, who was doing FaceTime on a laptop that had been set on a tray table by her bedside. Her father took her hand.

She wanted to speak. Ana had to force the words out of a bone dry mouth. "The three men in my life," she said. "What could be more telling? The man who birthed me, the one who hired me, and the one trying to incarcerate me."

CHAPTER 123

When Ana awoke next, first light shined on the window panels where Miller sat in the corner of the room, texting.

"Where's my father?" she said.

Miller looked up. "Breakfast shift."

He stood and approached the bed. He looked at the laptop, which still showed Landshark's office, but no Landshark.

"*I was thinking about buying a small ranch,*" he said, mimicking Ana. He shook his head. "Talk about smoke up their asses. I can just see you saving all those quarters, dimes, and nickels until you had enough for your own Hallmark movie ranch right here in sunny, tax burdened Southern California."

Ana raised her arm slightly to size up the pain.

"You were baited last night," said Jayden. "Was it your hotline? You want to see how close that shot was to trimming off the top of your skull? This is not about a gun shop robbery. This has weight."

She tried to sit up. To get her bearings.

"You think the wound on my cheek will leave a scar?"

BOSTON TERAN

CHAPTER 124

Two search warrants were issued. One for the Luis Velez apartment, on the grounds that sought property was evidence that a crime had been committed.

The second warrant was issued for Velez's mother in law's house on the grounds that sought property had been delivered to another for the purpose of concealing it, or keeping it from being discovered.

Landshark had called Ana to inform her, and against the adamant advice of her doctors, she left the hospital and got into a waiting Lincoln SUV.

By the time she arrived at the house, that warrant had also been served and a team under Miller was going through the residence room by room, closet by closet, drawer by drawer—no corner or suspicious cranny escaped them.

"What the fuck?" said Miller when passing through the living room—who does he see through the front window on the porch talking with Maritza Velez?

The first words out of Jayden's mouth when he came out onto the porch: "You look terrible."

"It's the light," said Ana.

"They let you out?"

"It's not the zoo."

"How you feeling?"

"Like I look."

"I won't ask what you're doing here."

As they talked, his eyes fell upon the house next door.

"We found a couple of prints in the Velez apartment that belonged to Andres. And the mail was stacked up since two days after the robbery."

160

He turned to Maritza. "Ms. Velez. The house next door, you said Caltrans owns it?"

"Yes."

"You've been in that house?"

"Yes…the old woman who lived there. We took care of her."

"You have access?"

She glanced at Ana, who nonchalantly nodded—yes.

"Yes," said Maritza.

"Would you allow us to search it?"

Again, Maritza glanced at Ana.

"She's not a lawyer, ma'am," said Jayden.

Ana nodded it was okay.

"I'll get the key," said Maritza.

Now it was just the two of them on that worn out porch with a clammy heat beating down.

Jayden took Ana's arm, looked the bandage over. Then he ran a subtle thumb along her skin.

"We're collecting quite an audience," she said.

There they all were. The usual crowd of neighbors, lookers, the unjustifiably nosy with their trusted cellphones.

"I'm gonna let you come with us next door," said Miller. "Because I'm hoping what I suspect isn't so. For your own good."

CHAPTER 125

Maritza led the investigators down the walkway to the back of her house and the chain link fence where she squeezed through the opening, the others following along like ducklings. Ana was the last of them and Miller hung back to help her through.

Maritza prayed for god's intervention as she undid the padlock on the rear door and the others followed her into a dirty and empty house with blacked out windows.

They had their flashlights on, panning rooms that had been severely vandalized, with holes in the walls, gaps where copper piping had been torn away, nobs and fixtures missing. Miller gave orders as to who would search where, all the while watching as well as he could both the Velez woman and an exhausted Ana Ride.

"There an attic in this place?" said Miller.

"No attic," said Maritza.

"A basement of any kind?"

"A full basement, sir," she said.

Miller came up to her and angled the flashlight under her chin, the uncertainty of her expression now stark in the extreme.

"You don't look very comfortable."

"I don't like these places."

"Who does?" said Miller. "Now…where's the basement?"

She led them through the kitchen to an alcove in the hallway under Miller's watchful eye. Maritza pointed to the door and stepped forward, past Ana, and opened it. Light flooded down a rickety stairwell and Ana and Miller stood there for a moment, him eyeing her. She knew he was giving her the judgment, that there was more to that look.

The basement was trash central and a rat heaven. The windows down there were also blacked out and the flashlights created long and dusty tunnels that passed over used furniture, crates, garbage, stacked cans of paint and turpentine. It was a fuckin' fire hazard of the first degree, and hell to grub through.

One of the investigators said, "I think I found something. Down there, sir. I'm seeing a hole in the floor."

Maritza looked across the darkness for Ana. The lights bore down on the hole. Then that same investigator crawled over a tottery pyre of ruin to look in the hole, cursing the stink.

"Anything?" asked Miller.

"Empty, sir."

CHAPTER 126

Susan Sarah Heyer lived on Milner Road, in the 6700 block. It was a narrow Hollywood street built in an era when Hollywood was a prized jewel. The house was just off Highland and the DeMille Museum. Spanish, built in 1921, it was now on the National Register of Historic Places. This is where Susan Sarah would pass away her final years.

More families than care to admit have a Susan Sarah among their numbers. That decaying figure who has outlived their worst impulses, who bears a secret life of disgraces and degradations, who was wicked and harmful, and who is still wicked, but harmless. And who lives in quiet, private depravity.

Susan Sarah was just such a woman and the house she lived in was bought for her by William Worth. You see, she was his aunt, and the only remaining family member alive. She was also the aunt, in fact, who took him to the movies and molested him.

He bought the house out of pity for her poverty, and because beyond his own personality, he was decent.

There was subtle payback through that act of kindness. You see, the award winning filmmaker Dean Harlan had died there, his violent passing being part of what became known in Hollywood lore as the Sunset Westerly Murders.

It was a popular landing spot for movie aficionados and "other forms of desperate movie losers," as Susan Sarah described them. The selfie freaks and YouTubers who invaded her privacy filming in front of her house or climbing the infamous Whitley Terrace Steps beside the home where once ran a river of blood.

Susan Sarah would scream at them, rant, insult, curse, threaten, even spit down on them, but still they came, this army straight out of *The Day of the Locust.* And if you don't think it gave Landshark a bit of vengeful joy, you are mistaken.

And this, Susan Sarah knew all too well.

CHAPTER 127

Ana had come to the house about a week earlier. It was an overcast night, the air murky. The house was not difficult to find. It was just across from the Hollywood Bowl on Milner. The house was built against a hill and beautifully appointed. Ana climbed the stairs, music played from beyond the blazing lit windows and their silky gorgeous curtains. There was a small grass patio where Ana knocked on the front door.

It took a while, the music was lowered. The peephole opened, a pair of eyes looked Ana up and down, then the peephole closed. A moment later the door slowly opened. A woman of about seventy stood there, well tailored, tall, lithe.

"Susan Sarah Heyer?" said Ana.

"Don't I look like her?" said the woman.

Ana knew what she meant. Landshark had said the woman looked like Loretta Young, the famed actress, when she was older. Ana didn't know who Loretta Young was. Worth showed her a picture of the two women standing together outside a downtown Catholic church, where all the washed up celebs came and prayed for the old days.

Susan Sarah came outside. "You didn't park on the street, did you? There's no parking on the street without a permit."

"No." said Ana. "I'm down the hill."

Susan Sarah went eye to eye with Ana. "Did William tell you about me?

"Yes."

"Did he tell you all about me, that is?"

"Yes."

Susan Sarah went back into the house for a moment and returned holding a set of keys, talking all the while. "William said you were a hard case. You don't exactly look like a hard case. Of course, a hard case can be deceptive. Take me for instance. Do I look like a woman who served seven years in Chowchilla?...No way.

"Now," she said. "Why don't you bring your car up here and I'll go open the garage. You can hide the satchels there."

"Yes, ma'am."

"By the way, William told you about the murders in the garage?"

"Yes."

"And you're alright with that? Superstitious wise?"

"As long as I'm not one of the victims."

CHAPTER 128

Susan Sarah was, that day, doing exactly as her nephew was. They were both at their computers, both logged into the Citizen app. They were both watching the scene at the Velez house and next door, which had been cordoned off by the investigative team. Landshark, you see, had paid one of his nightcrawlers to film the investigation from the street and stream it live on the Citizen app.

As Miller came out of the fenced off house, Susan Sarah said, "He doesn't look all too happy."

"You're seeing him through a chain link fence. He'll look a lot worse later," said Landshark.

"He's smart," said Susan Sarah. "And nice looking. Too bad."

"He was close," said Landshark, "but just a little late."

Ana and Maritza came walking out together, the look between them, even through chain links, telling its own story. Maritza did not understand; you could feel her confusion as Ana shushed what she knew was coming with a turn of her head.

"Your girl is holding up," said Susan Sarah.

"She has that extra gear," said Landshark.

"I wasn't so sure about her that first evening she came here."

"Miller worries me," said Landshark. "He's a blood in the water guy. And there's blood in the water."

"It would take a lot of blood to get from that wreck of a house to my garage."

CHAPTER 129

When they were truly alone, Maritza whispered to Ana, "What happened to—"

"You had a visitor. Enough said."

Back in the house, Maritza walked Ana to the porch where her mother sat quietly. There Miller closed in.

"They were down there, weren't they? The weapons?"

The two women lied with silence.

Miller looked to the old woman. "You want to see this turn out well for your daughter, don't you?"

"She knows what to do," said the old woman.

"I'm exhausted," said Ana. "I have to pay a visit to the hospital."

Miller turned to Maritza. "She didn't speak and she'll wind up in jail. You better speak, because if you wind up in jail, you will lose custody of your children."

"My husband can better answer you, Mr. Miller."

He cursed under his breath and Ana walked off. He followed at a distance. She turned once, he was there, then again when she reached her waiting car, he was on her.

"You're following me."

"Damn right."

"What am I supposed to be...that infamous deer in the headlights?"

"You are that deer in the headlights. Infamous or not. And I want you to feel that. I want you to feel my presence right there on your back."

"I can think of more interesting places to feel it."

CHAPTER 130

James Salamone had been approached to meet with a man who was a cheat, a liar, a con, and utterly phony. But beyond that, he was everything one could hope for.

Salamone had set the meet for a restaurant in the Water Market Tower. Faith and Flower was typical L.A. stylistic overkill, named after two streets from the city's star crossed youth. With sleek leather and designer fabric art, everything shined, everything reflected, everything spoke to the L.A. kind of success. Even the menus, for Christ's sake, would win an Emmy if there were such a category.

Philip DiNunzio was close to exactly what Salamone expected. He was that shiny type, suit with open collar, Italian loafers but no socks. He had served two years in the Army, in combat, which would smooth over some of that phony elitism.

They sat and drinks were ordered. It wasn't noon yet and the restaurant was still cool and somewhat quiet so you could hear the slight echo of servers moving the silverware around.

"So," said Salamone, "you dated Julia Domingo?"

"In college, and after. For a year."

"And you know for a fact she slept with her brother."

"You get right to it," said DiNunzio.

"I leave my pretense at the door, like a number of people all over the world do their shoes."

CHAPTER 131

"We'd been at it about a year after I got out of the Army," said DiNunzio. "She was always into politics. The busy little progressive. Meetings, rallies, voter drives, fundraisers. She had a long range plan—Congress, mayor, Senate, on and on.

"After her mother died, I had to take a trip to New York to hook up with some Army buddies. I took the red eye home to surprise her. I surprised her alright. She was in bed fuckin' her brother, who was a total headcase."

"She'll deny it, I'm sure," said Salamone.

"She can deny it all she wants. I talked to my shrink about it that very week."

"You were seeing a shrink?"

"The combat had burned my brain. My shrink will validate what I'm saying—I gave her the green light."

"What are you about?"

"About?"

"Yeah…Honesty? Transparency?"

"All those things," said DiNunzio. "The people deserve the truth."

Salamone listened, sort of. Mainly on his mind was: Would this Easter egg story hold up?

"What do you want?" said Salamone. "What's your work? What does the future have in store for Philip DiNunzio?"

As if on cue, DiNunzio said, "I've been driving Uber, but I'm trying to raise funds for a coffee table book. It's called *Cookin' for the Mob*…the favorite recipes of famous gangsters—"

"How much to properly develop this work of art?" said Salamone.

CHAPTER 132

Ana pulled up to the Carter and Ellison building on downtown Main Street. She was driving a pickup that Landshark had rented for her. It was the same locked down street as always. Buildings, as usual, with windows protected by corrugated steel shutters, and the Amtrak, when it sped past, was a loud, annoying pain in the ass you could feel right down into your teeth.

She rang the buzzer and smiled up at the camera. Carter and Ellison were glad to see her. She'd been on the news, her ruined truck, the scene of the shooting.

"Gents," she said, "I need a favor."

"I hate favors," said Carter. "Don't you?"

Ellison agreed. "Nothing worse. You lend a hand, you get sucked in, your life unravels."

"Fuck you both," she said.

"You did once, remember?" said Carter.

"That was a young girl who just happened to look like me."

She took two cellphones from her pocket. She went to speak when Ellison gave her the "keep quiet" sign—just in case.

He started down the hall. Carter fell in behind him. Ana knew where they were going. At the back of the building there was a large walk in safe where the boys kept their prized possessions. Carter closed the door behind them.

"Now we can talk," said Ellison.

"LAPD?" said Ana.

"Your very own Jayden Miller," said Carter. "He was here asking your whereabouts the night of the robbery and the week before. We thought it best to lay low about it."

"Not exactly a time we want to revisit," mentioned Ellison.

"Sorry," she said.

"We don't think they could get a warrant to bug us, but you know how slippery some of these badged boys and girls can be."

Ana held out the two cellphones. "There's about a dozen messages on each. My employer and I want you to find out all you can. Voice manipulation...localization via cell towers."

"You think one of them," said Carter, "is the shooter?"

"Number thirteen on that phone is the shooter. He...or she... set the meet."

"You sticking this one out?" said Ellison.

"You can't just let people get malign with you."

"Oh shit," said Ellison. "You're not reading *The Purpose Driven Life* or some other trash like that?"

"How do you feel?" said Carter, cutting off his partner.

Ana held out her bandaged arm and gave the air the finger.

CHAPTER 133

Engel sat across from Miller in a faceless interrogation room. Engel would be described by Miller as a dedicated young officer being suffocated by the status quo. A description, Miller believed, that would cover a growing percentage of duty officers...including himself.

Engel was a soft spoken kid, born and raised in San Pedro. LAPD was a step up.

"You know why you're here?"

"I'd rather you tell me, sir."

"Luis Velez…the Academy gun shop robbery…and an incident on Valley Boulevard where a civilian was taken from a squad car and put in a white van."

"What? I don't know anything about a Valley—"

"We'll get to the questions. First…" He looked over Engel's file. "You've been on the force nine years."

"Yes, sir."

"You have a superior record."

"Thank you. Valley Boulevard, sir—"

"What are your aspirations?"

"Sir?"

"Aspirations…in the force."

Engel looked suddenly discouraged.

"If I may, sir…my aspirations are…Get out soon, get out alive, and get out with my pension."

"That's not a very uplifting aspiration, is it?"

"I stopped a woman for speeding yesterday," said Engel, "doing fifty five in a school zone. She had a son in the back seat, about my boy's age. I said to the boy, 'You're a nice looking kid, you know that?' And he spit at me. Mother says nothing. I'm taking hits for every bad deed, real or imagined, some cop has done since the beginning of time. But that's not why you called me here, is it?"

"Not long after the robbery," said Miller, "you went to the Velez house looking for Luis."

"I went there because my wife suggested it. It was right after the shooting at the church. My wife and Maritza Velez sometimes work together at the church. She was concerned."

"But you also went to his apartment on at least two other occasions looking for him."

"Yeah."

"You aren't that tight with him, are you?"

"No."

"It was just...concern?"

"Yeah."

"Let's talk about Valley Boulevard on the night of—"

"I know nothing about this supposed incident. It certainly didn't happen on my shift."

"You were working alone that night."

"Yes."

"And your partner called in sick."

"Yes."

"Sick as in sick? Or sick as in fed up?"

"Both, probably."

"We had eleven squad cars on Valley Boulevard over the course of that evening. We're questioning everyone. Are you sure you didn't see something, anything, with a white van—"

"What does this have to do with Luis?"

"It's our belief that Luis Velez could well have been involved in the gun shop robbery and his disappearance is a direct result of that."

"You mean he split?"

"I mean nothing of the sort. We think this is a robbery that went off the rails after they killed that homeless man up in the park. And that Luis Velez has come to a tragic, but utterly predictable, end." He paused, then added, "With more tragic and predictable ends to come."

CHAPTER 134

After the meeting—or interrogation—Officer Charlie Engel went downstairs and entered the public bathroom. It was empty, thank god.

He went into a stall, locking the door behind him. And then, so unnerved, checked to make sure it was locked. He then bent over the bowl, and holding his hand against his chest, proceeded to vomit.

There were no comforting words, just that long runner of half digested food and bile splashing into the white bowl. The ultimate cry for help. *Too late, Charlie. You passed that turn in the road a dozen decisions ago. When you were too clever by half, and hadn't talked it out with life's ultimate bathroom attendant.*

He thought of all the questions Miller could have asked but didn't. Questions on his fingertips from experience. Questions he knew were left dangling out there intentionally for later, like the California earthquake prophecy that will take us all down.

He stood at the sink, despondent and pale. His courage back there in the bowl. He downed a couple of valium he always kept handy.

But, of course, there was no valium for what he had done. Unless you were trying to get to that hard white emptiness.

CHAPTER 135

They were in Landshark's office. He was at the bulletin board lining up new facts. Ana lay on the couch and rested. Her wounded arm stretched across her chest. She was transfixed by the ceiling with the streaks of sunlight and the shadows between them and how it all changed by the minute because of a cloud or the breeze upon the trees.

"Is the world we live in ever the world we live in?" said Ana. "I feel all this is expanding while we are getting smaller."

"Sometimes," said Worth, "the answer is not in the details, but in the design."

Ana moved her head a bit to see Landshark across the room by the bulletin board, pacing.

"I say the robbery meant nothing. Not as a robbery, not for the money the weapons would bring," said Worth.

"Andres and Velez," said Ana. "What were they?"

"Does it matter?" said Worth. "We've replaced them. We have the weapons. Possession is nine tenths of the law."

He pointed to the index cards with the names of all the players so far. "Every one of them is relevant to one thing...the 710 Corridor," said Worth. "The fight over who gets to decide the fate of these properties."

"The robbery may be the equivalent of someone dropping a dime," suggested Ana. "Is that it?"

"An act to make someone look corrupt. Ruin their reputation. At least compromise them."

"The way you lay it out...Julia Domingo is the likely target."

"Maybe," said Worth.

They were both quiet after that. The way Worth had said "Maybe" didn't sit well, not with either.

"You know that world we live in that you were just talking about," said Worth. "The one you wonder if you really live in?"

"Yeah?" said an uncertain Ana.

"It's coming after us," said Worth.

CHAPTER 136

Elias Ride came home from doing his obligatory shopping, all cursed out from the punitive food prices, thanks to what he saw as government induced inflation, only to discover his screen door partly open, the front door unlocked, and it, too, slightly open.

Not good. Not good at all. Not an Ana thing, not even by mistake. He pulled the snubnose he carried under his loose fitting shirt. He footed the door open slowly, keeping himself protected, before he entered.

Everything inside was as it should be. Nothing ransacked, torn loose, stolen, no cabinets or drawers tampered with, no closets rummaged. Nothing.

He went next door to his daughter's to find everything pretty much the same. The screen door open, the front door unlocked and partly open.

Was this a warning, a threat? What was the punchline?

He discovered the answer when he returned to his own place. It was right there in front of the computer—a saucer plate. And on the plate was a partly used pack of cigarettes. And what made that particular pack of cigarettes so eye catching—it was partly stained with blood.

He called Ana, who was still with Worth.

Then he called Miller.

While he waited he walked to the village office. Fidelma was working there that day, and she was never genuinely happy to see him.

"Check the cameras for the main gate," said Elias. "They're not working."

"They're fine," said Fidelma. "I checked them this morning."

"They're not working now. Check them."

Aggravated, she refused.

"Check them, you stupid old bitch. Or I'll come back there—"

She turned on her heel and went to the back room. She returned, more aggravated than when she had left.

"They're not working," she said. "And go screw yourself."

CHAPTER 137

Miller knocked on Ana's door and then entered. She had made coffee and was pouring her father a cup.

"They're almost done dusting for prints," said Miller.

Elias laughed at the thought of it.

"Want coffee," Ana offered Jayden.

He nodded that he did. "How are you?" he said.

"In no uncertain terms...fuckin' wasted."

"What do you both think?" said Miller.

"What's to think?" said Elias.

"Blood and DNA will tell us something," said Miller.

Elias put his cup down hard. "You don't need blood and DNA for this. The cigarettes, in case you hadn't noticed, are the same Ana smokes. And the blood...it could be dog's blood, chicken blood. This is plain enough. It's a message...My daughter is gonna be served up on a platter."

CHAPTER 138

After work Charlie Engel showed up unannounced at the Velez house. It was already dark when the front doorbell rang.

One of the boys looked out the window and called to his mother. Maritza answered the door and opened it but slightly.

"Hello, Maritza."

"Charlie...Why are you here?"

She looked past him to the street. He was not in uniform, not with his squad car.

"I know this might not be the best time, but could you spare me a few minutes?"

"This isn't a good time, Charlie."

"Just a few minutes."

"Tomorrow...tomorrow would be better."

He tried to press into the doorway, but she was not having it.

"I've got to help the boys with their homework before it gets late."

"I was questioned today about some alleged incident on Valley Boulevard where your husband was taken away in a van."

"I don't know anything about that," said Maritza. "Except what I was told today."

"It's not true, but I'm concerned about my job. The way things are, people react badly to suspicions."

"Tomorrow," she said, trying to close the door.

Engel had grown more intense as they talked, a reasonable sense of calm escaping him.

"Your husband lied, you know."

"No...I don't know."

"And you lied to the police."

"I did no such thing."

"You lied about the weapons."

"Untrue," said Maritza.

The older boy forced his hand into the opening and shoved at Engel. "Leave my mother be."

"You knew about them. You knew he sold them before. Did you tell that to the police?"

"That is a lie."

"I'm not going to be persecuted for you or your husband."

The boy kicked at Engel's legs.

"I said nothing about that to them," said Maritza, "because it is untrue."

CHAPTER 139

Later that night, with the children asleep, Maritza sat on the couch in the dark with her mother, resting against the old woman's chest, like she had as a child, for the child is never gone very far.

She would survive this, she promised. The lies and half lies and the deceptions under wraps. Because she had a purpose asleep in the room above her, on the couch there beside her, and within the walls of the house that protected them all.

But she was well aware of the social perils closing in. She was already fielding calls from members of the Tenants Association, curious as to why her house was cordoned off and searched and was her missing husband involved in a crime.

She had been one of the faces on the YouTube video plea with Julia Domingo addressed to the governor and a legion of California importants.

Dear god, she thought, *don't let them catch up with me.*

CHAPTER 140

Ana walked Jayden to his car. And if you think there weren't suspicious eyes watching from behind tweaked blinds, loose curtains, or little corners of the quiet dark, think again.

"Your father may be right," said Jayden.

"About what?"

"The blood and DNA."

"He's like that sometimes, the son of a bitch. Being right, I mean. God help us if he gets on a streak. He'll make us all look bad and we'll never hear the end of it."

At the car they took a moment. His car was parked right under one of the trailer village lampposts. Not exactly a perfect spot.

"Can I kiss you goodnight?" said Miller.

"That depends," said Ana.

"On...?"

"On where you intend to kiss me."

CHAPTER 141

Elias had the television on, but who needed the suffering? It was bad news upstaging bad news. The Uvalde school slaughter had devolved into a case of utter police cowardice. Turn the station and someone is being thrown down a flight of stairs, someone is being thrown in front of a subway train, someone is run over and then robbed. And the bad across the boards, all are being released without bail. The American legal system was becoming its own default button.

Ana yelled she wanted to come in. Elias shouted back that would be fine.

"I'm outta cigarettes," she said. "You wouldn't happen to have an open pack of mine laying around. Maybe one with a little blood on it?"

"That's not funny," he said in a moment of rage.

"It was a little funny," she said.

CHAPTER 142

Her father saw she'd had a pack of cigarettes on her when she took it out of her pocket. She'd come over to use his computer as she was having internet issues. A Zoom call had been set for her and Landshark to talk with Ellison and Carter, who had texted her they had news.

They were hoping for a breakthrough when Ellison opened with "Slick...clean. And a dead end."

"The deadest," said Carter.

Landshark kicked at something that went clanging across his office off camera.

"Don't rage against the machine too fast there," said Carter. "Cause we have one detail. One 'major' detail."

"Maybe major. With a heavy accent on 'maybe,'" said Ellison.

Ana looked to Landshark, crossed her fingers.

"One person," said Carter. "Left two messages. One on each hotline."

"Explain," said Worth.

"The one message on the hotline about the incident on Valley Boulevard with the van matched—"

"The one with the van in Kagel Canyon," said Worth. "Please, yes?"

"You got it," said Ellison.

"It's the same person," said Carter.

"We did voice checks," said Ellison.

"Then we checked the checks."

"And checked them again after that just to be sure."

"You have a marauder out there folks," said Carter. "A fully grown, intelligent, shrewd, well plotting marauder."

They went back and forth on every detail of the calls, and what they did not know and could not ascertain—were the calls actual incidents in and of themselves. LAPD still could not make that determination. Were they just smoke? A means to send the hunter down a wrong rabbit hole?

"A wise man," said Ana, "told me…It is not always about the details, but the design." It was her private salute to a thought that Landshark had passed to her. And truer yet.

So they began again, still the question outsmarted them. Except for that one—the caller had made two calls. Calls that fit together neatly.

Elias, who had been silent and sitting off camera listening, said, "You sound like a bunch of salesgirls, or whatever they call them now, selling douches."

He stood and leaned over his daughter's shoulder.

"I think Andres brought Velez into this," said Elias. "I think he was ordered or solicited to. Not because of Velez himself, or a talent, but because of his wife. And her connection to the Domingos. And the Tenants Association in the Corridor. This is not about a crime… it's about politics. It is an attempted assassination by association. Except something went off the rails."

"What?" said Carter.

"Does it matter…really?" said Elias. "Andres was scum. Velez not much different. You have the smoking gun…the weapons. Now you just need whoever pulled the trigger. Or who will pull it.

"For me…I don't want to see my daughter dead."

CHAPTER 143

When the call was over and everyone had gone to their separate corners, it was just Ana and her father. And him sitting again in his trusty old fart recliner with a beer, the portrait of cool dispatch.

Ana said, "Thank you, Mr. Ride."

"For what, Ms. Ride?"

"For having a damn sharp take on this."

"Ahhh," he said caustically. "I guess I'm like that warm quilt in times of disaster."

She cracked up.

He hoisted his beer.

On the way out, she added, "Thanks for not wanting me dead."

"Don't let that go to your head. I could change on a fuckin' dime."

CHAPTER 144

Charlie Engel had a brother—Freddy—who had been the original conduit between Charlie and the man known as ChiChi. Freddy looked like a castoff from a biker movie, or one of those Netflix imitations of the real world. Freddy was aggressive as he was injudicious, but built like he could carry around storm drains.

Freddy liked to say, "I'm a missionary in a scumbag's body."

"Charlie," said Freddy. "What do you want, my brother?"

"ChiChi."

"What about him?"

"I got to have the talk. And soon."

"I don't control soon, brother."

"Can you press? I mean press."

"Got to put the ad in Craigslist. I get a response…What do I tell him?"

"Valley Boulevard."

CHAPTER 145

Miller was just leaving his house for his car when he received a text from his commander to appear immediately at headquarters. "Immediately" was in caps. He knew this to be bad news.

When he arrived he was ushered right in. The captain turning toward him, the look on his face, confirmed the worst.

"You're being sued."

This he did not expect.

"For what…by whom?"

"I want you to see this."

The captain cued up a video. It was taken at night, on a cellphone. There was the fast food joint from a few nights back. And there was that crazy shit on the stone table, surfing.

"The nutcase," said Jayden.

"Keep watching," said the captain.

This was where Jayden Miller walked into frame. Where he flashed his ID and said, "Get the fuck off the table."

"This is where it starts," said the captain.

"Where what starts?"

The schizophrenic on the table pulled out a breadknife and began to slash at the air while ranting about the *Happy Days* television show and our crumbling America.

"You were off duty right there. And you should have had the foresight to call this in."

"Well…I thought I'd wait till there were at least a few bodies on the ground before—"

"Do you want comments like that used against you?"

The video played on with Miller using verbal insults like *crazy* and *nutcase,* demanding the *schizo* get the hell down from there and hand over the knife.

And when none of that made any headway with the star of this extravaganza, Miller pulled the schizophrenic from the table and disarmed him.

The captain began to read from the lawsuit. "When dealing with the emotionally distressed…Don't be insulting…Don't use strong language…Don't alarm them…Don't challenge them…Don't move aggressively…"

"In other words, just let them do whatever they fuckin' want," said Miller. "Of course, even when an officer is off duty, he, she, they, them, or whatever pronoun said officer goes by, is actually on duty."

"The Police League already has a copy of this. You will be assigned an attorney. As of this meeting…you are suspended."

"Can't we get around that?"

"The victim has a sister. Who works for the Department of Mental Health. Who happens to have gone to college with the mayor. And is one of his most ardent fundraisers. Need I say more?"

"You mean," said Miller, "I'm being flushed down the political drain."

CHAPTER 146

Landshark had gotten wind of the lawsuit from a former lover in the Police League. He wanted to tell Ana, forewarn her, but decided against it, leaving the decision to Miller.

As bad as that was, more bad news was barreling down the freeway. Of course, with all the traffic in L.A., nothing barreled like it used to.

The bad news was to come via a podcast known as DOWN AND DIRTY, CALIFORNIA, written by Dawn Newell, who had once worked for Landshark as a street reporter until she decided to try and dethrone the master.

Newell was a troll. The Nurse Ratched of the Woke Generation. She was born for cancel culture. Truthfully, any culture would do. She was part news, part malicious gossip. Call it a twenty to eighty split.

Lives that were shattered or swallowed, perfect. Lives that disappeared off the social map, fantastic. When it came to a body count, Dawn was utterly liberal minded.

CHAPTER 147

Bribery should always be disguised as good will. This way, any anxieties served up by the act will be appropriately served. This is something Landshark learned from his brilliant, albeit corrupt, parents as they exacted their stranglehold on the pharmaceutical industry, which is what gave the family its great wealth.

Dawn Newell had a computer expert who worked in her exclusive employ to handle internet issues. This young woman, it turned out, had aspirations of her own in the podcast field—relevant news influencer is how she liked to see herself one day.

The previous year she had ingratiated herself to Landshark by passing him a valuable tidbit insight on a former television star who now did videomercials. And so began a relationship of financial guidance for industrious information gathering. In this case—how did Philip DiNunzio and Dawn Newell come together?

When he learned it was through James Salamone, a design of criminal acts and good old fashioned public relations began to materialize.

CHAPTER 148

Dawn Newell called Julia Domingo directly. The call was intercepted by the loving brother.

Dawn politely blew him off with, "I need a quote from the lady herself for an upcoming podcast."

"I think I can give a quote as good as my sister."

"Better…That's why I want to speak with her."

"Alright. What's the question?"

"Do I talk to Julia or not?"

"I'll ask her."

She had him in a box and she knew it. "Shall I wait on the line, or until I've had enough time to drink one Bloody Mary?"

"Drink away," he said, and hung up.

CHAPTER 149

"Hello, Dawn," said Julia. "I'd have gotten back to you sooner, but I was on one of *those* calls."

"I'd like to start by saying I think your work on the 710 Corridor and the Tenants Association is to be emulated and admired."

"Thank you, Dawn."

She took a breath—that is, Dawn did. Julia could envision the bitch on loudspeaker, sitting naked at her desk, in a black mask and polishing up her cloven hooves.

"So," said Julia, "how can I be of service?"

"Philip DiNunzio has a few things to say about your brother and you…I'd like to know if they're true."

CHAPTER 150

Julia left the house in panic and misery. She walked up the huge empty backyard lot to the top of the hill, where the foundation of the original house still was, built by her uncle from his earnings in that television show back in the fifties.

Her brother had been following along behind her.

"Newell is a cunt," he said.

Julia paid him no mind. It was too painful for such high school barbarism.

"And DiNunzio…There's something in it for him. I can promise you that."

To hear this only made her sick. Then Daniel said, "I know it's my fault. I'm sorry."

"I can't believe it," she said, turning on him, "I can't believe it, nor can I bear it. After all these years, what you have to say in your defense is…This statement of fact…That you're sorry."

She shook him in despondency and disgust. "Do you know yourself at all?"

Taken aback, he said, "I know myself very well."

"Not a bit. You are a political animal. You are a tragic search for power, prestige, position."

"And none of this is you? It's you too. You are just better at the fraud than I am."

"And why is that?" she said. "It is because I have what eludes you. I have sincerity. I believe in what I say. You believe in what you figure to say that will impact others."

She pointed to that foundation of forgotten field stones, stones that had been graffitied at one time before she was a congressperson and had security.

189

"None of this means anything to you," she said. "This foundation. It speaks to my heart. It says our family has been here for a
century. Giving to, being part of, the culture. And we are its next
generation of aspirations." She pointed down the canyon to that
nightscape of a city. "That could be us...if we are not destroyed."

"We'll out fight them," he said. "Out fight them, out maneuver
them, out politic them."

"And I will tell you something else. There is no place in your heart
for 'Sorry,'" she said. "And I don't want to hear the word 'shame' ever
again. Because shame is not an excuse. It is not a reasonable means
to escape responsibility."

He did not answer. He did not know how, because what he was
after at this moment, the power of his own purpose, eluded him.
And so what does he say? What stupidity comes out of the mouth of
this unusually clever young man?

"I hate to say this," said Daniel.

"Then don't," said his sister.

"But mother is to blame, in part. Her death had a—"

"For what you just said...your Catholic soul should pay the
consequences."

CHAPTER 151

William Worth received a call from a crying and despondent Julia
Domingo. It was urgent, she said, that she come over, regardless of
the hour, to talk through a private matter that was about to break
publicly.

Landshark knew of what she spoke. He also advised that if she'd been drinking or knocking down pills, to let him send over a car. Knowing Salamone as he did, it would be no shock if he unleashed a few hired cellphone crawlers for what Salamone described as *rape PR.*

CHAPTER 152

William Worth guided an emotionally spent Julia Domingo to a very private den he had designed in the far wing of the estate. Appointed for comforting simplicity, the picture window protected by live oaks, the room soundproofed, and the lighting so subdued no one could see the tears running down the assemblyperson's face or hear her sobs.

She was vulnerable to the point of defeat. As children are defeated so completely in the moment. Landshark knew that kind of defeat. He had lived it, was living it. The ghost of one's past just over the shoulder till sometimes you awake damp between the sheets.

Julia was forthright in her explanation about how their mother had been such a powerful influence on the lives of her two children, the father having been gone from them. Their mother had been the matriarch of a social and political Latino community who had come through the welcoming doors of that home for years.

It was Daniel that their mother had political aspirations for and took him everywhere as if he were the anointed one. But it was Julia who carried the day with her beguiling simplicity.

She confessed to Landshark how Daniel had always been a little too sexual around her. It had been an ongoing issue, and with their mother's death, he became not only inconsolable, but sometimes unbearable.

He was the motherless son, then the failed son, then the one without a vision, a destination. Not only did he lean on his sister for support, but he also sought to dominate her and in that way become invaluable.

CHAPTER 153

Then they got into the subject of DiNunzio. She calmed some, the crying having exhausted her. She sat on a chair hunched over, one hand stuffed with Kleenex.

It was partly true what DiNunzio insinuated. Her brother, drunk and drugged up after their mother's funeral, had climbed into bed with Julia. Under the cover of much needed compassion, what he wanted was sex. But that did not happen. What did was DiNunzio.

"Tell me about him," said Worth.

"We dated for about a year. He was nice enough. Always scrambling. I thought I loved him."

"Have you seen him since?"

"Once, six months ago, he called to get together. At lunch he asked if I could help him. He was trying to raise money for some book scheme. Then the subject of my brother came up and the conversation veered into extortion."

"He could say you called him and offered him money to remain silent…considering your career rise."

"His call is registered in my office log and dated."

"You could have called him. And he called you back and you initiated money, for instance."

"I could have," she said.

"Would you take a lie detector test if asked?"

"I would…Would Philip?"

"Nobody gives a shit about him. This is about the 710 Corridor. And the Tenants Association. DiNunzio is just a messenger. And you're a perfect victim for Woke and cancel culture and rape PR. This is the work of James Salamone…who fronts for the DON Group, which wants that property."

She was utterly exhausted now. But her eyes—they, to Landshark, felt like droplets of poison.

"Why didn't you get rid of your brother along the way? You said earlier you covered each other's flaws."

Her answer was short and to the point.

"He's my brother."

"Good answer," said Landshark. "And bad answer."

"To throw him overboard is to admit the worst."

"Almost, but not completely."

"I won't do it."

Landshark was not sure how much of what she said was true, and how much left a lot to be desired.

"I won't cover for you. I won't back you. I'll print what you said and tell the reader to judge. I'll admit I'm not sure if you're lying or not. I will bring up Salamone and the DON Group. I'll bloody the water…that's what I do."

CHAPTER 154

Once Landshark was alone, and before he started writing the article, he put down a few flash thoughts he might use…Leonard Cohen's "Everybody Knows," steal a lyric or two. Questions, like all people, have a date with mortality…This robbery was about the well to do fighting over the barren wastes of the city they helped create…The man on the stone table out in front of the fast food joint surfing with a breadknife, use a shot of him as a standin for our world at large.

CHAPTER 155

Ana drove to the Hollywood Park Casino hunting for Jayden, figuring she'd find him all Adderaled up and blowing his money in some grand gesture of despair. But it turned out he was a no show.

She tripped it out to his place and parked. She could hear music blasting from half a block away and there were a couple of the neighbors gathered at the street gate to Jayden's house.

Ana was wearing fishnet stockings and chromish boots and a beret and cut a trashy Melrose Avenue figure.

As she made her way through that upset coterie for the gate, one of them said, "You a friend of Miller?"

"Me," said Ana. "No…I'm just a hooker."

That shut them up, sort of.

"Could you tell him to lower the music some?" said a heavyset matron in an old Dodgers jersey. "And change the song, for Christ's sake. For the last hour, over and over."

"Check," said Ana.

CHAPTER 156

She rang the doorbell, knocked a dozen times, louder, longer, harder. Pointless.

She peeked in the kitchen window. The only sign of a living person a dozen empties and a pizza box.

Forget this. She checked the door. It was unlocked. She waved to the neighbors down below and in she went.

There was music and it was loud alright and coming from YouTube. She gave the computer a look see. Eric Clapton doing "While My Guitar Gently Weeps" from the George Harrison tribute.

She didn't bother to call out because when she got to the doorway, there he was.

He looked like some version of a corpse stretched out on the couch, stripped down to stylish underwear, hands cupped behind his head and wearing a pair of sunglasses in a room that was already short of light.

It looked like a battlefield in there and Jayden was on the losing side. Things had been tossed, thrown, kicked, flung. There were more empties, a bottle of bourbon without a cap, and a joint in a crowded ashtray.

But the centerpiece to all this chaos was the coffee table. And why—because it was stacked with lottery tickets. Not fifty or a hundred...but it looked like hundreds upon hundreds. Maybe a thousand, two thousand, and they had spilled over to where there were at least a few hundred on the floor.

CHAPTER 157

Suddenly the body of Jayden Miller spoke.

"What the fuck are you doing here?"

"I came for an autograph," said Ana. "It's not often I'm in the presence of such an iconic troublemaker."

Jayden tried to sit up, but it was a major task. He listed a bit and cursed his way to uprightness. He swiped through the lottery tickets on the coffee table until he found a pen under all those possible winners.

"Give me your hand," he said.

She came forward and put out a hand, which he took. He then autographed her palm.

"Perfect," she said. "That's the hand I masturbate with. Mind if I sit?"

She sat down next to him. "The neighbors asked you to turn down the music."

"What did you tell them?"

"That I was a hooker."

He looked her over and nodded. Then he shifted gears.

"They're gonna make me go out at some point and do the whole Virtue Signaling act. That phony I'm sorry for being a pronoun phobic 'danger to society.'"

"How many lottery tickets you have there?"

"Seven thousand six hundred and whatever else was in my savings account."

"Daring move."

"I thought so."

He reached for the bourbon. Went to undo a cap that was not there.

"That was my fuck you money, and what good is fuck you money if you don't say fuck you from time to time?"

"They say you've been playing that one song all night."

Angry, realizing there was no cap on the bottle. Drinking, he then said, "I have been playing it all night and you know why? Because that's how I've felt all night long."

"That song is shit," she said.

"What…What did you say?"

"What am I, talking Chinese? The song is shit."

She got up, crossed the room.

"I'm turning it off."

"Leave it alone," he said. "I swear I'll throw this bottle at you."

She turned it off.

He threw the bottle.

He wasn't even close. It took out a fist of plaster.

"You missed on purpose, you pussy," she said.

"That's bullshit."

She hadn't actually turned it off, but lowered it some. Just enough so that mob downstairs didn't put in the 911 call and there they'd be facing a bevy of pissed cops—if they even showed up in Wokeland anymore for such things.

"You and I," she said, "are scheduled for a twelve round fight against parties as yet unknown. That fight is to happen right here in the phoniness capital of America. And that fight is going on as planned. Dig?"

He got it. Yeah. She'd been trying to shake him up, shake him loose, shake him out of doing something so ragefully stupid, like buying all those lottery tickets. Which he looked at now. Stared at, really. He grabbed up a clump of them, then let them just fall loose to the floor.

"Dazzling," he said to himself. And he sure did not mean it as a compliment.

He looked across the room at that dead serious chick in the fishnets and beret.

"Do we dress for the occasion?" he said.

"Darlin'...we are the occasion."

CHAPTER 158

Daniel sat all those hours on the second floor balcony, looking out over the city, knowing his sister was up there on Mount Washington, looking down upon the same scene, but from a different world view altogether.

He'd vomited and vomited again, and he'd smoked a joint to try and stone himself out, but little good it did. His past was riding him down, his past had all but materialized into a punitive masterpiece of selfish, ill conceived passions.

The same car that took his sister away brought her home again, and when she stepped into the street she looked up toward the house and saw him there. What she did not see, could not, was that his powers to focus, command, order, incite, dominate were lost to him.

She entered her part of the house in a state of exhausted silence and he had the audacity to say, "You told him everything, didn't you?"

She did not answer. He grabbed her by the arm and said again, "You told him everything, didn't you?" Her answer was to stare him down until he let go.

CHAPTER 159

Daniel set up a press conference at the Chamber of Commerce offices where he and his sister would address the Newell podcast, which had now evolved into a genuine news story.

She stood before the cameras with her brother just behind her and began, "My desire has always been to serve the people of Los Angeles, especially the minority communities, which have so long suffered from political disinterest...My brother and I know we can rely on your goodwill and excellent judgment."

Crying here and there, she repeated what she had told Landshark.

When it was Daniel's turn, he came forward and said, "When my mother died, I had, for all practical purposes, a nervous breakdown. My actions at that time were wrong. I have asked for my sister's forgiveness. I ask for your forgiveness. And I ask for God's forgiveness."

When Daniel was done, the first question thrown at him was from a ringer, courtesy of James Salamone, "Do you think your admission here today will compromise you and destroy the integrity of the Tenants Association property fight in the 710 Corridor?"

CHAPTER 160

Lily Vee drove to Vegas from Pocatello. She was to go to a diner in the Alta Decatur Shopping Mall where instructions for her employment would be hand delivered.

She had gone through endless cups of coffee when a messenger arrived, asked the door host for a Lily Vee, and was ushered to her table. He was carrying a manila envelope which, when he knew he had the right party, he handed over and left.

Lily Vee was about as unassuming as you could get. You'd need a real pretext to want to meet with her at all. But Rabel had pretext enough.

Her job was to clean up messes, smooth over mistakes and disasters, and stop hemorrhages before they started or spread. She was not a humane operation; she was in the business of victims.

Inside the manila envelope were about half a dozen names with photos, addresses, phone numbers, details. There was also an advance on services to be rendered. She looked all these over about as casually as one would a product catalogue.

She drove to Los Angeles through the desert and into a heavily trafficked sunset. She had been born and raised in that city. Venice, to be exact. In an apartment on Ocean Front Walk that faced the Pacific. It was now a drug rehab center of some repute. It should have been one back then.

She did not drink, she did not do drugs. She had sex only with women, women that she paid for their services. Men, you see, were like a tube of toothpaste—squeeze the last drop out of them, then toss. She was self destructive in many ways, but that was her personality structure.

CHAPTER 161

Charlie Engel got off the late shift at eleven, but he didn't go home. Instead, he drove to Long Beach, watching the headlights behind him, to see if he might be followed. In Signal Hill he parked on

Walnut and sat in the dark and watched and waited. Then, when sure he was not followed, he walked the two blocks to the Fantasy Castle.

His brother was at the bar waiting for him. Keeping his mind occupied on a couple of bored hookers trying to make enough to pay for a dream or two.

"You look pale," said Freddie.

"It's the paranoia. Did you do your Craigslist thing?"

"Yeah."

"And?"

"The eagle has landed, as they say."

"You know what's really got me freaked? The thought that ChiChi fed the hotline that information."

"You're paranoid on steroids."

Freddie got a text on one of the three phones of his that he lined up on the bar. He read it, then handed the phone to his brother.

"Read," said Freddie.

The text said:

Can't get together. It would have been fun.

"What's it mean?"

"It means that you are being followed."

CHAPTER 162

That old saying *Never bring a knife to a gunfight* leaves a lot to be desired. Sometimes a knife would have been a better way to go.

Charlie Engel kept a couple of well used revolvers in a small lockbox within the empty shell of an air conditioner stacked in the rear of his garage.

He made sure the gun was loaded. He even pocketed extra rounds, though more on the rage riding on the back of his paranoia. He realized he was acting like half the assholes he arrested, but he could not control himself.

When his wife said, "Where are you going at this hour?", he told her, "I'm not going anywhere. I'm in the garage cleaning up. If anybody should ever fuckin' ask."

CHAPTER 163

Engel had made his way up onto the porch landing by the kitchen door to Miller's place. He was sneaking a look in the window as Ana came to get a beer from the fridge. She had her back to the door. Engel had tried it and found it unlocked and he came bursting through. Ana dropped the bottle as she turned and had a revolver pressed up under her chin.

Engel shoved her back toward the entry to the living room as Jayden was rushing to find out what the hell had happened. What he saw stopped him cold.

"Let's have a talk," Engel said. "Alright…alright?"

Miller threw his arms out like *Alright, let's talk.*

"I'm gonna let her loose," said Engel.

"I'd say that's a good thing," said Ana.

"Don't get arrogant with me, girl. Alright?"

"No," said Ana. "I'll wait till later."

Engel shoved Ana right into Miller.

He made Miller sit on the couch and Ana in a chair at the far end of the room. He wanted space between them.

"What were you following me for?"

"What are you talking about?" said Miller. "I'm on suspension."

"You were following me...why?"

"You need diazepam," said Ana.

"You're on suspension," said Engel. "And you're out on bail. You were investigating her. And now here she is at your place. How you gonna explain this?"

"How are *you?*" said Ana.

"Why would we follow you?" said Miller.

"You damn well know why."

"I'm bleeding," said Ana.

She held up her bandaged arm. Some blood was seeping through the gauze. "I have to take care of this."

She stood. He flashed his gun at her.

"I need peroxide and gauze."

He cut her off.

"You should just get out of here," said an infuriated Ana. "Disappear, man. Otherwise, sometime soon, they'll be whispering a few comforting words over your grave."

He hung on the moment. He wanted to shoot them both but wished he hadn't come at all. He could see the bathroom at the end of the hall and shoved Ana toward it.

"Was it you on Valley Boulevard?" said Jayden.

"There was no Valley Boulevard incident that I know of."

Engel glared at Ana. She was at the sink. She had undone the bandage, gotten some gauze and tape. She had a glass with peroxide. She was coming back up the hall and said, "I need Jayden to help me with this."

He stepped back and as she passed him, she flung the peroxide in his eyes.

CHAPTER 164

What the peroxide did to his eyes, the blinding sting. He lost control of the moment. Miller threw aside the coffee table and charged. Engel was trying to wipe away the burn. Ana hit him on the side of the head with her fist. Miller rammed straight into him. The gun was no longer in Engel's hand. It hit the floor and the two men went scrambling for it. The thuds of their bodies on the parquet floor as they snaked over each other.

Ana kicked Engel in the face with her chromish boots. She kicked him and kicked him and the air shot out of her lungs and she made this hissing noise. She bloodied him up but good.

Then there was Engel on all fours, eyes tortured, sight blurred, his blood spattered on the wood floor. Miller was standing over him, as was Ana.

"I can't see," he said. "I can't see. My eyes."

Ana hustled down the hall to the bathroom and emptied the glass of peroxide, then filled it with water. She put the glass in Engel's hand.

"Rinse your eyes, genius," said Ana.

As Engel worked to clean his eyes up, Ana leaned against the wall and looked over the wound on her arm. Miller glanced at her and nodded, but there was an uneasy sense in each of them that their world was spinning out of control.

She walked behind Jayden and whispered, "I smell peril, man."

CHAPTER 165

Engel was sitting at the dining table cooling his eyes with a wet rag when Ana came from the kitchen with a couple of bottles of beer, their long necks between her fingers. She jammed one into Engel's shoulder to take it.

"You were following me," he said, taking the beer.

"Where?" said Miller.

Miller was sitting on the couch. The gun was on the coffee table, which he'd righted. Ana brought him a beer.

"Long Beach," said Engel.

"What's in Long Beach?" said Ana.

"You know very well. I hooked up with my brother Freddie at Fantasy Castle."

Ana laughed out loud. "That's putting your dick in harm's way."

"It wasn't us," said Miller.

"You're in the middle of the middle, boy," said Ana. "And you could very well end up being shipped home in an envelope. So you better plan up. What looks best. Make sure you got life insurance."

"I know I was being followed. And it was you."

"It wasn't us," said Ana.

"Maritza Velez said you went to her house and threatened her," said Jayden.

"I told her the truth."

"Whose truth?"

"That her husband was a thief. That he'd been involved in robberies in the past. That he was involved in this one...."

Ana picked up the gun from the coffee table.

"To know all that," said Jayden, "you'd have to be hooked in."

"Involved, as they say," said Ana.

"Tell us about ChiChi," said Jayden.

Engel took the wet rag from his eyes. "It's time I walk outta here."

"Maybe it's ChiChi following you," said Ana.

"My gun," said Engel, putting out his hand as he stood.

"The gun stays," said Miller.

Engel took the situation as it was and started out.

"Hey," said Ana. "I got one question."

"I don't know any ChiChi. There is no Valley Boulevard incident."

"That's not the question."

"No?"

She held up the revolver.

"What happened to the serial numbers on this gun?"

CHAPTER 166

Freddie Engel was in one of those Get It On Motels in Long Beach, a few blocks from the Fantasy Castle. The girl was hardcore and oxy ridden. She was good for the mileage, but not much more. Just another shade of making due, that's how Freddie described them.

Of course this was no she, except in her mind. All the rest of her equipment came off the shelves.

When a particular cell of his rang, Freddie knew it was his brother. He looked at the time. Cursed privately.

"I got to do this," he said to his bedmate.

Freddie sat up. "Talk to me."

"I just had a confrontation with Miller and that woman."

Freddie got up and went to the bathroom and shut the door.

"What do you mean, confrontation?"

"A confrontation…"

"Where?"

"At his place in Eagle Rock."

"You went there?"

"Yeah."

"Did you follow him or something?"

"I know where he lives."

"Did you bring a weapon? Please, Charlie…tell me you did not bring a weapon."

There was a pause, then dry breathing.

"God…no."

There was knocking now at the bathroom door. "I'm not gonna wait around here."

"Hold on a minute, Charlie."

Freddie surged out of the bathroom. Grabbed the girl by the dick. Led her in pain to the bedstand, then unloosed her, handed her a vial of oxy and some cash.

"You got one minute," said Freddie.

She was outta there in one minute.

He could pace now, naked, lit only by the bathroom doorway.

"The gun," he said. "Did you use it?"

"No. They…got it away from me."

"What was the confrontation?"

"I told them I knew they were following me."

"And what did they say?"

"What do you think? Velez's wife told them about me confronting her."

"You confronted her?"

207

"I had to try and smoke her out. She knew her husband was a thief. And that he'd committed other robberies. That he fenced some of the weapons from other—"

"God damn it. How did Miller and Ride both know about ChiChi? How?"

"I think Velez copped to his wife."

"Valley Boulevard killed all that."

"I don't want to hear Valley Boulevard again. I'm strangling on it."

"Where are you?"

"In the street. By my car. Just up from Miller's."

"You talking too fuckin' loud, alright? Let's be cool, okay? Okay?"

"Sure."

"They were both at Miller's?"

"Yeah. Him and the Ride cunt."

"Listen…stay where you are. I'm gonna make a call. I'll get back to you in a few minutes."

"What are you gonna do?"

"I'm gonna try and get to the end titles…understand?"

CHAPTER 167

He made a call. Burner phone.

Lily Vee answered.

"Where are you?" said Freddie.

"Where I planned to be."

"My brother—"

"I saw him go into Miller's. He went in like the lion and came out like the lamb. What is he about?"

"He is about one mistake after another."

"Can't have it."

"No...I need you to do something," he said.

"Yes?"

"I mean—"

"Yes."

"You can see—"

"Yes."

"He just can't—"

"No...he can't. Just keep him occupied."

CHAPTER 168

Freddie called his brother back.

"What?" said Charlie.

"Keep where you are."

"What are you—"

"Cavalry to the rescue."

"I'm sorry, Freddie. That I went a little out of my—"

"Forget it. It happens to the best of us."

"Freddie?"

"Yeah?"

"The whole Valley Boulevard thing. Then Kagel Canyon. I feel like I'm getting closed in. That I'm alone out there."

"You're not alone, Charlie. Now just wait. Get in the car. Keep it dark and quiet and wait."

"Alright...I'm getting in the car."

Freddie could hear the door open, the door close.

"I'm in the car."

"Right. I'm gonna stay on the phone with you, Charlie."

"Great. Do I know who's coming?"

"It doesn't matter."

"How you gonna do it?"

"We don't want another Valley Boulevard, do we?" said Freddie.

"It was all Andres's fault," said Charlie. "Andres or Velez...I don't know whose fault it was. Maybe Andres. I wouldn't put it past the bastard. But maybe Velez. Velez's wife is tight with Miller and Ride. And what they know they don't tell LAPD. They're up to something."

"Forget the fault thing."

"Sometimes I think—"

"What?"

"ChiChi let loose about Valley Boulevard."

"What would make you think that?"

"I don't know. I feel he's closing a door on the people that can point a finger."

"I love you, Charlie, you know that. But you got to tighten it up upstairs. Your mind goes in way too many direc—"

The glass shattered and there was a whistly pop, just like how a silencer would sound.

"Charlie—"

Charlie did not answer.

CHAPTER 169

Freddie sat back down on the edge of the bed and shut off the cellphone. He could see his shadow on the carpet imprisoned within the frame of the lit bathroom doorway.

So much of what Charlie had said was true, some of it frightened Freddie.

A flood of questions would be coming his way. He tried to think of something frivolous to clear his mind.

He'd let his own brother be slain—it was as simple and horrifying as that.

The air conditioner seemed so loud. Too loud. It made him feel lonely and isolated.

Freddie went and took a very long and very hot shower. He washed himself diligently. He wanted to make sure his dick was clean.

CHAPTER 170

"Did you hear a scream?"

Jayden was sitting on the couch with Ana. He had just finished rebandaging her arm. They were evaluating everything Engel had said, especially the Valley Boulevard incident and the claims he'd made about Maritza Velez that didn't exactly jibe with what she'd told Ana.

Ana repeated herself. "Did that sound like a scream?"

"Didn't hear anything," said Miller.

She listened harder now, so he listened harder.

"There," she said.

Again he just shook his head.

She got up, he got up. She went through the kitchen to the porch, he followed.

Standing out there in the night they could hear down below. It was a woman, alright. She was calling out, "There's been a shooting…we need help here!"

CHAPTER 171

There were about a dozen overwrought and panicked neighbors surrounding a sedan that was parked just up from the corner of Chicasaw and Highland View, in front of a house with a white picket fence.

People were taking pictures, of course, or moving about shocked. One of the neighbors was already on with 911.

Jayden made his way through the crowd holding up his identification. "LAPD…Please…Outta the way here."

Ana was just behind him. She could see the driver's window had been shot out. When they got close enough, what both surmised became imprinted on reality. Slumped over the console was Charlie Engel, and he sure didn't look anything like he had when he'd left Miller's place.

CHAPTER 172

Miller made everyone step back. He wanted to check the "victim's" vitals. He flashed on his pocket light. He reached through the shattered window and undid the lock. He walked around the front and entered the car through the passenger door. He checked Engel's pulse, his neck. All the while he was looking for something, anything, that might add to his investigation. There was a cellular still in Engel's hand. It had its share of blood on it. But there was another cell on the passenger side floor. And it may have well been a burner from the looks of it.

His first thought—do I take the fucker?

CHAPTER 173

Ana knew enough to hang back, work those shadows. You could hear sirens blocks away and coming on fast.

Miller quietly crossed the tiny street to where Ana waited. He passed her and nodded and walked on a bit and she joined him, looking back.

"Am I wrong…or is that a tsunami heading our way?" he said.

"We have to come to a decision and fast," she said.

"Get in your car. Get out of here."

"Not gonna fly."

"Go to Landshark's. You can cover there."

"Your neighbors saw me come in. And me claiming I'm a hooker. See what I mean?"

"You could say you left at any time."

"I did something like this once...and I ended up out on bail."

A police cruiser came sweeping around the corner.

"Too late," said Ana.

"It was a good idea," said Jayden, "while it lasted."

"Before this night is over," said Ana, "you know what they'll be calling us?"

"People of Interest," said Miller.

CHAPTER 174

They were brought in for questioning and separated. They had enough time, at least, to coordinate their stories—what to leave in, what to bury. Charlie Engel's claim that Maritza Velez knew of her husband's criminal activities and he was definitely involved in the Academy gun shop crime was at the top of the bury list.

Their statements both claimed Charlie Engel forced his way at gunpoint into the Miller residence. There had been a confrontation—a fight—and Engel had been subdued, then sent on his way. Within ten minutes they heard a scream and went to investigate. The gun that Engel had carried into the residence was handed over and would prove to have Engel's fingerprints on it.

By the time they had deposed Miller and Ride, they knew of the last phone call between the two brothers right up to the moment of the shooting.

CHAPTER 175

An exhaustive search was begun for the murder weapon. Warrants of Miller's home, his car, the rental pickup that Ana Ride was driving. A block by block hunt for video cameras took shape, starting at Chicasaw and Highland View out to Colorado and Eagle Rock boulevards, on the chance a third party had committed the crime. In concert or not with the people being questioned.

Both were released the following morning. Each had an attorney, each made a statement. The usual proclamation of innocence, of course. But claiming innocence is a feint position indeed, well populated with liars, fools, thieves, murderers, and the recently dead.

There were camera crews and crawlers lurking around the trailer park for Ana Ride to return. It was worse than before. There was a line of news trucks along Topanga. Most had been chased off the property. Elias had forewarned her and knew the moment she swung into the park.

She made it clear to her parking space before the mad dash was on. They were coming out of the woodwork, desperate for that top shot or quote. Elias was on them quick. He was carrying, of all things, a can of Raid, which he sprayed on them generously.

When she got inside her trailer, Ana crashed down on the couch. She was so shot that she couldn't even negotiate getting off her prosthesis.

"I'll do that," Elias said.

He knelt and took off her prothesis with some unexpected tenderness.

"Not exactly a rock star, am I?" said Ana.

"Not exactly."

"What's it like watching a daughter grow up and be shot to pieces?"

"It's a real page turner."

"I'm hurting, Elias…Need some pain killers. In the medicine chest."

Ana sat back and massaged the stump of her foot.

"We got oxy," said Elias, from the bathroom. "Percocet… tramadol."

"Any of those torpedo sized ibuprofen in there?"

Elias brought out a vial. Got a bottle of triple sec from the fridge. He passed them to her. She junked down four 600mg with a triple sec chaser for each.

"How'd it go with LAPD?"

"We told the truth."

"What's the truth?"

"It means we lied where we thought we'd get away with it."

"Learn anything?"

"Yeah…Valley Boulevard really went down."

"How do you know?"

"Charlie Engel was shitting fear just trying to deny it. And that's not all…I think they're killing off everyone who can testify against this fuck up of a crime."

"Where does that put you?" said Elias.

"Ground zero, baby."

"We got to do something about that."

"That's why I'm gonna ask a favor of you…a big time favor."

"I don't like the phrase 'big time favor.'"

"Sorry," said Ana, "but I need you to pack about a week's worth of clothes. A shotgun. A revolver. Ammunition." She thought a bit, then added, "And a baseball glove. If you still have one."

"Where the fuck does a baseball glove fit in?"

"I need you to play nanny."

CHAPTER 176

Ana called Maritza and told her she was coming over for a cold blooded heart to heart. When Ana pulled into the Velez driveway, Elias was right there in the truck behind her. She asked he wait outside as Maritza, at the screen door, watched.

"Who is that?" said Maritza.

"Former LAPD. Former Marine. Otherwise known as my father."

"Why is he here?"

"To keep you alive…if possible."

Maritza suddenly showed all the warning signs of panic. She told her mother in Spanish to watch out for the children and keep them with her. The two women then retreated to the kitchen, the door shutting behind them.

"You lied to me," said Ana.

"I don't understand."

"You damn well do. Did you see me on the news?"

"Yes."

"And the late Charlie Engel?"

"Yes."

"You knew Engel was deeply involved in the robbery, didn't you?"

Maritza sat staring at her hands folded on the table. Never a good sign. Makes goodwill go right down the toilet.

"You also knew, but did not tell us, that this robbery, which Luis was deeply a part of, was meant to embarrass, disgrace, destroy the Domingos…or at least compromise them when it came to the Tenants Association fight for their property. You knew it, didn't you?"

"Does it matter what I answer now?"

"Your husband, Engel, who knows who else…all dead. And more to come. They're gonna start with the low hanging fruit and work their way up. And you know what you are?"

"No."

"You're low hanging fruit. They're gonna kill off all witnesses. Because someone funded this operation, and it's going bad."

Ana put a hand under Maritza's chin, forcing her to look up.

"Has anyone approached you with a threat or bribe?"

CHAPTER 177

Elias cruised the premises while the ladies talked. He took the walkway down to the garage, looked over the backyard, the fenced off building next door. He was doing a quiet reconnoiter, amassing impressions of how best to secure the Velez house.

Ana came down the front porch with Maritza Velez and introduced the two.

"I hope this will all amount to nothing," said Ana.

"So do I," said Maritza.

Ana told Maritza she'd like a few minutes alone with her father.

"What do you think?"

"It's a disaster," said Elias.

"I'll see what Carter and Ellison can do."

"What happened in there?"

"She told me the truth."

"And what was that?"

"The truth is any lie you can get away with."

"Seems I've heard that before."

Javier and Jorge came sprinting up the street after school when they saw Ana. They were all over her with questions as they checked out Elias.

"Who's the old guy?" said Jorge.

"I'm your fuckin' nanny," said Elias. "That's who."

CHAPTER 178

The shooting of an LAPD officer not only made the news, as it should, but also played like crazy on the Citizen app and Twitter. You can always depend on a blown out skull for clicks. Also, the dislike and disregard for law enforcement in general made ideas of corruption easier to imply.

Exploiting this, James Salamone had people pump up social media volume, bringing in issues like the connection of Ana Ride—a person of interest in the murder of Charlie Engel—to the Domingos. What was the secret meeting in Lake Hughes with Daniel Domingo all about? And, by extension, Ana Ride's relationship to Maritza Velez, who was in the Tenants Association and part of the fight against the DON Group, for legal right to certain properties in the 710 Corridor. Add to that one Jayden Miller, a disgraced LAPD investigator and now a person of interest in the Charlie Engel murder. A murder that took place about a hundred yards from his residence.

Here is where Dawn Newell, fed high end rape PR from Salamone, fleshed it out in podcasts that she hoped would engulf the situation in political fire, and do her career the appropriate shine. She put it out there that Luis Velez, with the blessing of the Domingos, had robbed the Academy gun shop with the help of coconspirators, among them his wife, whose intention was to lay the crime at the feet of the DON Group and destroy their credibility against the Tenants Association.

CHAPTER 179

Death by social media. Death by a thousand comments planted in the civil discourse for poison's sake.

The Domingos, Maritza Velez, Jayden Miller, they were being run down. They also had their defenders, but this fight would not be won there. You just don't die as quick.

The internet is a walking loudspeaker in scenarios like this, and all that cancel culture is a smoke screen for the nefarious power of money and control. It is about an armed camp of gutless wonders who hide behind the anonymity of a cellphone, while assassins lurk in the shadows of a threat.

Los Angeles is a perfect place for such fraudulence, because the whole damn city is adrift in facade. You have to remember, the whole damn place, every street, every alley, field, going back over a hundred years, had been a location in a movie. And all that had really happened was one location replaced another, like one lie replaces another, and the Dawn Newell podcast outlining the crime and the reasons behind it had more lies and more truth in it than one might really guess.

CHAPTER 180

While Worth finished off his attack of the Newell podcast, Ana, who was in the office with him, said, "Newell is right…about what happened."

"Yes…the crime was to be laid at someone's feet…but it was not the DON Group."

"They meant to crash and burn the Tenants Association in their attempt to buy the property by corrupting the Domingos and Velez," said Ana.

"Only we can't prove it," said Worth.

"Same crime, different set of conspirators. They have more juice than us, so they have more veracity," said Ana.

"Newell didn't come up with any of this," said Worth. "This has James Salamone's imprint all over it. He handles all inbound and outbound for the DON Group. And he'll go beyond the beyond when it comes to bringing in someone to do this."

"We need bodies…breathing bodies who can cough it up. And there's at least two out there."

"Where do you get two?" said Worth. "You including Freddie Engel?"

"No…he's a useless wonder. I'm talking the shooters. I'm talking the man who made the two hotline calls. And then there's the woman who shot Charlie Engel."

"Wait a second," said Worth. "Where'd you get it was a woman?"

Ana lit a cigarette under the staring eyes of Landshark.

"I walked past the window," said Ana. "The angle of the shot… very low. Shooter was shorter than me. Maybe five foot three…It'll come out when forensics is done."

"Why not a man? Small? Same guy who made the calls?"

"Could be…but the rattlesnake in my head says different. There's someone out there who is making the calls…He's got us on the run. And he's gonna kill off all witnesses and threats. I believe he brought in a woman to close. I would have."

She had this unnerving silence framed by the dry, flat L.A. sky that had Landshark thinking. There was a hard gravity about her. Something outside the norm.

"You ever been involved in anything like this?" said Worth.

"You mean…when I was serving?"

"No. I mean…out there."

CHAPTER 181

"I know where you're going, Mr. Landshark…I'm like this city the way you write about it right there. Dig down you'll find one movie set buried under another.

"Shall I tell you a story?" Ana said, getting up and heading to the bar. "It's about a young woman asked by a private security firm to go into Mexico and help lure a gent of dubious character and perverse baggage back to the States.

"He was slick…had never been conned. But one thing finally got past his radar…a moderately attractive young woman with a prothesis didn't really pose a threat or danger. And she was eminently fuckable."

Ana made a drink, but only stared at it. "This young woman was just sitting in her car on the shore at night near the *Titanic* movie set and one leg dangling out the window…like a lure on a fishing line.

"What a fuckin' ploy, if I say so myself."

"No sooner had they entered the appropriately dingy motel room than he was abducted. The gent was tasered, bound, and gagged, then waylaid onto a boat for the inexorable date with his past...End of story."

She crossed the room and picked up the cigarette she had left burning in the ashtray, but then she put it down. Landshark saw she was far off in the private landscape of her life.

"Was justice served?"

"Is it ever?" said Ana. "On time, I mean. No...that's when it's simply called revenge."

"How did the girl feel about all this?"

"You mean does she feel regret? Remorse?"

"You could use those words," said Worth.

"I told you, Mr. Landshark, I'm like this city. Keep digging down and you'll find the remains of another movie set."

CHAPTER 182

There were people coming and going on Chicasaw, taking selfies at the chain link fence to Miller's house. When Ana arrived, she was recognized and people asked for a selfie with her, which she laughed off.

"Wait till I'm convicted," she said. "Then the photos should be worth something."

Miller saw her coming, and by the time she reached the deck, the kitchen door swung open. He waited inside.

"What are you doing here? You into punishment?"

"I have one question that needs answering."

"Just one."

"What was it you took out of Engel's car?"

"What are you talking about?"

"I'll bet it was a burner."

"You're like a wild dog."

"Worse. You didn't go into the car to see if Engel was still alive."

"That's procedure."

"He had a hole in his head the size of a softball. I could see that much. You went in to see if there was anything to rip that might advance the case...before LAPD got there. When you were crossing the street approaching me, I saw you slip something into your pocket."

CHAPTER 183

Ana left to the same fanfare on the street. She got into her truck and drove around the corner to Oak Tree Drive, which was the block on the hill behind Miller's place. That's where Jayden jumped a neighbor's fence and was into Ana's pickup unnoticed.

He was holding the burner that he had confiscated from Charlie Engel's vehicle. While they drove to Long Beach, Miller set up a recording app on the phone. Freddie Engel owned a warehouse down there where he sold exercise equipment. Everyone knew this was bullshit and a front for his criminal cronies.

They kept him under surveillance. The crowd that came and went was a who's who of shitbags and steroid junkies.

When Freddie was by his car, alone, Miller called the most recent number to see who might answer.

The phone rang and rang.

Then the phone was answered. But it wasn't Freddie who answered it.

A man's voice. "Freddie…?"

Miller grained his voice, like the connection was shoddy. "Yeah…"

A clipped silence. Then Miller again, "Last night…bad." He waited.

A long silence followed. It felt to Miller like a thinking silence. A cautious, weighing silence.

"I can't hear ya too good," said the voice.

"How 'bout this?" said Miller. "We have the weapons."

The line shut off.

Miller sat back. Took a long breath.

"You don't need a college degree to have that conversation explained to you," said Ana. "Miller…I think I just heard the door to your career slam shut."

"Ma'am, it's all in the perception. It could be a jail cell door."

Then something caught Ana's eye. She swatted Jayden's shoulder. "Check this out. I think you stirred it up."

CHAPTER 184

A call came in for Freddie. One of the cellphones on the dashboard of his Lexus rang.

"Yeah…."

"What happened to the phone I gave you?"

He did not expect it to be who it was on the line. He was still pretty shaky from the night before. "I…don't know…I…" He checked the dashboard, then the console, then the glove box. "I must have left it in Charlie's car."

"It isn't in the car anymore."

"What?"

"Someone called me on that phone to let me know they have the weapons."

"How?"

"How is not as important as who."

Freddie started to look around the parking lot and the street, like he feared he was being watched.

CHAPTER 185

Hunkered down in their secure office, Carter and Ellison did a check on the recorder app off the burner phone. It conferred what they all pretty much suspected. The voice matched the other two on the hotlines.

The marauder, as Carter or Ellison named him, had a long reach. And it was getting longer all the time.

"He's got to go," said Ana.

"Who?" said Miller.

"Freddie Engel, of course."

The three men were watching her hard now.

"Unless he can do us some good."

As they walked out, Ellison said to Ana, "Are you getting more cold blooded as you get older or what?"

She was flipping the burner phone, throwing it in the air and catching it. "It's the reptile in me, man."

CHAPTER 186

Jayden drove while Ana smoked and worked the music. She got a call from Landshark on a secured line. She put him on loudspeaker.

"Word is," said Worth, "tomorrow sometime you'll be under twenty four hour surveillance."

"Got it," she said. "And FYI...we told *him* we have the weapons."

"*Him? Him* who?" said Landshark.

"The same *him* who left the messages."

"How did you get to this *him*?"

She killed the line.

"What did you do that for?" said Miller.

"To fuck with his head."

He called back. She didn't answer it.

"They can't keep us under surveillance too long," Miller said.

"No?"

"Ever hear of 'defund the police'?"

CHAPTER 187

One of Freddie Engel's assets was a funeral home and crematory out in Sun Valley on San Fernando Road. The mortuary had lawsuits against it, complaints, fines, bodies had been discovered in cold storage for as much as six months, clients' ashes had been lost somewhere in the pipeline. The state was trying to revoke the mortuary's license. This is where Freddie brought his beloved brother.

It was past midnight, when the mortuary was closed, that Freddie arrived. He was alone with his brother's casket in a viewing room. The casket was closed, of course, the wound having been too devastating for restoration.

Freddie sat staring at the casket in the dark. It was like looking into your own future, and don't think Freddie didn't know it. He was so emotionally fucked up, so ashamed, so stricken, so guilty of facing his own sin, yet knowing he would do nothing about it, that he would kick it aside and keep on, survival first. He put some lines of coke on his brother's casket and snorted them. He actually cried while he did this, which made him hate himself all the more.

"You can't escape it, man."

This jolted him. A woman's voice from out of the ghostly nowhere of the mortuary.

"Who the fuck—"

Ana turned on the flashlight she was carrying. She put it under her chin so Freddie Engel could get a good look at her.

"I love the part," said Ana, "where you were actually crying on the casket. While you were snorting cocaine. Great shot...don't you think?"

Another light flashed on from across the room. Only this beamed in on Freddie.

"I was moved," said Miller. "Genuinely moved. There's nothing like men's tears in a situation like this that makes you want to vomit."

"That's harsh," said Ana.

Their lights closed in on Freddie.

CHAPTER 188

"If you think," said Freddie Engel, "that I'm gonna be taken down by a couple of pussies like you both, you—"

Ana hit him across the bridge of his nose with the barrel of her gun and down he went to his knees, grabbing at the air, bleeding, stunned.

"First of all, I'm not a pussy," said Ana. "I identify as an immoral force. A troublemaker. Who is gonna bring down the wrath on your ass."

Miller grabbed her and shoved her away. Cursing, she leaned against the casket.

Miller stood over Freddie. "I have something you need to hear."

He took a recorder from his pocket. Set it on PLAY. There was the first message from the hotline about Valley Boulevard...And then the one about the fight in Kagel Canyon around the white van.

"Now," said Miller, "this was taken off the burner left in your brother's car. I called the last number."

There was Miller's voice talking up the weapons.

"The same character," said Miller. "ChiChi...Yes?"

"I don't know any ChiChi," said Freddie.

"Let's see what Charlie has to say." Ana lifted the casket lid. "Oh man, your brother is looking bad, Freddie. Hey, are you gonna bury him or just hang him up in cold storage like you're being sued for?"

"I've done nothing," said Freddie.

"You wanna bet," said Jayden, "that you don't go to LAPD with any of this?"

Freddie stood. He closed the casket lid. He couldn't bear to look at his brother.

"We got nothing more for you, Freddie. It's not our life you can save," said Miller.

"It's dark money," said Freddie.

"What?" said Miller.

"It's all dark money running this. A guy connects a guy to another, who connects to me and I connect a guy and on it goes. There isn't any ChiChi. It's just a name. And he's not alone now. There's at least one more."

"How do you know that?" said Ana.

"Because you can't be in two places at once," said Freddie.

CHAPTER 189

"Why do you think he talked up the dark money thing?" said Ana.

"Desperate."

"Knows he's a dead man."

"The cellphone call did it."

"Turned him into that infamous crack in the wall."

"And you were right," said Miller.

"Was I? About what?"

"That there's two of them out there."

"I hate to be right about that," said Ana.

"He's selling his own out, as best he can. Trying to, anyway."

"He's a fool."

"Yeah…but he's got a choice of caskets at his disposal."

CHAPTER 190

They were practically invisible coming up the alley behind the Velez house. They went through the hole in the fence without a sound.

Elias was alone in the den where Maritza worked, as he faced the abandoned building. He sat in the darkness peeking out through the blinds until the door to the hall slid open and let the light cast upon him.

Javier entered. "Can I come in?"

"Yeah...but shut the door behind you."

The family was in the living room watching television. Javier slid the door shut.

"There's someone in the house next door," said the boy.

"And how do you know that?" said Elias.

Javier tapped his ear.

"I didn't tell my mother."

"Wise decision."

"Who do you think it is?"

"I'll tell you shortly."

"Can I wait here with you?"

"Why not?"

They hung together in the dark. Elias had the kid whisper, just to be safe. They covered endless subjects. Trivial, not trivial, big issues, nothing issues, sports, movies, the whole pronoun thing. Then Javier said, "My father was a shit, you know that, right?"

"I don't know anything about your father."

"Your daughter is pretty cool."

"She can put it out there."

"Were you a shit as a father?"

This stopped him cold.

"Why do you say that?"

"Curious."

Elias was too guilty to answer honestly.

"Do I look like a shit?"

"Not much one way or the other. You could be a shit."

"I guess I could."

"I think most fathers are shit."

"Is that the word on the street or your own opinion?"

"I could be wrong. But I doubt it."

The boy had waylaid him with a couple of modest sentences. The room being dark a good thing.

"I'm glad you're here," said the boy. "We all are."

CHAPTER 191

There was some vague noise. It could well have come from some night critter in the weeds. The boy heard it, Elias heard it. The boy raised a finger, Elias nodded.

"Somebody out there?" said the boy.

"I hope so."

The boy did not understand.

Elias turned his laptop so the boy could view the screen.

"We'll know in a minute," said Elias.

"What are we watching for?"

Split screens. Cameras had been set up in the empty house. One focused on the Velez backyard, one the front yard.

"That's our house."

"Right."

Suddenly one of the screens flashed on Carter in the backyard giving the thumbs up sign.

Elias responded by text. The last he saw of Carter and Ellison, they had started up the alley.

CHAPTER 192

The men had come and gone like the singular hunters that they were able to materialize and dematerialize according to the shadows. The only living thing they saw, or that saw them, was a homeless old witch bundled up by her shopping cart near the dumpster that edged the sidewalk.

Only this was no homeless old witch, but another kind of witch altogether.

CHAPTER 193

The City of Hope was having one of its seasonal fundraisers in the Grand Ballroom of the Beverly Wilshire Hotel. There were always a lot of celebrities at these affairs wearing their best retail smiles. The same for the city's political class. Among that crowd were the Domingos.

Daniel was still taking social heat for his "past actions" and social media rape PR was hot on his tail to step away from his sister's political campaign.

Of all the people who should come up to the Domingos and share a civil camera moment was James Salamone. But what looked innocent enough was plotted public relations.

CHAPTER 194

At the end of the fundraiser, the Domingos crossed the hotel's porte cochere to a private elevator where Salamone awaited in a suite. Little time was wasted, urgency disguised as cool dispatch ruled.

"You need to achieve a goal," said Salamone. "I may be able to serve up the solution. The 710 Corridor properties are your goal. Which are, as of now, clouded with conspiracy and doubt.

"You have a hundred tenants making claims they have the first right to buy certain single family homes or apartments they have lived in and paid rent on for decades. It is a paperless claim. And a conflict that could go on for years while needy multifamily dwellings are desperately desired throughout the city. So…remain in stasis or solve the conflict."

Salamone looked from brother to sister, letting them both know he saw Julia Domingo as the seat of power, and the brother on the verge of being expendable. For that quiet slight, Daniel would have liked nothing better than to slam Salamone's face into the suite wall.

"Tell me what you have in mind," said Julia.

"Each tenant in the association turns over their claim to the DON Group, and for this will be granted a twenty year lease on a two bedroom apartment at the rate of rent they are currently paying."

"The tenants are leaving a lot on the table," said Julia.

"Yeah…a lot of maybes, possiblys, could bes, a lot of legal wrangling, lawsuits, countersuits, pleas like you put on YouTube while the properties keep decaying.

"For a guarantee of twenty years with the rent prices they are paying now, which are a decade behind the times, the tenant would be saving one thousand to fifteen hundred a month for two hundred and forty months. That's worth almost half a million dollars. And they have no upkeep to deal with."

CHAPTER 195

"That's gonna be a heavy lift," said Daniel. "People have expectations."

"I can help you there, too."

"Yeah?" said Daniel.

"Two words."

"Which are?"

"Dark money."

"Really," said Daniel.

"A fund has been put together," said Salamone, "and it has your name all over it." He was addressing Julia. "It will turn you from a congressperson to *the* congressperson…Especially with your dedication and passion."

He now addressed Daniel. "It will help you with your other conflicts…Velez, for instance. Her husband…Was he involved in the robbery? Was this all to be laid at the DON Group's doorstep to damage them in the 710 Corridor? That has got to be cleaned up."

He then turned to Julia. "If anyone can clean it up, you can."

When the Domingos left the suite, Daniel was diminished and angry. Coming down in the elevator together there was no hiding the fact.

"What he meant he wanted cleaned up," said Daniel, "but wouldn't say...is me."

"It has to be dealt with."

"It?"

"You, alright?"

"He's testing to see if I can be thrown to the wolves."

"Is he? Maybe it's quite the opposite."

Daniel hit the STOP button. The elevator jammed to a halt. Then there they were, looking at themselves and each other in the glass panels.

"The question is," said Daniel, "are you gonna sign off on this... With all your dedication and passion?"

"No...the question is can we get the Tenants Association to sign off on it. That's where all our dedication and passion need to be channeled.

"And something else...the best fight can be the one you walk away from."

She hit his fingers with a fist where they covered up the STOP button.

CHAPTER 196

They didn't have much time. Landshark cooked breakfast so Ana and Jayden could clear out before dawn, when surveillance was supposed to kick in. He relayed all he knew about the meeting at the Beverly

Wilshire Hotel. A secret meeting where the leaks were already being carefully prepped. One thing for certain—time was slipping away. One of the guilty had to be put on their backs and cracked open like a crab.

Landshark led them to a gate at the far end of the compound. He unlocked it, then started down through the heavily grottoed hillside. It was less a trail or path, and there were occasional bottles hung by ropes from branches to guide them.

He led them to a wall surrounding a home that fronted Mount Washington. There too Landshark unlocked a gate. When he closed it behind them, he explained.

It was the office of an accountant and bookkeeper who handled certain of his affairs. In the garage was a vehicle that had been specifically placed there for their secret use. He handed the keys to the vehicle and the gates to Ana, who passed them to Jayden.

"Give me a minute with our friend here, will you?" she said to Jayden.

Jayden took the keys and walked around the house to the garage.

"I'm curious," said Ana.

"Yes."

"You had no trouble leaving the property and coming down here. No agoraphobic anxiety, no panic attack. What gives?"

His face took on a sphinxlike stare. "I'll tell you about that one day...when this is over."

CHAPTER 197

Jayden sat behind the wheel, of all things, but a Ford Econoline cargo van, with a faded white paint job. It had healthy tires and a jacked up engine that would give it a real boost. It could be, by description, the same type van as described in the hotline calls about the vehicle on Valley Boulevard or in Kagel Canyon.

When Ana climbed in the shotgun seat, what was the first thing Jayden said?

"What do you notice about this van?"

"Yeah," said Ana.

"Was he trying to be strategic...or ironic?" said Jayden.

"Both...probably."

CHAPTER 198

Elias watched over the kids on their way to and from school. The rest of the time he set up post in that little room. One eye on the front yard, the other on the laptop with the surveillance cameras cued up.

You give it a day or two and you pretty much see the same dull faces over and over. Except for the shitbag drive bys with their cameras, the illiterates, the insulters, the gross condemners. Maritza still had a landline and you could Google her number so the unmercy was endless.

Death sometimes comes with such ferocious simplicity it is more of a shock than death itself. So it was with Elias looking out the window and this raggedy thing of a woman, an innocent tragedy, and her shopping cart heaped with the pathetic state of life plodding along.

He had seen her how many times, walking along hunched over. Only this time—

What's wrong with the picture...Something is wrong with the picture.

A moment later he saw the scenes on the laptop had glitched. Was it a glitch? The images there, then gone. The screen was nothing.

Elias stood, reached for his handgun and shotgun, the years of hardwiring in his head tripped. This was his version of the rattlesnake telling him—it's gonna be now, you stupid human ass, and it's gonna be bad.

CHAPTER 199

Elias ran into the hallway, calling out, shouting to Javier, who was on the upstairs landing moments later.

"Everyone in the basement like I showed you...Now!"

They had what was called a California basement, which was nothing more than a small flat square of concrete flooring, maybe ten feet wide, where they kept the water heater.

Elias helped Maritza's mother along. The women were panicked, their speech wild and in Spanish. Elias saw that patch quilt fraud of some homeless woman coming up the front yard firing an automatic rifle.

The windows were coming apart, sections of ceiling satelliting off across the room. Elias was herding the women along, Javier at the head of the basement stairs helping his grandmother and mother to safety. His little brother was crying and Javier dragged him toward the door.

"Lock the door," Elias shouted, "and stay down there till I tell you otherwise!"

Bullets struck the room he had been in. Shards of plaster and choking smoke everywhere.

Elias got down on one knee and shot at the windows that faced the walkway along the side of the house because that is where the woman was coming from with her automatic rifle and its monster magazine.

The firing between them so fierce, so relentless, so loud, in those tiny quarters the house shook. In the darkness where the earth had settled around the foundation for decades it now turned into long strands of seeping gravel and sand that began to drizzle down on the Velez family huddled up together.

Then they heard Elias shout and the sound that came out of him was as if his throat had been cut loose—and then he wasn't shooting anymore.

CHAPTER 200

"Do you know what a cistern is?"

Miller did not.

Ana had him drive out to the Village Trailer Park. Just across Route 118 and the trailer park was property once owned by the Iverson Movie Ranch. That property had been sold to the trailer park, but had never been developed. It was a stretch of barren countryside in the middle of the hills.

A cistern was a below ground tank about the size of a large swimming pool, all roofed over and boarded up, for storing water. It was there in those remote hills in case of fire or drought.

She was testing the water with a stick to see how deep it was, and it caused the water to give off a putrid stink. Then she looked over those old crates that must have been there for years.

Jayden was about to ask what she had in mind when he got a call.

It was Landshark.

"Ana with you?"

"Yeah."

"Don't say it's me. But you've got to get her to Keck USC Hospital right away…There's been a shootout at the Velez house."

CHAPTER 201

"I lied to you," said Jayden.

He had told her he'd been requested downtown for further questioning. They were about a mile from the hospital when he fessed up.

The rattlesnake in her head said it all. "Elias…?"

He nodded. "There's been a shooting at the Velez house."

Everything around her just shut off. The traffic, the light, the noise. It was as if the generator for the world just died. Then she heard a woman who sounded very much like herself shout…"Is he dead…? Is he dead?"

CHAPTER 202

The parking lot outside the emergency room was a madhouse. Squad cars, news trucks, every story hound possible, and the curious who just happened to be there at the right time for getting a little of their bloodlust satisfied.

Ana plowed her way past any form of opposition—LAPD, doctors, aides, hospital security, admitting nurses. "Elias Ride!" she shouted. "He was brought in here from the shooting…He's my father!" Right there in the middle of the corridor, she shouted, "Where is Elias Ride?!"

Then he heard someone who sounded very much like her father shout right back, "I'm right fuckin' here."

She turned and there he was lying on a gurney in one of the emergency room stations. He was being treated for a bullet wound along his shoulder blade. She could see there was a Kevlar vest on the floor.

"You had a vest," she said.

"What do you think, I'm stupid?"

She started to cry. She wanted to go to him but the staff kept her out of the way.

"You must have saved up all those tears for the last twenty years."

"Go fuck yourself."

CHAPTER 203

The Velez family was in two adjoining stations. They were being looked over and treated for cuts and scrapes. Mostly it was fear.

When Javier saw Ana, he rushed over and held her.

"Your father saved our lives."

Jayden got Ana's attention. Jutted his chin toward a circle of investigators around Maritza Velez.

"Do you think," said Miller, "that she'll cough up she was threatened and offered a bribe?"

"No," said Ana. "She's not gonna toss that contract with Landshark aside. She's not that honest."

CHAPTER 204

Considering they were "people of interest" in the Charlie Engel murder it made remaining in the emergency room a real task. They learned what happened piecemeal from the Velez family and investigators friendly to Miller.

The shooter, they believed, made their way up the alley to a car parked there, one waiting with a driver.

The first descriptions didn't even have the shooter's race down, nor age, nor sex, for that matter.

Ana had a Zoom call with Landshark out in the parking lot.

"You're not mad at me?" he said.

"For what?"

"I told Jayden to lie to you."

"And he did an admirable job."

Ana could see the Velez family was being escorted to a couple of squad cars.

She angled the laptop so Landshark could get a look.

"Why do you think they wanted her dead...right now?"

"Because dead bodies close deals," said Landshark.

CHAPTER 205

Ana managed a few minutes with her father before they wheeled him up to surgery to extract the bullet in his shoulder blade that had just skimmed the Kevlar vest he was wearing.

Elias held his daughter's hand and had her lean down so he might whisper in her ear. Jayden watched from the doorway what was a profoundly human moment, one they clung to until it was time.

When she was with Miller watching from the hall, Ana said, "We almost forgave each other…we were that close."

As they walked away she started humming some song, to herself really. Something like *"I'll meet you in heaven if you make the grade."*

"What is that?"

"One of Elias's old favorites."

She looked at Miller now from a place of deep silence. Then she smiled in a way she had never smiled at him before.

CHAPTER 206

Elias Ride died on the operating table.

Ana and Jayden were in the cafeteria, discussing their next moves. Ana had been right about a second shooter, beyond the one in Kagel Canyon. And that second shooter being a woman.

The surgery was to take two and a half hours, so she was surprised when a call came through.

She screamed out so suddenly, so painfully, Jayden dropped his coffee cup. It shattered, coffee and bits of crockery scattering everywhere. The cafeteria went silent, eerily so. People stared.

"What?" said Jayden.

"Elias is dead."

He had suffered a massive coronary during the procedure. And it had nothing to do with his wound.

She rode up in the elevator in shock. It was like going to the gallows. He had made the fight. He had won the fight. He had kept the Velez family alive and unharmed.

"We were that close," said a crying Ana, holding her thumb and index finger a breath apart.

CHAPTER 207

Ana disappeared. She and Jayden were outside of surgery talking to the doctors, and then she was gone.

The last she was seen, she was walking down a long corridor. To the bathroom, Jayden thought. Or just to steal a little peace and quiet. But it wasn't so. It was as if she had just faded from the moment. Like someone kidnapped.

Miller went to the garage where the van had been parked. It was gone.

He called William. He was shocked by the news about her father, but he had not heard from her.

She had disappeared into her own peril…this is what Landshark thought. She carried the will for complete destruction around with her. And this was just the scene for it.

CHAPTER 208

Freddie Engel was asleep in bed when he was hit in the mouth with a hammer. He came up spitting out parts of his front teeth and plenty of blood to boot.

He was just conscious enough to drag his naked body to the floor before he took a hammer blow square to his back.

"Move again," said Ana, from in the dark, "and I end you."

He remained flat on the floor. She handcuffed him from the back, then she shackled his ankles.

"Get yourself upright," she said.

And to help him along, she pressed the handle of the hammer well up into the flesh behind Mr. Engel's balls.

She walked him at gunpoint, naked, chained, out his kitchen door and into the back of her waiting van, where she cuffed him to the cargo van wall slats. She did this all with a ruthlessly cold efficiency.

He was too busy swallowing blood to say much. He was looking at the van floor and out the window at the neon signs along the freeway that flashed by.

The first that Ana spoke was maybe twenty minutes in. "Tell me about Valley Boulevard."

He did not know what to say. What to lie, what not to lie. She slammed the hammer against the metal door frame to get his rapt attention.

"I'm in a war mood, fella...My father died tonight...He was murdered, in a manner of speaking...So I could go nuclear at the least provocation. I mean the hormones are amped up...and just hovering on red alert."

She hit the hammer against the doorframe.

"I'll flush you away, boy."

CHAPTER 209

She learned what little Freddie Engel could tell her. Velez had been on Valley Boulevard to keep clear of this ChiChi. Charlie came along in his squad car and offered Velez a ride home. It was the lure in. Charlie tasered Velez, the van rolled up, and it was the last seen of Velez.

Whatever happened to Andres or the weapons, Velez never gave it up. The robbery was supposed to happen a week later under the charge of this ChiChi. Andres and Velez were to be foot soldiers under him. And they would be disappeared promptly afterward. Which they must have guessed and decided to rock on.

"And instead," said Ana, "I'm here...and you're there. And things don't look so promising."

The van swerved off the freeway and onto some nothing asphalt where Freddie could see out the window that it was good and dark.

"You can hear the crickets out here, man," said Ana. "Which means your screams will fall on deaf ears."

He had no idea where he was until she came to a mean stop on a dirt road, then saw ghostly dust rising up around the windows.

When she swung the door open, there it was—the cistern.

Freddie looked around. Nothing but high brown summer brush and a few singular trees growing up out of a vast silence.

She got him out of the van. His bare feet on the hard earth painful, just like she intended.

"What is that?" he said.

"A cistern."

He was talking funny because of the shattered teeth and was wobbly from the beating.

She shoved him toward that decaying structure using a flashlight to guide the way. She shouldered the heavy door which she had earlier loosed from the lock. And there he was, a foot from the stinking pool, the air dense.

"What...is this?" he said.

"The courtroom," she said.

CHAPTER 210

Freddie Engel, fucked as he was, screamed out because he knew what he was in for. He was about to take the dive into that stinking, infected pond. Just him and all those contaminants.

"Who is the woman?" said Ana.

"I don't know."

"You know the woman, otherwise you would not have known there was a woman."

He tried to get out a few pathetic evasions, but she didn't give a shit. In he went.

His manhood tested was found lacking. He was swallowing water, choking, gagging, trying to keep his head upright with her forcing him under, again and again. Toxins leaking out through his broken teeth.

"Drown, you prick!" she shouted.

A searchlight suddenly panned over the structure, with long veins of light through the rotting wallboards. Freddie screamed out because he saw this was his survival.

Ana shouted, "Fuck!"

Freddie kept yelling, "Help me!...Please!...Help me!...I'm being murdered!"

Ana knelt down and tried to force him under. Freddie was crying now, his voice choking on fear and that crap water he was swallowing.

The cistern door kicked open. A tunnel of light through the doorway bearing down on Ana drowning Engel.

"I knew you'd come here," said Jayden. "Let him go."

"Let him drown."

He pulled Ana loose and Engel went under, and if it weren't for Miller grabbing him, Engel would have been a corpse.

"You were gonna kill him," said Miller.

"I think of it more as a calling," she said.

Miller had pulled Engel from the water and he lay there in the dirt, pleading, the searchlight Miller carried flaring right over Engel.

"You're LAPD," said Freddie. "You can't let this crazy kill me."

He put the light right in on Engel so he had to look away. His flesh had whitened from the glare and he was sure a picture of the poor naked slob.

"I'm not gonna let her kill you. But I might do worse."

"What are you talking...you're LAPD. I could help clear you. Get me outta here and—"

"I want the woman," said Ana. "And I won't keep repeating myself."

"Well," said Miller. "There you have it. She wants the woman. Give it up...or I let her take it from you."

"I prefer to take it from him," said Ana.

CHAPTER 211

Ana sat in her truck in the parking lot of The Hideaway Bar in Kagel Canyon. She had her truck back in the darkness of the trees by the mural of John Wayne and characters from *The Wild Bunch*. She wore the crucifix that Landshark had given her. She was filming the wait. And that's what she called it—the wait.

She and Landshark had not really talked since before her father went into surgery.

"I wish I could say something," said Worth, "about you and your father that would have meaning. But I don't know how to express—"

"The Elias Ride Show," she said, "was cancelled in midseason due to unforeseen circumstances. The drama that will replace it features a revenge laden young woman and former Marine with a prothesis and no literary qualities whatsoever."

"You frighten me sometimes," said Landshark.

"Me, Mr. Worth? Why I'm just your basic handful of atomic dust. Nothing more, nothing less."

And so she waited. The night passed, the day passed. Young women that might fit the description arrived with their boyfriends and husbands, came alone or with girlfriends. Most harmless enough...then came one on an old Yamaha 350.

She was not leathered up, not tatted. This was a plain Jane model. Almost intentionally so. With hair cut supershort, so any type of wig or makeup would really alter her.

Ana had been talking to Landshark and he could see what she was filming from the crucifix camera she wore around her neck.

"I think we have something here."

"What makes you think so?"

Ana slunk down in her seat. Held a telescopic sight just over the rim of the dashboard so she would check out the shoes the rider was wearing.

"Elias told me something before he went into surgery. The shooter was wearing black nylon boots with a yellow star. He thought it a little too good for some homeless woman. He told me to log it. Guess what…same kinda boots."

CHAPTER 212

Ana gave Landshark the plate number, both figuring it would come back clean and untraceable as to who this woman really was.

"Do you think there's something about this Kagel Canyon?"

"I can sure tell you what that first night was about," said Ana.

"Do you think they have any idea what's happened to Engel?"

"You mean do we have the upper hand or do they?"

"You haven't heard from Miller?"

"He'll call if there's something."

"If this is the woman, and she was in the bar that first night, watching, she'll know you on sight."

"I'm so unforgettable looking, how could she not?"

"I keep wondering…why Kagel Canyon?"

"Freddie Engel had no idea. He just said this is where they'd planned to meet if it became necessary."

"Do you think they have a place up there?"

"You mean somewhere they could stash the weapons?"

"Maybe you should wait on Jayden."

"Sorry, William."

Landshark knew what she intended. He could hear that cold, smooth death in her voice.

"We're leaving the law behind, aren't we," said William.

CHAPTER 213

Freddie Engel had a two story house that backed up to Amtrak just past the Artesia station in Long Beach. Miller had him in lockdown in a nothing den behind the living room. Engel was still naked, still handcuffed and shackled, but add to it now he was chained to a couch. Miller kept the house dark and the shades drawn.

He robbed a beer from the fridge and moved about watching the street from one window and the depression where the train passed through the neighborhood from another.

It wasn't long before a burner phone of Freddie's began to ring. A couple of rings, then nothing. A couple of rings, then nothing. It went on and on like that.

"You should have turned me over to LAPD."

"I am LAPD."

"This is fuckin' kidnapping."

"You're talking funny...Something wrong with your teeth?"

The phone calls kept coming and finally Jaden noticed something peculiar. There was this cadence to the rings. Orderly and precise... Three rings, silence...One ring, silence...three rings, silence...two rings, silence....

"It's like Morse fuckin' code. You got something happening, Freddie?"

"I can't talk to you right now…I'm too busy spitting blood out of my mouth."

Miller called Ana. He stepped out in the hall as he did.

CHAPTER 214

When her phone rang, she knew.

"Fill me with good news," she said.

"I think they know we got him. At least someone does. What about you?"

"I'm sitting here with John Wayne looking over my shoulder."

"You're at The Hideaway?"

"Yeah. I believe the chickie is inside."

"Freddie Engel's phone kept on with that ringing tell."

Freddie shouted out in a slack garble, "Tell that bitch girlfriend of yours she's got payback coming!"

"What was that?" said Ana.

"Freddie sends his love."

It was dark and windy in Kagel Canyon, keeping Ana's emotions on a knife blade.

"How can everything down there be okay if you think they know you got him?"

Freddie's phone was making Jayden quietly crazy.

He kept looking out window after window.

"I don't like your silence, Mr. Miller."

"I'm not crazy about it either. Listen…if anything goes bad, just cut me loose, alright?"

"The same goes for me," said Ana.

Another uncredited silence.

"There's that fuckin' silence again," said Ana.

CHAPTER 215

There was a crew already closing in on the house. Two of their number crossed the tracks, then scaled the concrete wall that flanked the Amtrak. From there it was you could crab your way through the high weeds to a crawlspace under the kitchen. A third would fence hop from down the street to a crawlspace by the fireplace. The fourth would come from up the block, slip under the front porch to another crawlspace. There was a trap door under the house that led up to where the water heater was in a storage closet.

The four were young, relentless, and weaponized. Street shooters, car jackers, upscale robbery, murder for hire, no crime was out of their orbit. And this one was, as they say, body specific.

CHAPTER 216

There was a candlelight protest around the now badly damaged Velez house. People wanted her out and shouted so, some with bullhorns, others had preordained placards.

They wanted her out of the Association, out of the neighborhood, out of their lives.

Dawn Newell was there gathering material for her podcast, culling through them for the most infuriating comments against the

Velez family.

She intended to come down hard, pushing the idea that what happened at this address was a symptom of the inescapable violence infecting every aspect of civil life and discourse. And that Maritza Velez was a living example of this disease. She was the clandestine face of crime and as guilty as her missing husband, and possibly more so.

Their conspiracy against the DON Group, and that company's attempt to buy and develop the property and fulfill the city's long standing need—multifamily affordable dwellings—was in and of itself an act of racism and white supremacy.

And the reasoning—who financed the initial crime, who financed the ongoing attempt to make the DON Group the guilty party? Someone with privilege and money and connections. Dawn Newell would add one caveat to her podcast, one that James Salamone gave her on deep background—a possible deal was in the making between the DON Group and the Tenants Association. A deal that would confront the racism and white supremacy. And that would be good for all involved.

CHAPTER 217

A squad car turned the corner and started down the street to where the houses backed up to the Amtrak. A call had been put in about a disturbance...Possibly shots.

The house belonged to one Freddie Engel. The squad car pulled up and ran its searchlight across the front porch. The house was dark, the front door wide open.

They put in a call, then got out of their car. They started up the walkway and unloosed their weapons. They called out but received no response. They rang the bell, they knocked on the door. They were greeted by only silence, so they entered the house, carefully, knowing they were part of that hated America, where dead cops were the prize.

Freddie Engel was a well known badass so you could expect almost anything. The house smelled of weed and stale men's clothes. There was nothing to see but moonlight on gaudy furniture. There was nothing to confirm the call. Until one of them saw in the den behind the living room what would qualify as a nightmare.

There was Freddie Engel. Lying on the couch as he had been, still handcuffed as he had been, still shackled, still chained to the couch. His shattered front teeth a mark of violence, the small bullet hole to the skull the confirmation of death.

CHAPTER 218

Ana sat in the truck in the dark till the goddamn bar closed. Till the last of the bar hounds and drunks filed out, laughing it up, doing their goodnight thing, then they walked or stumbled to their rigs and off they went. And that was that. The lot was empty, the lights went out. Pretty soon it was just Ana and Duke Wayne.

But no chickie.

Ana got Landshark on the phone and explained. She was talking it through, trying to come to some idea about what happened.

A call came in. This one from a number she did not recognize.

"I got a feeling," she said to Landshark. "Talk to you later."

When Ana answered, what sounded like a woman said, "It's a beautiful picture, isn't it?"

"What?"

"You waiting for me. I could have killed your ass."

"You didn't crawl out of the woodwork for no reason," said Ana. "So give me the edited version."

The woman came from back behind the bar where a dance floor door opened to a smokers' patio. She was coming through the trees like this was all nothing.

Ana shifted a semiautomatic from the shotgun seat to her lap.

"You got enough in you to follow me," said the girl.

"I've got enough to run your ass over," said Ana.

The girl got onto her Yamaha and revved it. She swung out into Kagel Canyon with Ana right behind her.

About a mile up the girl slowed and put on a blinker—she actually put on a blinker and turned onto a dirt road that slanted off into the woods. A road you'd have to die on to know it was there.

CHAPTER 219

The Yamaha was well ahead when Ana suddenly pulled off into a stand of trees, flipped off the headlights, and shut the engine. She tucked the semiautomatic into her belt and then she pocketed a few little goodies she rummaged out of the glove box. She stepped from the truck and started up the shadows, keeping clear of the road.

Well ahead Ana could make out the motorcycle taillights slow then stop. She heard the engine kick off and saw the lights go out.

Then the girl yelled back, "I'm here to talk, girl! Make a deal! Not kill your ass."

Ana did not answer. She just continued on and pretty soon she could make out a corrugated warehouse against the moonlight and, of all things, three boats on trailers.

Ana heard the warehouse door on rollers open. A light went on from within. It was some kind of repair shop with the usual hoists and racks and clutters of equipment.

Ana used the boats as cover to close in some. She flashed on that night in Mexico. It was that night all over again, only she was playing a different part.

The girl was standing under a single light. She looked perfectly harmless. And that's always the worst kind.

Ana thought of her father, and the girl's part in his death. She was not prepared as yet to deal with the fact she had asked her father to watch over the Velez family.

Ana would need no pretext to kill this girl good and proper, that was a certainty.

"Are we gonna talk...or are you gonna stalk about?" said the girl.

"Both," said Ana. She kept close to the boat hulls but worked her way closer. "You need the weapons back because your handlers have to clean this mess up. The dead have to be...very dead."

"We can fight it out, you and I," said the girl, "but you should know Freddie Engel has joined the recently dead. And your bedmate is hanging on by a threat. You won't believe me. Call him."

Ana came on slowly, waiting for signs of anyone, anything. Once at the doorway, where the shadows ended, the girl saw Ana as clearly as she saw the gun at Ana's side.

"Call him," said the girl.

Ana leaned her head in and looked around the dusty interior.

"In a minute."

The girl stretched out her arms. "There's no threat here."

Ana glanced at the girl's shoes. She could hear her father's voice for what would be the last time.

"Let's make that call," said Ana.

She came forward. They were now just separated by a few feet.

Ana reached for her cellphone but it wasn't a cellphone she took from her pocket. It was a World War Two era stiletto. A nasty piece that Elias had actually given his daughter for a birthday present—some fuckin' present.

It would come in handy tonight.

The girl was shocked to find she was stabbed. She stumbled backwards and landed on the dirt floor. She was not five feet from where the two Mexicans and Luis Velez were buried.

"You should know," said Ana, "I've just cut open a couple of your vital organs. You're bleeding to death. And you probably have just enough time to sing your favorite tune."

CHAPTER 220

Whatever happened out there in Kagel Canyon Landshark did not know. Ana had been prescient in turning off the crucifix camera she wore when she stepped out of the truck. He assumed the worst, but William Worth was an expert at assuming the worst. He had made a life of it, and a career.

He tried to call Ana, he got no answer. So he waited.

He watched the news on the bank of screens. Everything was focused on the Uvalde shootings still, all these weeks later, and it was telling a very different story than in those first days. Instead of being brave lads, the police and sheriffs in that dusty border town were, it turned out, flawed, confused, compromised, and failures at their duty. Possibly even cowards, who let the children die in vain while they waited in the hallways.

No story is complete until the last body is buried. Even then, cast your lot with doubt. Landshark's mother had told him this many times, and how he hated his mother.

CHAPTER 221

It had started to rain a little before she walked out of that bleak warehouse. Spots of dirt on the windshield turned to muddied eyelets. She sat in the truck and looked at the blood on her hands. She wiped them clean as best she could on her dark shirt. It was raining hard by the time she drove down Gravity Hill. That is when she just broke down and started to cry.

She pulled off the road and into a flat landscape of wild grass. She shut off the engine and the lights. She watched the rain stream down the windshield. An image seen endless times by endless souls, at endless moments such as these. An old image, for sure, yet new for the one suffering it.

It hit her hard that her father was gone from her for good. There would not be another moment, another scene, another quarrel, another incident, another threat, another drunken confrontation, another fight...yes, fight. Especially a fight. Something tangible in a fight.

What do you do when the war is over, but isn't done. Where do you go when you're chasing questions that outrun the answers. Where do you go when you can never really catch up with forgiveness.

There was lightning in the far, far distance.

She got out of the truck and walked well into that muddying field. "Strike me dead," she said to the lightning. "Strike me dead. Come on…strike me."

CHAPTER 222

Ana had expended it all by the time she returned to Mount Washington. She put the truck in the garage of the other house. She had Landshark turn off all the lights and security cameras and she made her way up through the din of overgrowth to the back gate.

Landshark had clothes for her and she undressed in a workshop out back. He was there with her, keeping his silence until she was done.

"There's what I need to know," he said, "and what I'd like to know."

"What you need to know?" She took out the antique stiletto and triggered open what had to be a seven inch blade. She stuck it into the top of a work bench. He saw there was blood on the blade.

"What about Jayden?" he said. "Do you know anything?"

She gave a long, cold blooded sigh. "I might have cut him loose."

"You don't know."

She held up two phones that were once the property of the late Lily Vee. One was a burner. That would be her first call.

CHAPTER 223

Once they were hunkered back down in Landshark's office, Ana made the call. She had the dead girl's two phones. She started with the burner. The other, she slid across the bar. "Have Carter and Ellison turn over every phone number."

She took the burner and called back the most recent number. The phone rang until voicemail kicked in. She waited, she hung up.

"You didn't leave a message," said Worth.

"I left a message."

They sat at the bar and waited. Landshark made drinks. Ana was bearing what the day had brought.

When the phone rang two hours later, they both jumped.

Ana took a breath. She answered the phone and said right off, "You know who this is."

"Does it matter what I say?" said the voice.

"No," said Ana. She stood now, stretched her back muscles as if she was ready to strike a blow. "I have the weapons. You need them back. At this point because the deal on the 710 Corridor property is about to close. You were hired by Salamone and you need me and those with me…dead. I'm gonna give you the opportunity. As far as Jayden Miller goes…none of this 'We'll trade one for the other.' I've cut him loose. Not interested. Kill him if you choose. I'll run you down either way. Arrange the taking."

She ended the call.

She stood there, very alone.

"The unchartered waters of fury," said Landshark.

"Yeah. You'd be surprised how well they're chartered."

"You'd let him die?"

"He might well be dead already."

"Yeah...but you don't know."

She walked up to the bar, looked at Landshark so he knew and understood.

"It wouldn't change anything. And besides...he'd cut me loose. You see...we'd agreed to it."

CHAPTER 224

The hill behind the Domingos' house overflowed with members of the Tenants Association and the tenants themselves involved in the 710 Corridor property dispute.

Julia Domingo had posted an email from the Don Group outlining the terms of the settlement. The gathering today was to talk out the deal and come to some possible resolution.

The conflict of the last few weeks, the robbery, the shooting, and assorted political insinuations had left everything in a state of chaos, which was, and is, the perfect breeding ground for successful corruption.

A microphone had been set up on a makeshift stage where everyone with standing could vent their opinion. The deal, when simply laid out, was compared to selling the property outright, for thirty cents on the dollar.

But the caveat, of course, was there would be no legal fight through the court system, no appeal upon appeal. No years of rambling, waiting for money. Julia Domingo compared their situation to the movie *Erin Brockovich*, where how much is it worth to wait and wait instead of settling and going on with your life.

There was also the governor's silence on the matter and that inevitable phrase leaking out of his office: "We need to look into the matter further."

Landshark had people there filming. He watched it live in his office on a series of computer screens. The people there were at the microphone, their voices, opinions being carried out onto that Los Angeles neighborhood. There were refreshment stands all set up, where they had balloons. It could have been a high school rally or a local carnival.

And down below, on the street, another microphone set up in the back of a pickup truck where a woman spoke, pleading for the people not to make the deal. That it was a corruption in the works. The woman was Maritza Velez.

And it wasn't long before Landshark watched security invite her down from the truck and walk her away.

CHAPTER 225

Perch was an outdoor restaurant on the roof of the Pershing Square Building on South Hill Street. Once L.A. got itself a skyline, rooftop restaurants became vogue. They helped make everything seem bigger, more important. And god knows, people need that, or at least a pretext of it. Besides, they're a perfect place to leap from after a disappointment or two.

James Salamone sat with two attorneys from the DON Group. He had set his laptop up on the table so they could watch what was happening at the Domingos' place, courtesy of a crawler Salamone hired.

While they watched and ate, a bottle of champagne was brought to their table along with a note. The note was addressed to Salamone. They all wondered what little mystery came with it, but Salamone read the note privately.

This is what it said:

Don't congratulate yourself too soon.
The vote is not yet in on you, this Chichi,
or is it Rabel?

Salamone put on a bold smile and tucked the note back in the envelope. "A little precongratulation congratulations," he said.

He waited an appropriate minute or so and then excused himself. He went to the men's room and took up in a stall and made a call.

His heart was not doing him any favors, the way it raced.

Rabel answered.

"She's here," he blurted out.

"Here where?" said Rabel. "Who?"

"The Ride woman. She's here at the Perch and...what's the difference. She left a note." Salamone read the note. He was almost done with it when someone suddenly was kicking at his stall door.

The kicking was merciless so he was forced to unlatch the door and open it. Fearing the worst is exactly what he got.

"And that kicking was with a prosthesis," Ana said. "I was afraid you might have left without as so much as a hello. So I thought—"

There were a few people in the men's room doing their best to only innocently stare or eavesdrop. An embarrassed shell, Salamone walked out without a word.

Ana followed.

"I love fast walkers," she said. "Means we'll get to the close a lot quicker.

She was virtually breathing down his shirt.

"Hey, remember this," she said. "Every place is the same...when you're dead."

She did not follow him but stopped at the elevator. As Salamone went back through the doors to the rooftop patio, Carter passed him.

Ana got on the elevator. Carter followed. And a beat later, coming from the bar, Ellison joined them.

"Well," she said to them.

"We got it," said Carter.

CHAPTER 226

Landshark was at his computer when Ana returned. He was caught off guard by her pale and rather shocked expression. She was also carrying a small bundle of wrapping paper which she set on the desk.

"What's wrong?" he said.

"I have to show you something...but be prepared."

Her eyes went to the wrapping paper, his eyes followed.

She explained, verbally stumbling along. She had returned to the house on Mount Washington and put the truck in the garage. The phone had rung. Ever vigilant, she had kept to the dark and answered it.

Right off, she said, "We're closing in."

Rabel did not answer.

"What do I call you?" she said. "Rabel...ChiChi...Does it matter?"

"Through Mr. Worth," said whoever he was, "I will send you a plan with the appropriate means of exchange...The weapons and my safety in exchange for Mr. Miller and your safety."

"I've cut him loose," said Ana. "I told you that."

"Yes, I know. But I haven't. At the rear of the garage, the filing cabinets. On the top of the last one nearest the door is a bundle of wrapping paper. Open it in good health."

Landshark listened, staring at the wrapping paper.

All the while, he was so afraid, so shaken he was going to ask Ana to open it, but instead he mastered his own fear. At least enough for that.

The paper crinkled as he carefully opened it. And what he saw....

He could barely get to the bathroom fast enough to vomit.

Wrapped in bloody men's underwear was an amputated index finger.

CHAPTER 227

They all gathered at the Landshark estate when he received an anonymous email. The son of a bitch outlined his proposal with a schoolteacher's precision and included a detailed map with Google images of the exact locations. And besides Ana Ride, he emailed Carter and Ellison.

"He's sticking it to us," said Ellison.

"How do you know this Rabel is a he," said Ana, "and not a she? We never confirmed that. Rabel could be a...they."

It was true, Rabel was an unread book. And every door of information they opened, so far, had closed another. Their one major crack were the phones being tied to James Salamone. There would be questions from that, hard to answer—not impossible—but hard.

"Do the weapons still have this much power to queer the deal?" said Landshark.

"It's us he wants," said Ellison. "The weapons just validate what's all gone down."

"It's Ana he wants," said Carter. "And he's gonna want her even if he beats us at this."

He turned to Ana. "He's gonna keep coming after you, like you are after him. It's never going to end."

"Elias used to say…Never give death a second look."

CHAPTER 228

They went to pick up the weapons. Carter and Ellison guarded each end of Milner Road. Ana backed the pickup into Susan Sarah's garage. They kept it dark except for the flashlight Landshark's cousin was carrying. Highland was flush with activity that night and very loud. Long streams of headlights marking the Cahuenga Pass.

After Ana finished getting the weapons on board, she said to Sarah, "This is where the body was buried in that Hollywood murder William told me about?"

Susan Sarah pointed her flashlight at a spot of concrete flooring. "It's great," she said cynically, "to be a part of Hollywood lore."

Ana went over, knelt down, and rapped her knuckles on the spot. Then she got up.

"What was that for?" said Susan Sarah.

"For luck!" said Ana.

CHAPTER 229

Del Sur was a nothing community in the Mojave Desert. Endless powerlines and scrub are its iconic landmarks. And you can't forget the few faceless housing developments plucked out of the sand, and none the better for it.

Following instructions Ana made her way through this unincorporated wasteland of L.A. County. One of the markers was a vast solar farm. It went on forever and looked like a lake.

California wants you to think it's the heartbeat of cutting edge energy. But when you drive through places what you see is the capital of wasteful stupidity.

At the barren corner of Avenue J and 90th Street West there was an RV park. A dozen or so vehicles called this blistering patch of gravel home. There was a small building that had been a bar and a church. Its claim to fame was that ZZ Top once played there.

"They must have been mighty fuckin' desperate," said Ana. She had an open line to Landshark, who had her connected to Carter and Ellison, who were trailing her pickup about a mile back.

Her instructions were to turn north there on 90th and make her way to the Sparrow Ranch Motel and All Faiths World.

CHAPTER 230

The desert in these parts gets a real human potluck of types, oddities, eccentrics, outlaws, zealots of the flesh. It also turned out this was Rabel country. Carter and Ellison had worked the night tracking phone calls though every technological smokescreen to their cellphone towers. Most of Rabel's calls had come from within a mile or two of Del Sur.

Sparrow Ranch and All Faiths were pretty much a nondescript Tex-Cote home, a trailer, a warehouse, and a huge array of office furniture baking in the sun. Beyond that there was scrub and fencing, lots and lots of fencing as far as the eye could make out through all that glare.

Ana had been directed to wait at sign by the entry under a spread of trees. The sign said: LAMBS, SHEEP, EGGS?

CHAPTER 231

Ana sat in the truck with the engine idling, the air conditioner full blast. Los Angeles was going through its worst heat wave in years. The air like something brewed in a pot. She was left there waiting for nearly half an hour. Landshark was moody, sure there was something wrong here. Carter and Ellison were not far behind in their judgments.

The door to the little house opened and a man stepped out into the bleached daylight.

Carter could just make him out through a long lens. He was tall and reedy. Wore beat up jeans and boots and a straw cowboy hat. His skin was deeply lined.

"I'm being approached," said Ana.

The man had a slow, easy walk. When he was close enough to the truck he motioned for Ana to open her window. The hot air coming through practically choked her.

The man leaned down. "Are you, by chance, Ana Ride?"

"Not by chance."

"I got a message for you from one of the Rabels."

"You do?"

"Yes."

The man told Ana she was to go across the road, pass around that mess of solar panels. From there you could see the remains of the old Bohunk's Airpark. Rabel would meet her there.

It had all been written in a note that Ana took.

"Do you know Rabel?"

"I know the Rabels. Number of them. Half dozen live out there. They own that RV park. And this ranch. They put up the money for All Faiths."

"Do you know which of the Rabels left me this note?"

The man eyed her oddly as she slipped the note into her pocket.

"You're more likely to know that than me, Miss. I was just told there's a delivery out there for you."

Ana smiled, "I just wanted to know who exactly to thank."

CHAPTER 232

As the man started away, Ana closed the window. The others had heard everything. "What do you think?" she said.

"This is feeling off," said Landshark.

Ana started up the truck.

With his long lens Carter could see the remains of the dirt road the man had spoken of.

Ana swung the truck around and started up past that sea of solar panels.

"You guys see anything?" Landshark said. "I'm gonna start to run down every Rabel there is…I don't think he or she is a Rabel."

"It sure feels like that," said Ana. "You guys see anything?"

"It's pure, flat nothing," said Carter, "and for a good mile maybe. Then there's something…a shimmer. Maybe the remains of a hangar or sheds."

"Old time desert airpark…We'll follow you out," said Ellison.

"Not too close," said Ana.

CHAPTER 233

While they were talking, of all things, a small plane, a single prop, came riding the thermals from Lancaster and passed right over Carter and Ellison. It had come in low, damn low. Ellison stopped and Carter used his long lens to check it out. "I believe it's a taildragger. A single prop. A Maule maybe," he said.

"A real desert rat plane," said Ellison. "Land that jukebox crate anywhere."

It banked and headed west, where there were half a dozen other planes along the horizon, above Castaic Lake.

There was a bad fire starting up along the lake which flanked the 5 Freeway. With the heat and the dry brush, this could become a fierce disaster that would last for days.

It might even shut down the freeway and bring that whole section of L.A. County to its knees.

Her truck rumbled along, the heat coming off the desert floor like a scorched pan. She reached what had been the dirt runaway and from there she could see the shimmering steel sheeting of a half fallen to hell hangar and corrugated sheds with heaped garbage, rotted wood. A pile of toilets, the remains of a few cars.

She stopped. "No need to come closer," she said.

Carter and Ellison slowed, but kept on a bit. "I just got to get close enough," said Ellison, "so Carter can keep you in his sights."

She sat in the truck and scanned the landscape, the rotted buildings.

Landshark said, "Ana."

"What?"

"Nothing," he said.

"It's fuckin' grim, gents. I'm stepping out of the truck. And I'm weaponed, like we talked about."

"Be careful," said Landshark.

"I wonder how many people are buried out there," said Ana. "Think you could Google that for me, William?"

CHAPTER 234

She had her cellphone and kept the line open so they could all talk. In her other hand Ana held her semiautomatic. She steered pretty close to the truck, searching the landscape for some telltale sign. She spotted the remains of what had been a dog or a wolf, now the sand filled in around the ribs where there had once been flesh.

What no one noticed at first—

"That plane," said Ellison.

Carter grabbed his camera lens.

It was coming their way from the direction of Lake Castaic.

Carter checked it. "It's the same plane."

It descended, even more so than last time.

It came in lower, then lower, and it headed right for Ana. She pressed against the truck. The plane could ride the thermals and wasn't but ten feet above Ana and she could just begin to see a face in the window and the dust kicked up and blew over her, it blinded and choked her. Then the plane went on and started to bank.

"What's happening?" said Landshark.

"I think this is it," said Ana.

"I'm getting pictures of the plane," said Carter.

"This could be the dance," said Ana.

The taildragger banked and came in low, dead on with that once upon a time runway. The pilot smoothed it, the drop was a little rough, the tail end really biting at the hard rock.

The taildragger landed and slowed and the prop got closer and louder and the air a sweep of dust until it was about fifty yards from Ana's truck.

The plane came to a stop but the pilot did not quite get out. Instead the pilot kept under the shadow of the overhanging wing.

"It's important you know this," said the pilot, raising a hand in which Ana saw a device of some kind. "I can blow this crate apart and your friend there with it."

CHAPTER 235

Ana took a few steps. She had to cover her eyes against the dust being kicked up from that engine prop. It was Jayden alright. But he could be as dead as alive.

"You better tell your groupies to keep their distance," said the pilot.

Ana yelled into her cellphone. They heard alright.

The pilot stepped back, opened the side door and storage panel.

"Put the weapons in there."

"I want him out of the plane first."

"Go to it," said the pilot. "He's just weight now."

Ana walked around the plane. She could shoot the pilot. But if true about the device, she'd be killing herself and Jayden. If he was dead, it would be a different story altogether.

Jayden was braced to the seat. He was beaten to the point that if he was not dead, he was sure giving a serious rendering.

She put a hand on his. "Hey Miller...Can you hear me, boy... This is the evil one checking in."

It was a long nothing before he finally found enough in the tank to exact some pressure against her fingers.

"Alright, boy...We got some business here. I'm gonna get you off this plane."

She undid the ropes, shouted to the pilot. "I'm undoing the ropes!"

Lifting himself was out of the question, he could not even get his arm around Ana's shoulder, he could not get out words. He was a catastrophe of dead weight that she had to literally lift and drop onto a roadway, in a cloud of dust from the propeller.

"You'll be alright," she whispered. But she had no idea. Saying that was no better than an outright lie, in fact. She stood and started around the taildragger to try and confront the pilot without all that dust between them and when she did, she saw—

The pilot wore a pullover mask, and underneath it, some kind of plastic mask. There was no way to tell if it was a man, a woman, or something other. Even the hands were covered with gloves. And the device that pilot gripped.

"Load the weapons," said the pilot.

Ana did as ordered. First one satchel, then the second. Evaluating all the while could she make a sudden assault and get that device free.

She loaded the last satchel and the pilot shut the storage door.

"Get in," said the pilot.

"What?"

"You're coming with me. 'Cause I don't know any other way of keeping those groupies of yours from putting out the alert."

"Gents!" Ana shouted into her phone. "In case you didn't hear... I'm taking a little trip...Hold all calls!"

She walked around the Maule and climbed into the passenger seat. The pilot shifted the device to its left hand and shut the door.

The pilot then edged the plane onto the old runway. The pilot studied Ana.

"I go where you go, motherfucker," said Ana. "And that's not good news for you."

The pilot just sat there staring at Ana.

"Come on, man," she said. "I got to be back in time for dinner."

The pilot throttled it.

CHAPTER 236

The small taildragger came climbing out of the dust, the wings see-sawing a bit from the thermals and then the plane just took a pretty little lift and Carter and Ellison were forced to watch it sweep right over their heads, close enough to almost touch, heading west toward the Sierra Pelona and the billowing smoke from the fires along Lake Castaic and where after that who the hell knew.

The taildragger lifted and rose, pressing the sky, on toward those hard California hills, toward smoke spiring up through dark canyons and along sunburned slopes toward the lake. It was loud in the cabin and the plane shook from the heat with the fires and the pilot was connected to nothing, connected with no one. The pilot's chin was sunk down onto his chest in a terror of determination.

"Gonna die today," said the pilot.

"Been there," said Ana.

The pilot looked at her. Something in that creature's eyes was burning dimly.

"Yeah," said the pilot.

"Go ahead," said Ana, "blow this shit box. Send us on."

The pilot held the explosive device away from her and up against the door window and screamed. The kind of scream one could hear at the other end of the world.

Ana knew, the pilot knew, this was about the unseen power of who can bear death better than the other.

The plane was suddenly crossing a ridgeline and then banked into a vast rising wave of smoke and ash. You could feel the heat coming from the earth. The plane just clearing the burning treetops and you could see more trees and brush on fire, endless acres of fire, for endless miles, and crews of firefighters making their desperate way along rocky trails and police choppers in the sky and transports dumping blood red retardant. The world before them was coming undone. The plane was struggling now against this firestorm and burning bits of bark spattering violently against the windshield so it was impossible to see and the sky around them a toxic yellow. The pilot leaned into the throttle.

Ana shouted, "Where are you taking this plane?"

"What's the difference?" the pilot shouted back. "You're not gonna live to see it."

The lake came out of the smoke in all its beauty with the shoreline ringed by fire. The lake still as glass and flags upon flags of wild smoke across the waters.

If I, she thought, *could bring this plane down and crash it into the lake, they would find the weapons. The lake was no more than two or three hundred feet deep. They'd find the weapons and they'd find the bodies and the story would be the story at last.*

Ana did not give it a moment's more thought. She took out her knife and lunged at the pilot. She got one hand around his shoulder and grabbed the gloved hand with the detonator. She needed just a little time, just enough, and she put the blade deep into the pilot's throat.

The plane dropped. The tail end caught the tree tips along the ridge and the tail shattered.

The plane rolled. Ana lost her grip on the hand with the detonator.

The plane was out of control. It skimmed the crystal blue waters, pouring out black smoke. The pilot lost consciousness from lack of blood and let go of the detonator.

Ana felt it come loose but was a moment too late. She flashed on her father and that glary look he had. The hand device detonated.

There was a burst of sparks from the engine, and then an explosion. The propeller was flung across the sky. The engine was blown all the way to Suicide Point, where it would later be found.

The cabin skimmed the surface of the water for a hundred yards at least. And then the cabin itself sunk. There, then gone, under the beautiful blue waters.

CHAPTER 237

Footage of the crash got into the pipeline almost instantly as there were news trucks and choppers at the site, and locals all along the dam at the south end of the lake.

The reason for the crash was another story, to unfold in shocking bursts of conjecture and information. Only Landshark was witness to the plane's final moments of distress, courtesy of the crucifix camera Ana Ride wore around her neck. He alone knew the truth of it, or at least until the moment when the cabin went underwater.

CHAPTER 238

Carter and Ellison had followed as best they could being fed information from Landshark. The roads around the lake had been cordoned off and ultimately the two men had continued on foot avoiding the park rangers, the police, and worsening fire.

By the time they were looking down upon the Castaic, men were in the water. The cabin and part of one wing had ended up in about ten feet of shallows along Government Cove. Where the wing was sticking up, there was a boat. Carter could see through the camera lens they were lifting a satchel of the weapons, water streaming out of its seams. There was already one satchel on the boat. It was open and a man was pulling out what looked to be an AR-15.

The smoke across the lake grew thicker and the heat from the flames on the ridge above them more unbearable. Carter kept wiping at his eyes to see if somewhere there was a sign of Ana.

He was just about to tell Ellison he was done, his eyes were burned out, when he saw one of the men in the water. He was pointing up toward the far end of the lake. With so much dust Carter had an impossible time to sight where the man was pointing, so he slowly panned the lake and he panned the shoreline and the lake again. Up by what was known as the Hawk's Nest he saw there were two rangers standing on a rocky crag that jutted into the water. They were waving furiously for help. Trying to get someone's, anyone's attention. Then one of the men leaned down and Carter could just make out, "There's a body up there."

CHAPTER 239

Landshark was the first to get the news out about the crash and that on board a cache of weapons had been discovered that may well have been stolen from the Academy gun shop robbery. He also named Ana Ride as one of the two people on board, and that he had it from a good source that she was taken under duress, because of her ongoing efforts to uncover the truth behind the robbery.

CHAPTER 240

The Castaic fire was the news now, and what put it over the top was a downed plane and two possible fatalities, added to that the seizure of weapons.

Carter and Ellison had been forced from the lake back up to the road by rangers and LAPD. All the while they tried to solicit, beg, plead for information from anyone, everyone, about the crash and survivors.

They got nowhere. It was all a confusion until they overheard an officer on his radio talking about a body being taken from the plane cab. A body—not a survivor.

Too much smoke, too much haze for the camera Carter carried.

Then a helicopter came crossing the ridgeline and closed in on the Hawk's Nest. It was clear enough for Carter to make out this was an air ambulance and it was now hovering over the rocks where the body had been discovered.

An air ambulance meant someone was alive. And then paramedics started to drop a stretcher and Ellison was on his phone to Landshark.

CHAPTER 241

Landshark could professionally massage or, if flat out necessary, bribe his way to the answers to his questions.

What he got from an air ambulance dispatcher—

The body taken from the plane appeared to be that of a male. The survivor being airlifted appeared to be a woman. The nature and extent of her injuries was yet unknown.

Landshark then decided to take a cut at Salamone's confidence and his vulnerability.

He knew Salamone would take the call. He was always chasing aspirations or escaping desperations. Landshark told Salamone he had a reliable source claiming the pilot of the plane that went down in the Castaic with all those weapons aboard may well be a dubious character by the name of Rabel...And that he might not only be involved in the Academy gun shop robbery, but may be indirectly connected to the DON group regarding the 710 Corridor property deal. And did Salamone know this man, or know of him.

It did not matter what lies Salamone would toss out, Mr. Worth just wanted Salamone to know bad news was around the corner.

CHAPTER 242

Ana was flown down the Newhall. She was diagnosed with, at the very least, fractured ribs and a punctured lung.

The pilot carried no identification, and was finally identified by fingerprints as he was a convicted felon by the name of Lenny Conrad. Landshark had a team gather everything they could on this Conrad, and to uncover if he was connected anywhere to someone named ChiChi or Rabel.

Ellison and Carter reached the hospital when Ana was in surgery and they hooked up with William by phone. They also got word that Jayden Miller was in stable condition after suffering an assortment of wounds from a severe beating.

CHAPTER 243

You start to think you have a grasp on everything, but you don't. You believe answers are falling into place when in fact they might well be falling apart.

William Worth received a phone call from Maritza Velez. She told him she had been in her den working when the boys rushed in and demanded she come see the television.

It was about the crash in Castaic. There was one victim being airlifted. Then there was a police picture of Ana Ride, "a person of interest" in the slaying of one Charlie Engel. And now the survivor in a crash of a stolen plane, a plane that was carrying weapons believed to be the ones taken in the Police Academy gun shop robbery.

And then there was a police photo of Lenny Conrad—the pilot killed in the crash, a convicted felon who served time for armed robbery and kidnapping.

"I know that man," said Maritza. "I saw him once with my husband weeks before the robbery," she told Worth.

"Was he involved?"

"I don't know. I do know this…He was dying. He had cancer and was desperate for money for his family."

CHAPTER 244

The next day Landshark gave a punishing indictment on his podcast of the deal pending between the DON Group and the Tenants Association, based on this new information from the crash stating that no deal of any kind should be consummated until and unless the weapons could be positively airlocked to this mysterious character named Rabel and was working in concert with the DON Group, through an attorney by the name of Salamone. Or was he being fronted by the Domingos to subvert the DON group and better their own position of power.

He included nothing about Lenny Conrad.

Landshark did include one additional thought to the podcast—Los Angeles is a most disjointed city. And a disjointed city breeds and favors disjointed people and their disjointed ideas, and who live out their disjointed lives and who either commit or unravel disjointed crimes.

Myself, accordingly, he included.

CHAPTER 245

Ana Ride came through her surgery not nearly as wrecked as she should have been. Six fractured ribs, a punctured lung, concussion, the previous wound on her arm retorn open to the tune of twenty plus new stitches.

The six broken ribs she thought a complete laugh. The number six symbolizing love, balance, and harmony.

Ana agreed to be questioned by LAPD while in intensive care. Her attorney, Paige Hughes, was there beside her. Ana answered all questions honestly, except for the ones she did not. And the most important of all—how did she come to be in possession of the weapons? She was advised she would be arrested upon her release for withholding evidence. Paige Hughes advised the district attorney all bail would be guaranteed by her firm.

So there was Ana, alone in the dark, and she gets a call on the phone she would not have been allowed to have in intensive care.

It was Jayden.

"First thing," he said, "thanks…again."

"For what, I left you in the fuckin' desert."

"But…at an airpark."

"Why don't you come down here and fuck me with all that optimism."

CHAPTER 246

An ambulance brought Ana to the Worth estate when she was released, and where she settled in, it being too painful and too lonely to go right back to the trailer park.

They sat in the office late that first night. The office had become like a second home to Ana. She and Worth drank and he kept the office quite dark, so the nightworld of the city below dominated. The investigation had intensified as LAPD was trying not only to connect Lenny Conrad to the robbery, but to either James Salamone or the Domingos with regard to the 710 Corridor.

"Was this the man known as Rabel?" said Ana.

"Conrad was dying of cancer," said Worth.

Ana stopped the drink she was about to take.

Worth told Ana what he'd learned from Maritza Velez. That she'd met Conrad, that he was connected in some way to the crime, and that he was dying. None of this Maritza related to the LAPD.

"Conrad had a mother and son in Calexico. Across the border in Mexicali there are a lot of late stage cancer treatment doctors…."

"How does this fact out for us?"

"I have people who've done investigating for me down there. I have proof Conrad was getting treatments at the same time he was trying to kill you up in Kagel Canyon."

Ana set her glass down gingerly on the table, thinking, realizing. Conrad is not Rabel…. "So Rabel is still alive."

"And out there somewhere," said Landshark.

"Somewhere," said Ana. "Covers a lot of ground."

"My guess," said Landshark, "Conrad was paid to do you and get those weapons. And the risk…None. He was dying. How much do you think his mother really knows?"

"She's got a convicted felon for a son," said Ana. "Money shows up on the doorstep, she's not talking. Not to the law and order crowd anyway."

A look passed between them. A silence they had seen in each other and learned to read. They were a step ahead of everyone at this moment.

"He's gonna come after you," said Landshark.

"Us," said Ana.

"Yeah. Until the Corridor deal is closed, anyway."

"It won't close," said Ana.

"No?"

"You won't let it."

CHAPTER 247

They talked until they had exhausted every thought, but their teeth were already good and sharp for the next go round. William crashed, Ana stayed up alone. She sat in the dark studying that big island of lights out there in the night, the Los Angeles that taunts your dreams.

He was out there somewhere. She looked at the phone on the desk, the burner she had contacted with him. She was tempted to make the call, to let him know she was coming. That she would hunt him out. But he would know, he knew already...because she was alive.

CHAPTER 248

William had thoughts of telling Ana about the house down the hill, and his feelings of being safe there.

It had belonged to his family, even when he was a boy, serving as an office then, of sorts. When he was under threat of being molested by the perverse friends of his even more perverse parents, he would suddenly disappear.

Under the cover of darkness he would stealth away and hide in that silent empty house with a lone flashlight as his only friend.

And there he would be free of the torments of his life, for a time anyway, hiding in the cellar, the garage, a storeroom closet. He would read by that light. He would read and read and read, and little by little Landshark was being born, broken as he was.

CHAPTER 249

In the morning Landshark came into their office with coffee but there was no Ana. The only clue to her whereabouts being a note she left taped to the computer screen:

William—Gone hunting.
Borrowed the truck. Be ready.
Ana

CHAPTER 250

Landshark had an SUV delivered to his house. He stood in the driveway and signed the papers of ownership. He was pretty good and certain where Ana had gone. Landshark had a forged driver's license which the deliveryman took a picture of for the dealership.

"I love that new car smell," said the deliveryman. "Don't you?"

"Not one fuckin' bit," said Landshark.

The deliveryman didn't know how to follow that up.

Once alone, Landshark walked the car, looking it over. Then he stared up that long, long driveway to the street beyond.

The living world out there had become the embodiment of every paranoid fear he had forever been tormented by. The terror he emotionally suffered more alive in the day to day existence down below than he could have ever imagined. He and the world were about the same.

He opened the car door and sat in the driver's seat. He turned on the engine and listened. A car engine always spoke to him of either freedom...or death.

In his pocket was a little present Ana had left behind for him. It was the stiletto her father had given her.